# The Winter-Blooming Tree

# the winter-blooming tree

## Barbara Langhorst

Palimpsest Press
1171 Eastlawn Ave.
Windsor, Ontario. N8S 3J1
www.palimpsestpress.ca

Printed and bound in Canada
Cover design and book typography by Ellie Hastings
Edited by Aimée Dunn
Copyedited by Theo Hummer

Palimpsest Press would like to thank the Canada Council for
the Arts and the Ontario Arts Council for their support of our
publishing program. We also acknowledge the assistance of the
Government of Ontario through the Ontario Book Publishing
Tax Credit.

ISBN: 9781989287859

*for the nine*

# 1

Ursula's thoughts were remarkably vivid, awake or asleep, as rich in dreams as in nightmares. She had learned long ago to conceal them; it was how she got by. Whenever she tried to soothe her memory or even subdue it, small things lingered, bright hopes and dark doubts and denials. So what if her fancies and fears left her distracted, if she forgot this and that? She had a lifetime of things to remember. She had no one to confide in now, certainly not Mr. Perfect, Andreas. And, as dear as their daughter was, Mia had once accused her of being unfeeling, of lacking imagination. She knew this was not true, but it didn't lessen the sting. How could a young woman understand the rich and varied states of her aging mother's inner life? And how could that quack of a family doctor insist that she waste a perfectly good day, translating her mind into a set of numbers, a table of calculations, for some stranger's file?

She had been dreading this moment for a full six months. Here she was, alone, in a peculiar office. The February sun shimmered in through the wide wall of windows. Ursula found herself seated on a teal linen sofa, a white woven rug with broad gray stripes beneath her feet. The hardwood floors were dark, and a black spotlight that looked like it had been lifted from a movie set guarded one end of the couch. A white ceramic lamp stood at the other on a mid-century walnut stand, the matching coffee table long and sleek and modern before her. What type of a doctor saw patients in a place like this? Still, something about the space was familiar to her. The memory dodged her—and there was that feeling again, that strange emptiness, everything blank, so impenetrable and dull.

Suddenly it came to her, all in a rush. Her father had once confided that he kept a comfortable office so that his patients would find themselves at ease when receiving what was often the worst news of their lives. The room around her was as grand as the one she had imagined as a child, the day her teacher had asked her to draw a picture of her father's office, that mysterious place Babbe went to every day, the one she had never even seen. Anyone as important as he was must work in a fancy room, so she drew a chandelier, a beautiful starburst of yellow wax-crayon. She had topped his long black desk with an enormous pea-green typewriter, her father behind it, wearing his lab coat and stethoscope. A squiggle of black hair for his brush cut, then she had drawn in his horn-rimmed glasses and laid the floor, a checkerboard of black and bright-green squares. The whole room had looked splendid.

After supper, when Babbe was in his easy chair, reading the newspaper, she had taken it to show him. How he had chuckled as he looked at it. He had pulled her onto his lap, patted her cheek and pinched it softly, calling her *Schätzli*, his little treasure. And somehow, she had not felt foolish at all. He had smiled at the chandelier and said her likeness of him was very good. He asked what she had studied that day, and how she liked young Mrs. Gottlieb, her teacher, and then he told her to change into her pajamas and fetch their story. And they had read an extra chapter of *The Secret Garden* that night.

How she missed him, all the stories he told her of Basel. She missed both of her parents. Forty years had passed since Mamme had died, and still, whenever she thought of her mother, still she ached. Even the joy of meeting Andreas and falling in love the next spring had not eased her pain. Whenever she somehow managed to forget, whenever she felt the slight ease of normalcy, suddenly the memories would flood back, leaving her feeling more bereft than ever. But she had survived, and now she and her siblings were busy with their own lives. They were all busy, practical people; Mamme had made sure of that. And after their mother's death, Kathrin and Norbert had never mentioned the questions that could not be answered. Only Babbe had sensed Ursula's particular grief, and he had always made time to call her, every single day of her adult life. How she loved to speak Baseldytsch with him, the language of all her memories.

And then he too had died, just a year ago last December. Ursula had never allowed herself to break down, not even once. Nowadays, given her symptoms, her lapses of memory, it was more urgent than ever to maintain her intellectual focus. She demanded fluency: second languages were supposed to keep the mind young. There had been a time when even little Mia understood the beautiful tinkling words, though that had had less to do with her mother's Saturday lessons than with the fact that Ursula had insisted on discussing all grownup—and therefore all interesting— decisions with Andreas in the old tongue. But when Ursula spoke it these days, Andreas replied in English, cheerfully ignoring her old-fashioned ideas. She knew what that meant. To him it only made sense to adapt sooner rather than later, but for Ursula it was not a simple calculation. Some concepts simply did not translate. Yes, she had been teaching in English for almost her entire career. But for real communication, well, Canadian English was unmusical.

Still, despite all of Ursula's efforts to cajole or entice, now-adays Mia rarely bothered to try to speak the old language unless there was some special favour to be gained by trying to please her mother.

Ursula stared out the doctor's window, longing just to leave, to run away, to bury herself in her books, her research, but she had to see this through. She had to find out what was happening to her. She scanned the room, searching for clues. It really was the strangest office. There were no certifi-cates or diplomas. The light-gray walls were bare, except for two huge line drawings, abstract, hanging symmetrically above the sofa. There was a padded black leather Eames recliner with matching footrest. That alone was worth a small fortune, she knew. Business must be brisk; there was hardly a lack of Alzheimer's patients these days, with the tsunami of boomers washing ashore, drowning in the sad-ness of their sedentary lives.

Ursula came to with a start. She could hear voices, a young woman murmuring and a deeper tone too, and then the hall door opened and in walked Andreas, tall, white-haired, fit, as magnetic and well-groomed as James Bond stepping off a Learjet. His smile surprised her. What did he have to be happy about? Some new toy, some new friend he'd met as he wandered around Midtown Plaza, while she had been struggling through those endless exhausting tests? He walked over to her and just stood there, looking down. Why was he wearing his public face, the charming one, even though she was the only person there to see it? You could always count on him to look so—what was the word? He was still handsome, yes, he had always been very attractive, but that wasn't it. The exact word she wanted was somewhere beyond the tip of her tongue. He had a certain look when strangers were involved. She was surprised to feel a small frisson while looking at him, a little jolt of the old longing. For a half-second she forgot to wonder what he was up to.

Before either of them could speak, there was a quick rap-tap-tap at the side door and the neurologist entered. His receptionist slipped in behind him and set down a tray on the coffee table, then exited, closing the door softly behind her. Ursula remained seated, willing the great man to walk over to her. She was a bit unnerved when he did precisely that. He seemed awfully friendly; was he bearing bad news? The young doctor introduced himself, shook their hands, and encouraged Andreas to take a seat beside Ursula. Then he settled himself into his trendy recliner, swung his feet up, and began to consult his tablet, scrolling through screen after screen.

Ursula was so tired of waiting, she wanted to scream. But she knew an outburst would hardly help matters. Her eye caught the tray with the tall blue-striped carafe on the coffee table before them. There were three white mugs, apparently intended for the three of them. She reached over, loosened the lid, and lifted the carafe. Her right hand shook as she poured the coffee, but no one seemed to notice. She paused a moment for the steam to subside, spooned sugar into Andreas's cup, stirred it briefly, and handed it to him, adding cream and sugar to her own. The doctor's she left black, setting it near his end of the table, with the cream pitcher, the sugar bowl, and a plastic spoon on a paper napkin.

The doctor was chatting about the weather. Andreas seemed relaxed, nodding at what the other man was saying, his arm resting along the back of the sofa behind her in what anyone else would read as a show of support, a gesture of protection. Ursula knew her husband was simply making himself large, asserting himself in these strange new surroundings. She sipped her coffee, careful not to burn her tongue. She remembered her father explaining the real reason why doctors spoke to patients outside the examination room: it was so important to set people at ease, let them relax before they had to focus on the diagnosis. Ah, that explained it. The office was designed to produce every sensation of comfort; only the plastic cutlery seemed out of place, and, of course, Ursula herself. Right on cue, as if to prove she didn't belong in these polished surroundings, her stomach growled, and she pressed her palm firmly against her abdomen to silence it.

The doctor was explaining why there had been so many cognitive tests. "We have to expect changes," he nodded. "Growing old is a nuisance, but the alternative is so much worse." He paused to smile at his own joke. Ursula was in agony. Why didn't he just come out and say that she had failed every blessed task she had fought her way through that morning? She had been lost so much of the time. Who could remember those absurd pairs of words, the nonsensical lists, spliced by demanding, unrelated tasks? But the great man just prattled on and on and on, with Andreas inserting what he thought were intelligent questions at every turn. Damn them. They were showing off like grad students, jostling for position. Get to the point! As much as she feared what he would say, how she needed to know what was wrong with her.

She was trying so hard to pay attention. She'd never been able to concentrate on mellifluous tones. Take the nightly weather report, for instance. Those smooth-talking meteorologists began in some important urban centre, Ottawa or Toronto or Vancouver, sashayed to and fro, waltzed back and forth between major cities around the country, and long before they made it to Saskatchewan, Ursula would be wondering what groceries she needed to pick up tomorrow or whether the homework exercises she had assigned would prove too complicated for her students. By the time she came back to the moment, the announcer was always finishing up with the latest storm bearing down on Newfoundland.

Ursula was desperate to know what was happening to her, but Andreas was prattling on and on, questioning the significance of this metric and that, the norms and standard deviations. She could hardly bear it. What irrelevant detail were they stuck on now? She couldn't stand one more word. Her eye lit on the glossy coffee-table book that was spread just so beside the carafe, the pages branching with five thin limbs of gorgeous apples, each one different, an array of yellows and greens and reds, each fruit shapely and perfect. There had been a time when she had known every variety by sight. Hmmm… Honeycrisp, Goodland, Norland, Parkland? What was the other one? Norlands don't keep as long, she thought, and then, as the men laboured on and on, probing the statistics, their voices receded to a distant hum, and her mind simply lifted, and she was away.

She hadn't thought about that tree in ages, not since the second summer they'd lived in Humboldt, almost thirty-five years ago now. Ursula had fallen in love with a pretty little five-grafted apple tree at the grocery store, of all places, on the very last day of their parking-lot sale. The tree had stood tall and thin, nearly two-dimensional. It hardly seemed too much to ask that a fit young man—her fit young man—dig one more hole and help her plant it. But Andreas had been so charming, so adept in the logic of his procrastination. And Ursula had not been so surprised, after all. He hadn't refused outright to help her (a good husband would never do that), but while the tree waited on the deck, its long branches flicking against the wooden lattice, at last she thought she understood. Andreas never would find room amidst his fine calligraphy of nursery specimens for what was, after all, just one of his peculiar little wife's peculiar little whims.

But because she loved him so, Ursula pushed that thought away, and soon they lapsed into routine—not the routine of home, of Switzerland, no, never that again, but the new routine—the one they built to fit those days, to enfold their hours up there, in Humboldt, Saskatchewan, Canada. Each afternoon they had laboured together in the garden, digging and planting, so in love, so wordlessly in sync, until at last, exhausted and weary, they headed back in to fetch their evening meal. Even their diet was different here; *when in Rome*—, Andreas joked, and all that free-roaming Saskatchewan beef was really good. They were reborn as carnivores, grilling thick steaks topped with tangy gourmet barbecue sauce. And when it was time to eat, they sat side by side in their new slatted teak chairs, sipping Zinfandel and talking the day through, all while the pale-yellow light flooded the northwest and the blue sky above gave way to indigo, punctuated with bright stars and luminescent pink contrails. When at last the darkness was all around, they fed tall bonfires and delved deep into the stories of their lives. And at midnight they retreated into the comfort of the house, climbed the stairs, showered together, made love, slept peacefully. By nine a.m. the boreal forest was calling to them through open windows, the day simmering with birdsong and lush with the vibrato of insects.

Each morning, after coffee and croissants, they prepped lessons, tidied rooms, shared a quick lunch, then fled with the joy of truants into the garden once more. It was all so new, that first July and August in Humboldt. By the time the long summer slipped into fall, the apple tree was just one more deck ornament, even to Ursula. And in October, when the first snowstorm hit, helping Andreas haul the heavy pot downstairs seemed no less natural than stowing away the patio umbrella or folding the lawn chairs. How easy it was to ignore.

And yet one day, when she had gone down to throw in a load of light wash, at last Ursula saw it, its graceful, espaliered limbs alight in a single struggling beam of sun. The room was thick with scent and pale petals and even a few spindly apple-green leaves. And miracle of miracles, some of the flowers had set, and small green fruit had formed. When she called Andreas, he had been just as astonished as she, and for weeks they spoke of it. Had they reinvented Eden, opened a portal into time, if time could exist before consequences?

But thirst and gravity must have their way. Ursula had consoled herself as she gathered the first handful of their never-to-be apples from the concrete floor. When the real orchard, the one in the backyard, budded out in all the ecstasy of May, she knew that if the universe had tried to teach her anything, it was that hard work brought prosperity. So when at last Andreas had hauled the little tree upstairs, the slim branches lathered with petals and chartreuse leaves and elongated filaments troping towards the light, she was determined. It would not be too late. He would plant the thing tomorrow.

But when he repositioned the base in its familiar water stain on the deck, she felt an emotion she could not name—and then the fresh wind stirred, and oh, how the dried blossoms blew.

The faded petals were streaming before her when suddenly her eyes refocussed. There was the coffee table, the large book, its photos of stunning clarity, the slender branches heavy with rounded red-and-yellowy-green apples. The doctor was speaking. "…with academics, the decline can be as sudden as falling off a cliff. In most cases, the minor confusion of MCI, mild cognitive impairment, appears first."

Andreas replied, "And when family members notice this mild confusion—?"

Ursula swallowed hard. Was that why she was still functioning as well as she was? But she'd read about mild cognitive impairment: according to MedLine, she had all the symptoms. To hear Andreas just pleasantly relating that he had been observing all her mistakes, in his superior way, well, that was too much. She couldn't breathe.

The doctor continued, "Patients score 24 or less on the MMSE. Those with dementia decline until they stop tracking time and space. But even before they reach full-blown disease, MRI or PET scans can help to confirm the diagnosis—and rule out brain tumours."

*Confirm the diagnosis.* Confirm what diagnosis? Stop tracking time and space? Did she have MCI—or dementia? Ursula blinked. She wanted to weep. She wanted to scream. She could hardly ask them to go back and explain, or let on that she had entirely forgotten to pay attention to what they were saying. Why on earth had she let herself daydream, right when it mattered? Why couldn't she have listened, just this once?

The doctor turned towards her, his eyes searching. "Ursula? You're very quiet. Are you with us?" he prompted.

And yet, somehow, despite everything, the right words came to her. She didn't even have to pause to think. "Such an odd question, doctor. Of course I'm with you. This is not a séance," she smiled.

And the doctor's face creased as he smiled back at her—he was not so young as he had appeared, after all. He shook his head, saying, "A séance? That *would* be remarkable." He turned to Andreas. "Your wife has quite the sense of humour. Excellent," he smiled. "That will make all the difference. Enjoy yourselves as often as you plan—"

"Plan?" Ursula shook her head. "Our lives have been planned since we were seven years old. The Swiss—"

Andreas corrected her quietly, his voice melodious as ever, "As often as we *can.*"

The doctor didn't notice. He stared at the electronic chart as if it were an oracle, channelling all the mysteries of the cosmos. "Life in—where is it? Ah yes—in Humboldt must be quite the project for you," he said absently, tapping and scrolling, "after growing up in Europe. Your family doc can monitor her condition; of course, you or he can contact me, if—" His voice trailed off.

"When?" she prodded.

He met Andreas's glance, cleared his throat, and then continued. "If Ursula exhibits any more of the symptoms we've described."

"Certainly," Andreas nodded.

If Ursula hated anything, it was being treated like a child. "I will monitor my own condition, thank you, Dr.—" she corrected them both, pausing for effect. "Dr.—"

And then there was… nothing.

Her mind was utterly vacant, a white space grayed with shadow, that place she had found herself in over the last year whenever her thoughts and words deserted her. The walls of her mind curved and warped, pure and blank around her. All that emptiness, that nothingness. She searched but there was not one single clue, not one blessed word. She'd been so caught up, so certain she could prove her own capacity, that she'd forgotten the bloody doctor's name. She could feel Andreas looking at her, waiting. The great man himself, the neurologist, was looking at her, too, with a type of interest, at last. She could hear her own breathing.

Andreas casually finished her sentence: "Dr. Paul."

The sun's angle had changed, leaving her in shadow. Ursula felt cold, rigid-tense. She had to say something. She could see the steel filing cabinets, rows of them, in the office in the high-rise across the parking lot. She found herself studying the people over there, standing by the water dispenser in the window. She had to say something. Dr. Paul. Paul McCartney was her favourite Beatle. How on earth had she forgotten that?

"Of course, Dr. Paul," she purred, rolling the *l* for effect.

The men exchanged glances.

"We're grateful—" Andreas started to say.

Ursula was anything but grateful. She couldn't bear Andreas's people-pleasing, not at a moment like this. She stood up, spoke a little too firmly to compensate. "Yes. Of course. Thank you for your time, doctor. We really must be going." She looked around the room for her things. Where in the world had she left her coat?

The doctor swung his feet to the ground and rose smoothly from his recliner. He looked into her eyes for a moment longer than she expected, then glanced at Andreas, who had risen beside her. "The most important thing now is to get some rest. The MRI will confirm my diagnosis; I'm ninety-eight—" he paused—"well, ninety-five percent certain. And there's nothing like worry to impair memory and increase deficits. Now might be a good time to retire. Even a leave would help. But keep busy, find a hobby that uses your mind. You can call my nurse." He paused, glancing from Andreas to Ursula. "No, better yet, your family doc can supply the paperwork. If you're interested," he said, looking down at his tablet again, "there's a nice support group in Aberdeen."

Andreas nodded. "Only an hour away."

"Only an hour *each way*—" Ursula fell silent. It was certain, then: she had dementia. Why else would they need a support group?

"We'll look into it," Andreas spoke again. She saw him turn and bend, retrieve something from the end table beside the sofa. It was her ski jacket, the one she had found on sale last week, that deep, rich fuchsia colour. She was surprised to feel a fine surge of pleasure. She had completely forgotten it. He held it out for her, and she slipped her arms into the down-filled sleeves while he guided the collar. She drew her gray mitts and knitted toque from the pockets while Andreas pulled on his dark woollen coat.

She was looping her scarf around her throat when she heard Andreas talking to the doctor once more.

"Time off sounds like a good idea. And we'll have company around the house soon. Our daughter will be moving home at the end of next week. Perfect timing."

Mia, moving home? This was the first Ursula had heard about that. She felt as if she had stumbled into some parallel universe. Her face went taut, then blanched, and all at once the blood rushed back, and finally, at last, she knew what she was feeling: she was enraged, absolutely furious. Of all the ridiculous ideas—why in the name of Heaven would a journalist move home to a one-horse-town like Humboldt, where the most widely prized news items were the obituaries? And why in God's name would Andreas choose this moment to blurt it out in front of a stranger, when he had not yet had the courtesy to tell *her?*

She knew what he would say when she asked him, that patronizing tone he always used—the one she loathed—the one he always used nowadays: *We discussed this. (We discussed that. We discussed it.)* His superior tone made her want to spit. Well, they hadn't discussed a blessed thing, not this time. She stood absolutely still, stiff, raging inside, *I'm not ill. I'm NOT. It's the stress, the students, the isolation. I AM NOT ILL—* Her mind tried a new tack. *I'm busy, yes, too busy, I'm burnt out, absolutely, isn't that how everybody else explains these types of problems? No one in my family has ever had dementia—*

She knew she must not give the men any more information; they had already guessed far too much. She would not reveal her terror. She straightened herself, walked silently across the room, turned the metal handle, pulled the door towards her, went through the doorway, and set off down the dim hallway. She could hear Andreas's voice rise before the door clicked shut behind her. For a moment she walked in almost complete silence, the rustle of her jacket the only noise, then the door opened again and closed, and she heard him hurrying behind her, his stride heavy as he laboured to catch up. They were at an intersection of several hallways when he reached her. He tried to take her right hand.

She pulled it free, stood absolutely still.

"Darling, I only want to help," he said, bending down, trying to make her look up at him.

She stared away, refusing to meet his eyes, took a breath before she spoke. "By ordering our daughter to move home and be my nursemaid? I can't deal with this now, I can't. For God's sake, Andreas, what were you thinking? There's no life for Mia in Humboldt."

He opened his mouth. "Don't be ridiculous. It was her idea. It won't hurt us to help her out."

She could not remember ever being this angry. "Help her? You want to help? By all means, big man, help. Lead the way." How she longed for the life they used to share. She could almost hear the deep frustration she was sure he experienced when dealing with her nowadays. But he would never chide her, never reveal what he was really feeling. Not Mr. Perfect, not Prince Charming, he-who-knew-no-weakness, he-who-had-no-empathy. Whenever she tried to point out that she was right, he'd simply say, *That didn't happen.* And if she pressed him, he'd say, *And if it did, it wasn't that bad.* And if she still didn't cave, he'd smirk, *And if it was, it wasn't my fault. And if it was, I didn't mean it. And if I did, you deserved it!* He acted as if gaslighting were something to be proud of: he thought the whole bloody narcissist's prayer was a joke. He truly had no idea how self-centred he was. Oh, how she longed for him just to get angry, really angry, right there, and let her in, show her what he felt, step out from behind the damned curtain, that wall he'd built around himself. Where was the man she loved, the one she thought she knew until a year ago; was he even still in there? She was so angry she wanted to slap his ridiculous smile off his empty face.

# 2

Andreas had no trouble finding the way out through this maze of corridors. He always knew where he was; it was one of the things Ursula loved about him, or so she used to say. As he caught up to his wife, Andreas reached for her hand. When she pulled it away, he smiled. He wasn't put off, though he could see her rage, her fury, even. She hated to be wrong—who didn't? But surely she was relieved, too? He was jazzed enough for both of them. He wanted to shout out to strangers as they walked by, "Praise the gods that don't exist! It's a miracle—my wife doesn't have dementia!"

He thought back to his long morning, wandering aimlessly around Midtown Plaza, browsing through shops of overpriced clothes he didn't even like and buying raffle tickets on cars and cruises he didn't want, searching for any little thing that might stop him from worrying about her "condition," as she always called it. He couldn't say when it had started, but for ages, for months anyway, Ursula had been in some kind of trance. She couldn't remember the smallest things. Who could say what was causing it? He had to admit that he had entertained the fear that there really was something wrong with her.

But the doctor had been certain, ninety-eight percent certain, it was nothing. She was fine, and soon enough she would calm down, he rationalized, and recognize the bullet they had dodged. In the meantime, he would simply do as she asked, and set about navigating their way through the dark maze of corridors. At last they reached the bright glass-enclosed bridge that would take them back to the hospital proper. It must be quitting time; the pedway was packed, people crushing against one another, and for a few moments it took all of his concentration just to keep track of her elbow as they worked their way through the crowd. He wondered what he could do to help her relax.

Surely they could do that now, at last. Surely she knew how ridiculous she was being; surely some small part of her aware that she was overreacting. She felt like a fool, of course. She'd been so certain she had dementia, was perched on the edge of oblivion. Well, she was wrong, that was all. She could thank her God for that. He almost wished he believed so that he could thank Him, too. The doctor had said there was nothing wrong that a little time off would not correct. And if—or when—she admitted how ridiculously freaked out she had been, he would tell her how terrified he had felt, too. That would only be fair. But Ursula was nothing if not stubborn.

*Relentless*—that was a better word. She always tried her best—how he had loved that about her. He remembered the way she had forced him to keep applying for tenure-track jobs when they had first come to Canada and everything had seemed so hopeless. Now that was a bad situation, a day neither of them would ever forget. They had stepped off the plane just as the worst blizzard of the decade was starting, blasting them into what no one had told them would be the worst recession in Canada since the Dirty Thirties. By the time they'd wrestled their luggage off the carousel, the position he had been promised at the University of Saskatchewan had been axed in the latest round of budget cuts. Their so-called sponsors had wined and dined with them for three full days (at the newcomers' expense) before abruptly depositing them in a rundown townhouse, the rent due in a week and only the *Saskatoon Star Phoenix* to kickstart their job search.

But that hadn't stopped Ursula; she was fearless, at least about his career. Of course, she should have found a position, too; her research was just as viable as his. She was brilliant and funny and sweet in those days—the whole package. She had sent him marching down to the Math Department, where, it turned out, there was plenty of work as a tutor; that was simple enough. But she had simply, inexplicably, given up after her first and only visit to Botany, had instead insisted that she wanted to become a high school teacher, arriving home with a part-time retail job at Fairweather and a T-shirt that boasted, "I got my degree in B.Ed."

For two long years they had lived on love and as little else as could be managed, and somehow, she always paid their bills on time. It was no wonder they had felt such hope that day in May when they drove their rented car east for his interview at St. Peter's College. They were young, they were strong, and the town was welcoming. She loved how rustic and quaint it was, and he had smiled indulgently at her delight. Although it was not nearly urban enough for his taste, it was a sessional teaching job, so much better than what they had been getting by with, and there would be more courses at colleges around the province. He liked to drive. Even he had accepted their new life with gratitude and plenty of hope.

Whenever Ursula most wanted him to believe in the support of the universe, in capital-D Destiny, she would remind him of that trip, of how curiously right everything had been, as unlikely as success had seemed. Even the landscape had been perfect: the wild forest the high-way rushed through, the tall dark spruce and waving pines, the pale ribs of aspen and papery birch that braced the hills as they rolled towards town. And when the car had rounded the last corner, there was a billboard, a veritable sign out in the wilderness, a jaunty visual *ta-da*: "Welcome to Humboldt, Population 4,028." Although he didn't know why, Andreas had felt the hair rise on the back of his neck. Of course he had never told Ursula that. She always babbled on about the charming welcome, so poetic, so precise in its detail. Even had they known then that the figure was never adjusted, not for births or deaths or defections, it would hardly have mattered. As Ursula told it, any caution they might have felt had washed away in the long steep hills before the town, some roller coaster swooping them up and down towards Fate.

Whether he believed that or not, the trip had truly brought a new momentum into their lives. There was no moving allowance, but real estate in Humboldt was dirt cheap, at least compared to the prices they had known in Basel and Saskatoon. In no time they had fallen in love with a neat sixties two-storey, fronted in glass and with gleaming blond wood floors throughout. It was everything they had hoped for, so airy and modern. The mid-century furniture he loved would be perfect. And though garden chores, especially weeding, had always made him grumble back home, they both looked forward to landscaping their new double lot. Andreas got out his drafting tools, and Ursula memorized the inventory of garden centres that would deliver, and together they designed an orchard of winter-hardy trees.

The days slid by, and soon it was Canada Day, July 1, and they had driven their new used Volvo out east to take possession. The movers were already at the house, unloading, and Ursula had roamed from room to room, giving instructions. While Andreas assembled furniture, she fetched him tools and unpacked the kitchen, setting up the espresso machine for their first morning coffee together, the two of them cheerfully sharing the work of settling in.

She liked to say that the long summer had floated by like a paper napkin in a breeze. That much was true; he hadn't even had time to engineer a way to plant her delicate apple tree, the espaliered one she found at the grocery store. Still a bit shy with her English, Ursula had let him make all their purchases, and because she was good at finding bargains, soon he found himself chatting up all the locals. Everybody knew him, from the gas station attendant to the girl in the drive-through window at the burger bar. The townsfolk had nice country manners, no one could deny that. On Saturday mornings, as Andreas and Ursula sat leafing through the newspaper, the phone would ring with an invitation for coffee the next day. The ladies served saskatoon pies and apple cakes and strong coffee with thick farm cream to new friends and old neighbours alike.

And once she had settled into the routine, Ursula was happy teaching chemistry at the high school. He didn't know how she could just walk away from something she loved as much as botany, but he couldn't fault her instincts; her teaching schedule did give her summers and Christmases and Easters with little Mia, who arrived the year after they had settled in.

And even now, despite her moods, still he longed for that old connection. It had been uncanny. Even now, her mind seemed to follow his to their youth; she looked up into his eyes and said, "This reminds me of the year we met."

He was about to wrap his arms around her shoulders in a hug when she said, "Remember how I always got lost in the university in Basel, even when I was twenty and perfectly fit?"

"You're perfectly fit now!" he wanted to shout. Instead he just said mildly, "We hadn't met when you were twenty, Sweetheart, remember?" He clenched his jaw. His head throbbed. As they walked off the pedway, he guided her to the right, fighting off the frustration that washed over him. He forced himself to look around, to smile pleasantly at all the truly sick and suffering, the pale dishevelled patients walking by with IVs or rolling past in wheelchairs or sitting slumped on motorized scooters. These people had problems, real problems. As he might too, soon enough, if his doctor had been right about his heart.

He forced himself to keep smiling, but he felt his face go taut, thicken into a mask. He felt alone, helpless-alone, with this malingerer. This self-obsessed hypochondriac. She wasn't ill. The doctor had guaranteed it; she was fine. Was she never going to give in and admit to being relieved?

She spoke again, more loudly. "You know I can't navigate inside. I need—"

He wanted to scream, but he gave no sign. There was nothing left to say. He wasn't going to feed her neuroses, not this time. That might infuriate her, he knew, but he wasn't going to let her convince herself she was frail or delicate or in need of cossetting. The doctor had said it all. She was stressed out, maybe even a little crazy, but physically she was fine. All they needed was the blessed MRI to prove it.

As if she knew what he was thinking, abruptly Ursula turned her body to fit between the people ahead and slipped down the hallway. At least, he thought, her garish new pink jacket would keep her visible as she bobbed in among the people wearing dark coats or pastel scrubs or hospital gowns and robes. He lengthened his steps and easily caught up to her as she reached the elevator. This time he took her hand firmly. He kept his face utterly calm, as he always did. He knew she would interpret his silence as acquiescence rather than the protection it was, the same tactic he always used to preserve the harmony between them. At least she rode up in silence. He held the door as she exited the elevator, and they made their way over to the next pedway, the one to the parkade.

While they walked, he thought back to the appointment. There had been that one moment when the doctor had seemed to think Ursula wasn't paying attention. She had seemed vulnerable, a bit lost, in that instant. No wonder she had trouble focusing. She always let her mind, so full of fears, carry her away. She was terrified of losing control; maybe that was well and good, at least now. The last thing he wanted was for her to flip out right here in public. If he could keep her calm, if she could hold it together for ten minutes longer, they would be in the truck and on the way home.

He was exhausted. The new early-morning runs and all the sleepless nights had taken their toll. If she said one more infuriating thing, even his good manners might not save them. He shook his head silently. It was so ridiculous. They should be dancing in the streets, celebrating.

Even in her high-heeled boots, Ursula was still a good thirty-five centimetres shorter than he was, and she was flushed now, winded. He glanced down. For a moment he had forgotten how hard it was for her to keep up with him when he walked. If he could somehow talk her into stopping for food, he might find a way to make her laugh. Dr. Paul had said that humour was the best tool they had. That only confirmed what he had learned long ago, early in their marriage. All they needed to defuse stress was a sense of humour, and relaxation, and sleep. And fine food and regular sex, of course. Good health stemmed from nothing more complicated than that. And, as Dr. Paul had pointed out, she needed to see a real psychiatrist, someone to taper her off those ancient meds, the ones their family doc had prescribed to elevate her mood and help her sleep. Surely they were affecting her memory. Still holding her hand, he lengthened his stride, just thinking of it.

# 3

"Mia? Could you step into my office for a moment?" Ed's always affable face looked strangely serious as he paused at her cubicle.

Mia nodded. What now? Another gallery opening to cover? The spring poetry festival? She rose and followed him across the noisy newsroom.

He held the door for her as she went through, then closed it firmly. She settled into one of the black vinyl chairs in front of his desk.

He went around and sat down, then opened the file before him, shuffling the papers in it. At last he looked up, staring at her over his glasses. "Mia, it isn't your work ethic. I want you to understand that."

Mia's eyes widened. "What's wrong with my work ethic? I'm here early most days, I stay late—"

He held her gaze for a moment, then looked down and jotted the date, then signed the form on the bottom. He spoke without looking up again. "Listen to me, Mia. I've just said it isn't any of that. But you were the last one hired—"

"What are you saying—the first one fired? You're joking, Ed, right? This is a practical joke?" Mia's already fair face blanched in disbelief, her lip trembling.

Ed shook his head and looked up at last. His eyes met hers. "I'm sorry, Mia. We'll call it a layoff, so you can claim EI. It's nothing personal—oh, don't cry, for God's sake." He pushed the box of tissues towards her, then glanced away out the window, towards the empty condo tower. "Times are tight. We have to cut somewhere. In this line of work, you have to prove yourself, show you're something special. You've been here a year already. When we hired you, you had so many ideas. Maybe now, when you're not tied to the arts desk…" His voice trailed off. "Your last day will be Friday."

"You can't fire me! You can't. I'm scheduled to start my vacation then. How am I supposed to pay my rent, my bills—?"

"Mia, listen to me. We're not firing you—we're laying you off. If something opens up, your file could be the first one we look at. And you'll get your vacation pay. That will help you get back on your feet. Consider it a bonus."

"A bonus? The vacation days you owe me?"

"Look, you're not making this any easier on yourself. If you don't want to get a call when things pick up—"

Mia could only sit there, looking like an idiot, she knew, crying, blowing her nose. She was acting like a child, blubbering that way. It was ridiculous. She wasn't sad; she was enraged, furious. Not knowing what else to do, she took a last tissue, wiped the mascara she knew was running down her face, and blew her nose noisily. Dad always said, "Never leave a job angry—word gets around. Poison one well, lose the whole aquifer." She had to get a hold of herself. What she really wanted to do was tell him off, then run from the room and never go back.

At last she forced herself to stand up, reach across the desk, and shake Ed's hand. She had to act as if it wasn't his fault. But what was she going to do?

Ed came around and sat on the corner of his desk. "Make sure Sharon knows where we can reach you. You'll find something soon, a bright girl like you. You just haven't hit your stride."

She faked a tight smile, said, "Thanks for all that you've done for me. I appreciate it, truly."

Back in her cubicle, she stared at her desk. She'd never find another job, not fast enough. She'd been living hand-to-mouth; her rent was $1800 a month, which didn't count utilities, or gas, or student loans, or food. Even if she could sublet or break her lease, the only place she could go was—

Oh. No. Not that. She wouldn't. She couldn't.

Even the thought brought pure panic.

Slowly she made herself face the facts. If she couldn't find anything else, if there was no other way, she'd truly have to move home. Humboldt. She shook herself; she had to calm down. Surely she could find some other gig—she had to. But where? She'd worked every connection she had to find *this* job. She turned to the internet. After an hour of searching, she hadn't found a single lead, even a whisper of possibility.

At last, she had to face facts. She made the call, and Dad assured her that he and Mamme would be delighted to have her move home, though he was sorry she had to go through this, of course. He knew she would have to make the best of it: she might die of boredom, but at least she could count on the peace and quiet.

# 4

Ursula sat in silence as Andreas circled the truck down through the dingy parkade. She was bone weary, worn out: the tests, the stress of the last few years, Babbe's illness, and though it had hardly been a surprise, his death. Nothing could have prepared her for that loss, and now it had been confirmed: she was losing her mind, truly. Honestly, how much more could she take? She needed to relax, no matter what anyone else thought. At least Andreas wasn't trying to make casual conversation with her now. She rubbed her neck, rotated her shoulders. There was nothing more anyone could say. When they reached the parking booth, she held her peace as the king of chit-chat bantered cheerfully with the young cashier, paid the fee, and their truck rolled through the red-and-white gate. As they pulled out into the street, Ursula stared through the passenger window. She was so tired, numb with worry. It would be good to be home at last.

Her stomach growled loudly again. Andreas surprised her and said, "You wouldn't happen to be hungry now, would you? Didn't they feed you?"

"The nurse brought me a bowl of lukewarm pea soup," she said. "And some salt-free crackers."

"That must have been ages ago."

It was true. She had eaten at noon, and now it was nearly five o'clock. To the west, the February evening sky lingered pale blue above a wash of butter yellow, a band of orange-red clouds obscuring the horizon. The streetlights flickered and lit.

"It will be an hour before we get home. Should we stop somewhere for a bite first? What do you feel like?"

"I don't know. It doesn't matter. Really. I can wait until we get home."

"You know what? The Station Place might be open by now. I hear they've renovated. I could go for a little lamb souvlaki. What about you?"

Ursula considered. There was her lesson prep, their lunches to make for the next morning, and the cat would be waiting for his supper—but all of a sudden, she saw his attempt at kindness, and something like the old feelings surfaced. For once he really seemed to want to take care of her. Her stomach rumbled again. "Alright," she said. "After the day we've had, souvlaki sounds wonderful. Thank you, Andreas."

"And let's not forget the baklava," he added. "And some wine, and a nice shot of ouzo—not necessarily in that order—and maybe Opa!"

She turned towards him, half-afraid he was mocking her, but he was smiling at the road with what seemed to be genuine pleasure. She had to admit that Andreas really could charm the birds from the trees when he wanted to. Not fifteen minutes ago she'd been completely in shock, her worst fears realized. Now all she really wanted was a little Greek music, a skewer of souvlaki, some tzatziki and pita bread. Maybe she could just let herself forget everything for a few moments. Of course, she would forget; that was what she always did, she told herself grimly. Well, what could it hurt, at least for tonight?

They parked behind the restaurant and made their way across the crowded parking lot to the front entrance. White lights filled the trees on the boulevard and framed the old railway car that established the restaurant's theme. When they walked in through the expensive new foyer, they were greeted by the rich scents of meat roasting with garlic and rosemary. The sense of welcome was instantaneous, as it always had been, but better—it was like coming home, not just in space but in time, to those first evenings they had enjoyed in Canada.

They could never afford a complete meal in those days. They used to go for coffee and dessert, linger to watch the people. Once, a tipsy tourist had even clambered up on top of a table to dance while the others linked arms with the line of staff, the crew of servers, and many of the guests, slowly snaking and swaying their way around the restaurant, all shouting "Opa!" as they smashed thick white plates on the stone floors to bring good luck. Ursula was too shy back then, could never have smashed a plate herself, but she thought that tonight, of all nights, if the chance arose, she would let go. If ever she'd had need of capital-L Luck, it was now. They would all need that.

Andreas removed his coat and she slipped off her jacket. He took it from her gently and handed both to the coat-check girl with the long black curls. He made small talk, as always, and the girl smiled back at him as she gave him the coat tags. At the entrance to the dining room, a waiter with wavy brown shoulder-length hair took two leather-bound menus from a stack and said, "For two? If you'll follow me this way, please—"

Andreas nodded and took Ursula's hand, and the young man led them to a roomy table for two in a leather booth. A heavy blue tablecloth flickered in candlelight. The waiter held a tall-backed leather dining chair for Ursula, then poured water over the side of the glass jug, splashing plenty of ice into the footed glasses. He set these on the table in front of them, handed them their menus and, with a smile and a little bow, turned and walked away.

Ursula looked around. The renovation was impressive. It was the strangest sensation, to feel at home in a place where so much was new-rustic and expensive—moody light fixtures, heavy stonework, handsome décor, textured hangings. Memories of those days when they had been young, poor, and so much in love came to mind. But how could anything be familiar when she and Andreas had altered in so many ways? Could they ever be those people again? She looked around at the tables of animated guests chatting and eating, some of them even holding hands.

Andreas might have been reading her mind. He said, casually, "You're so lovely, Ursula. What a day this has been. And this place looks better than ever."

Ursula blushed at his sudden compliment, followed his hand as he gestured around the room. The famous railcar gleamed in black and brass, animated guests talking and laughing within. Rich decorations and new antiques looked as if they had been there forever.

He smiled into her eyes. "It feels like old times tonight, all the evenings we had here. Except that there isn't a starving student in sight."

"It's true." Her eyes met his. "Everything looks as though it was meant to be this way. It's hard to imagine that the addition is new. But I'm afraid I don't see any lamb souvlaki on the menu, after all. Roast lamb, rack of lamb, but the only thing on skewers tonight seems to be the chicken."

He smiled. "Oh, I can make do with rack of lamb, Sweetheart, if you can?"

She smiled back, his eyes on hers still. There was something there, that frisson again. Feeling odd, shy somehow, she lowered her gaze to the menu.

"You go ahead. I think I'll have the moussaka. It's not like we have vegetarian options Humboldt," she said, glancing over her menu at the prices. If he was going to have the most expensive item on the list, she could balance things out. "It'll be like the old days, when we couldn't afford meat."

"It's a good thing we're not reliving the old days. New prices to pay for the new décor. We couldn't have afforded a thing on this menu, not even the coffee," he laughed.

She looked up, smiling. "True. We'd be in the kitchen washing dishes for weeks to come."

"Now there's an expression I haven't heard in ages. Remember how confused we were when we first heard people here say it? Washing dishes to pay for a meal. Do you think anyone ever really did that?"

"They might have, here in the wild wild west. Remember our first year in Canada, when you went to Manpower and over four hundred people had applied for one job as a dishwasher?"

"I ran as fast as I could, but it was filled long before I got there. Remember how I wound up holding rugs for display at the auction every Saturday? I thought my arms would fall off, those things were so heavy. But I survived, we survived. And then the tutoring worked out, and the sessional jobs, and now look at us."

Their eyes met across the table, smiling. Ursula felt that new-old sensation, the one that they hadn't shared for a very long time. He reached across to take her hand in his. For a moment, she felt as if they were the only two in the room, but almost immediately the waiter arrived and Andreas dropped her hand to pick up his menu. Ursula blushed. She pretended to study the wine list while Andreas gave the order. By the time he was finished, someone had turned up the Greek music, and conversation was no longer a possibility, so they sat there smiling at one another and watching the other diners. Before long, a platter of succulent dolmades and keftedes arrived. Andreas must have ordered those—she didn't recall asking for them. As she bit into the tender grape leaves and savoured the tasty meatballs, she found she really was hungry, after all.

The evening was more relaxing than any Ursula could remember in years. The wine was dry, the food was perfectly spiced, and between the music and the vibrant atmosphere, Ursula felt as if the painful past year had never happened. They were back in the time when all things seemed possible, as long as they had one another.

As the music played, Ursula forbade herself to worry. Soon enough she would hardly remember anything, not even pleasant times. Still, she told herself, you never knew how things would turn out. Take this evening, for instance: once again, Andreas had worked his magic, just as he always seemed to when all hope was lost.

She let her thoughts wander back to when they first met. She hadn't had any inkling how her life would change then, either, that long-ago afternoon when she stared down from her lab at the old city. After the worst winter anyone could remember, Basel had been wrapped in rain for the entire month of May. The late afternoon light, the landscape, its human figures striding along—everything seemed muted to grayscale beneath the low sky. Pedestrians hurried along the narrow streets, pausing only to fold-shake their umbrellas before stepping swiftly inside, the grandeur of the tall old buildings clearly lost on them.

Ursula remembered feeling lonelier than ever. The old fossil, Dr. Waldner, had already spoken to her about her constant sighing. "Odd," he had mused, "in one so young." It took all her self-control not to retort: she was not *so young,* she was *small, petite,* and, her mother had always added, *with a mind like a steel trap.* If only Mamme hadn't—no. She couldn't think about that now. She scanned the hills in the distance. What she wanted, what she needed, was a walk in the woods, but, even as she stood watching, the day's gray light gave way to evening.

Any day now the weather would break, that much was certain. And indeed, by week's end, summer had glimmered in. Under sunny skies, the flowerbeds waved irises of deep purple and light blue, crimson and white roses and peonies beside them. Even the puddles seemed to bounce with light. People gathered on bright café patios to sip strong coffee, linger over rich pastries and fresh gossip, but Ursula was not among them. She was out with a group of grad students on the bus to Langenbruck, where their hike would start.

The day was perfect, and as they disembarked and made their way along the trail, Ursula felt her heart lift. Deep in the forest, deer and foxes slipped by, brief shadows in sunlight. The fresh breeze in the treetops whispered of comfort; the sharp scent of spruce and balsam fir calmed her. Everything would be all right. Of course it would.

After an hour, they met a lone hiker, and the tall girl next to Ursula murmured, "You should see this one." She nodded in the young man's direction. "So dreamy."

Ursula had peered up through the group; she could barely see the stranger. He was standing with his back to her, apparently nodding towards their stunning blonde guide. *So predictable*, she thought, but said nothing, just smiled and slowed her pace, letting herself lag a few yards behind the pack.

They were nearing the edge of the forest on Chellenchöpfli when her bootlace had come undone, and she crouched to retie it at the edge of the path. The other students were already filing into the open, sharing binoculars and pointing at the birds soaring high above or swooping down through the valley below. Eager to catch up, Ursula stood quickly and walked through the last few trees, stepping onto the loose scree. The clearing opened before her like a new sky, and there stood the stranger, not two meters away, his profile as perfect as a young Greek god's.

As she was reminding herself how she hated clichés, she tripped over a stump and fell flat at his feet. Blushing like a sunset, she struggled to stand up, but the young man, who turned out to be Andreas Niederhauser, bent quickly to help her. Grimacing, she assured him she was fine, but he lifted her, nonetheless, and brushed the rock dust from her anorak. As she tried to bear weight on her injured foot, she couldn't help gasping. Without so much as a by-your-leave, Andreas picked her up and ported her over to a large rock. Ignoring her small protests, he untied her hiking boot, pulled off her woollen sock, and inspected her ankle, already purpling and swollen. His kind gray eyes mesmerized her when he smiled, said, "Stay put," and strode swiftly away. In moments he was back and wrapping her ankle with a tensor bandage from his well-stocked rucksack. And in his charming way, Andreas had insisted that she lean on him, all the way down to the Alpenblick bus stop.

As satisfying as the meal was, as warm as the once-familiar atmosphere made her feel, the hours flew by, and before Ursula knew it, Andreas had passed his credit card over to pay their bill and was chatting with the server. When they were finished, she stood reluctantly and walked with Andreas to retrieve their coats from the coat check. Smiling, he thanked the girl and put a generous tip into the jar, but the young woman brought the wrong coats, and he had to politely point out the correct hangers. So even the young couldn't always remember, Ursula told herself. At last, she arrived with their things, and Andreas smoothed away the mistake, full of thanks, as he held Ursula's jacket for her and then slipped on his own. They went through the door arm in arm, smiling as they stepped into the cold February night.

# 5

Outside, it was wet and dark, and Andreas soon realized there was no way to prolong the gracious mood that had enveloped them inside the restaurant. The snow was falling thick and heavy, and the enjoyment of the evening vanished in the wind as they hurried to the truck. The roads were slushy and slippery, and once they reached the highway, conditions were worse. He'd have to concentrate on driving, keep his attention focused. The bank of clouds blowing in from the west must have brought this snow; he'd seen them when they'd left the hospital, but it hadn't occurred to him to worry, not when celebrating Ursula's clean bill of health had seemed so important. They'd needed a way to mark their rare shared moment of relief, at last to start making some new memories, ones they could cherish.

He was deep in concentration when Ursula barked, "Andreas! You're almost over the yellow line—"

She was exaggerating, of course—she was always such a cautious driver—but he nosed the truck further into the middle of their lane. He slowed down a bit, drove even more carefully. If they were stopped by police, there would be the wine to account for, although he didn't think he was over the legal limit. He kept his eyes on the road.

Ursula was saying something, but her tone had changed completely. She was complaining about her students' poor grades on their last exam. What on God's earth made her think he would want to talk about that now? Did she think she could fool him, after all these years? She hated to be wrong, he knew that, and this afternoon must have been pure humiliation for her. She was upset with the doctor, he supposed. She wasn't one to give in gracefully, not when she must feel like a fool after all these months of being so sure she was about to lose her marbles. But seriously, he asked himself, how in the world could she even have thought that? After teaching high school for thirty-five years, her mind was still formidable, as deadly as a Gorgon. That was what had drawn him to her after their trek down the mountain—her remarkable intelligence and her piercing sense of humour.

His mother had seen it, all those years ago, when he took her home to meet his family. She warned him later, the night he had called to tell her they were engaged: Ursula's strength would be her weakness, she said. It was proba- bly her high-flying family's fault, but the reason made no difference. The unattainable standards she set for herself, those exhausting aspirations, would prevent his little bride from ever allowing herself, or him, any slack, any reprieve whatsoever. At the time, Andreas had dismissed his moth- er's fears, certain that he could never resent a girl who was oh-so-sharp *and* oh-so-sweet. Yet lately he had come to see that, as usual, his mother had been right. She had said that Ursula would both crave and resist attention. Well, atten- tion he could provide. He reached over to squeeze her hand. She pulled it away, saying, "Andreas! Hands on the wheel."

No slack whatsoever.

But nothing was going to spoil this sense of relief. Sure, he had been worried, not that he could admit that to Ursula. Trying to be supportive, he had half-jokingly asked the doctor, "Don't all women lose their memories during menopause?" It was risky, bringing up the change. He was a little surprised that Ursula hadn't flinched; even as the words slipped out, he knew she would surely see his question as just another dig where he wanted to "mansplain" her problems away, as she always said these days. But the neurologist had simply assured them that Ursula's memory was normal.

That part had been a little worrisome. His wife's memory had always been phenomenal, nothing normal about it. But it was clear that the doctor meant she was fine, normal for her age and profession. If there had been any trouble at school, surely she would have complained about it. Andreas glanced over at her. She was staring straight ahead, eyes apparently fixed on the road. She was thinking something peculiar, he was sure of it; he just couldn't say what.

Just then an SUV zoomed by, passing them. Its strange plate gleamed in his headlights: *Wild, wonderful West Virginia.* Why would anyone from so far south drive up here at this time of year? It inevitably snowed more in February than it did for the entire remainder of the winter. "Now that's crazy," he said.

"What?" She turned to stare at him. "Who's crazy?"

"It's nothing, Sweetheart. The vehicle that just flew past us. I was wondering what they're doing, driving up here, vacationing in central Saskatchewan in the middle of winter, of all times?" He paused briefly. "Speaking of vacations, that wouldn't be a bad idea, not at all. What do you say? It would do us good to get away. We can go to Corfu or Crete, then on to Basel. I haven't been home in years. We could see the family."

A vacation abroad should excite her. They could visit all their old haunts, live like civilised people, savour their favourite delicacies. The meal tonight had reminded him of how much he missed real food. These days, Ursula was always worn out when she came home from work. She'd given up cooking proper meals most weeknights, just threw together simple stuff, open-faced sandwiches or oven-baked meat, dry and tough. He knew better than to say anything. It was either her food or fast food, and the doctor had said that the so-called preservatives in fast food were deadly, would kill you more quickly than smoking. But there was nothing enjoyable about desiccated pork chops with baked fries and microwaved green beans from a can. He could almost taste the treats his mother always made, the food that Ursula used to cook when Mia lived at home, rich with cream and butter and cheese, the European-style bread that she had done her best to imitate with Canadian flour. Yes, she always did her best, but these days, she took no time to cook. And time was the secret for real food—time, and love, and plenty of care in sampling. Maybe he could pitch in, start making some of the meals, now that Mia would be coming home. That would please Ursula. And Mia could take care of the home place while they were away. They wouldn't even need to rent a car in Europe; they could sit back on the train and watch the scenery, take a real vacation for once. He could feel his face relaxing into a smile, just thinking about it.

"You haven't heard a word I said!" he heard her say harshly.

A semi-trailer passed them just then, spraying the windshield with slush. Andreas flicked the wipers on to clear the windshield. He couldn't see a thing. There was no washer fluid left. All of his plans disappeared in a flash. He was tired and frustrated, but as usual, he kept it to himself. Was he really going to have to stop on the side of the road in this bloody storm? That was the way people got killed. He blamed her. She had his truck yesterday while her vehicle was having its brakes repaired. She could never stand the smallest speck of dirt on the windshield; she must have used up all the fluid. He held his tongue, refusing to say anything that she could interpret as criticism. There was nothing to be gained by tossing gasoline on a fire.

He pulled over onto the shoulder of the highway and stopped, forcing himself to act calmly and do what needed to be done. He pulled the interior latch to unlock the hood. Pushed the truck door open into the wind. Got out and opened the muddy crew cab door, reached in, and retrieved the jug of washer fluid. At least there was no one coming. He shook his head silently. Christ, he needed a vacation. But unless he could convince Ursula to take some time off, she would be teaching until the blessed end of June. How was he ever going to last?

Well, he thought, maybe Mia could persuade Ursula that they needed a vacation. The three of them used to be so close. And Mia still called her mother, though these days Ursula was always up to her eyes in work or reading and didn't have time. Lately Andreas was often alone, working from home, when Mia phoned. He cursed his luck for forgetting to tell Ursula about Mia's call yesterday.

Mia had been so embarrassed, had assured him she would only stay for a few weeks, maybe a couple of months, just until she could find a new job. With the recession in the oil patch, everything was drying up in Calgary. The pipeline to the West Coast that the Feds were promising to build, if it could be built, might bring some of the work back, but with BC fighting it and the Indigenous vote split, the chances didn't look good. The prairies were never going to be the land of opportunity for a young journalist. And in cities where the jobs were, like Vancouver or Toronto, rent was unbelievably expensive. Even those new micro units with their fold-away kitchens and bathrooms, beds jammed into living rooms, whole flats smaller than a tiny house, were still too expensive. He wished he had looked into the market before Mia had started her master's: what were they thinking, letting her go so far into debt?

He finished his task and got back into the truck, and soon they were underway again. They caught up to the idiot who had been in such a hurry to pass, now going 70 km an hour. Andreas slowed down and backed off. That was what he always had to do, just like with the trouble with his teaching gigs lately: let all the world go its own bloody way. At least Mia had always had a real talent for happiness. Despite all the difficulties she faced, she didn't see the world as bleak. It would be nice to have someone around who could be counted on to be cheerful.

# 6

"What a clusterfuck," Mia muttered as she looked around the little apartment, remembering how happy she'd been priming the crayon-dingy off-white walls and painting them a fresh light aqua, the trim a bright crisp white. Her black-and-white photos, her images of the architecture she'd loved in all the cities she had lived in, looked amazing against the old red-brick feature wall, the space that had drawn her eye from the first moment she had seen the place. Just thinking of the plans she'd had for her life here made her sad all over again. Shaking her head, she lifted the frames down one by one, carefully leaning the stack against the doorway to bubble-wrap later.

She shook her head, muttering. Just what she needed: one more mess to clear up. She'd been trying as hard as she could for as long as she could remember, but for all her efforts, Calgary had turned out to be no more than a pit stop. And the trail she had been praying was her road to success was leading her right back to— Christ. She missed city life already.

At first, she'd thought maybe she was just stuck in some script, replaying the hard luck her parents had had. But life was always hard for immigrants, and even Dad and Mamme had found permanent positions eventually. Things were different for millennials. For the past ten years, she might as well have been playing whack-a-mole, only with jobs. She'd criss-crossed the country, landing stints here or there on radio in small towns while trying to break into television, but no project could be more hopeless than that. The pay for radio was terrible. She'd been grateful for contract work, magazines and newspapers, making the best of any experience she could find, anything to build her skills and flesh out her résumé. But as the Internet expanded, the market changed, and now every idiot with a smartphone thought they were a journalist, thank you very much, YouTube. Any rando could make a TedTalk or a Tik Tok or some form of faux-show. Reporters were going the way of the polar bears. It didn't matter how well you could hunt; when the climate changed, you were fucked before you ever got started. Time to retreat to the familial ice floe, whatever good that would do. One thing she did know: you could only hang out with your parents for so long before they'd drive you certifiably insane or make you as old and eccentric as they were.

Calgary had been alright; it wasn't Vancouver, but there had been people to meet, things to do or see, everything you could want. And all the walking she'd done had been better than hiring a personal trainer. She was pretty buff, if she did say so herself. Now *that* would hardly last back home. God. The food they ate, the cream and butter and cheese and potatoes. The rich Swiss fare bastardized with the worst excesses the prairies produced. Every meal organized around some huge chunk of good old Saskatchewan beef. Ugh. You'd think her parents were human cats, obligatory carnivores.

She walked over to the stack of boxes, reading the red felt-pen inscriptions; they hadn't even been there long enough to fade. *Mixing bowls, salad bowl, utensils.* She sorted through the pile, chose the ones she wanted to pack next, and carried them through to the kitchen. There she looked around and sighed. This was going to take forever, even if she did know what would fit in every box. Thank God she'd kept them this time. She must have known things wouldn't work out, even though she had never felt so sure, so safe, as when she landed the contract here.

That kind of optimism was always swiftly punished.

Well, as Mamme always said, *three moves are as good as a fire.* And at least her possessions had been edited, she thought wryly. She fastened her blonde hair back with an elastic and ran her hand along the spines of the books she had kept. One caught her eye: *Franklin's Lost Ship: The Discovery of the H.M.S. Erebus.* That was a book she was never going to part with; she'd dreamed of going up North, working her way into the Franklin story, ever since she was in grade school. She and Ryan Thomson were always plotting, scheming about how they would go and find his ancestor's bones, solve the mystery of the lost ships. But she'd been working every angle down here, unable to do more than cover gallery openings and live theatre at a time when most Calgarians were worrying about their jobs, not the broadening effects of culture.

She'd done everything she could to get ahead.

What the profs didn't tell you, even after all the mind-numbing summer jobs, not even when they knew you'd taken out six years of student loans, was that your timing sucked. She and all her classmates had been forced to watch as newspapers and radio stations folded and the jobs they'd been assured they'd find dried up like waterholes in the Godforsaken Kalahari, all their high-flying dreams scattered like sand.

# 7

"What are you thinking about?" Ursula asked as they got ready for bed.

Andreas continued undressing but did not respond. She knew he had heard her, and suddenly she felt furious. This silence, the endless mystery she'd once found so alluring, was rudeness, pure and simple. He could stop this charade. He had been so calm since the visit to the doctor. As usual, he was repressing his fears, acting as if there was nothing wrong. Yes, the task ahead of them was unpleasant, but now that they both knew for sure that she was ill, they had plans to make. They had to deal with the dementia, and better sooner than later. Andreas stood studying his reflection in the mirror, his belly sucked in, looking almost as attractive as when they first married. She shook herself. If he thought she was going to roll over and let him make all her decisions, he could think again. She plumped her pillow and lay down, her back squarely to his side of the bed.

For a moment she felt tears rise but, as always, nothing came of it. She was too bewildered even to weep. She was certainly not going to give up, not while she still had the wits to help him prepare. She knew she had to calm herself. Dinner, the restaurant, all of it had made her feel like old times—but now, when she needed him most of all, where *was* that man who had held her hand and gazed lovingly into her eyes not three hours ago?

A thought came to her. Maybe it was the food that had helped him remember that tenderness, the intimacy they knew so well when they were young. She felt better immediately. After all these years, if she couldn't whip up a dinner to get his attention, she would be a monkey's uncle. Conjuring one menu after another, at last she fell into a deep sleep.

At 3:00 a.m., Ursula woke suddenly, her mind as sharp and agitated as a mouse facing a ferret. She was dreaming about real events again, but this was no premonition: it had already happened, a week ago yesterday.

*Noreen had asked where the Science Fair entries would be stored this year, and Ursula replied, without thinking, "Plenty of time to figure that out. It's not until February."*

*The odd look on the young secretary's face made her feel like a stranger. Noreen paused a long moment, her face full of something like pity or fear as she said, slowly, "But this is February."*

*Time spun out, elongated, stretched like some enormous twanging rubber band. Ursula was all alone in that smooth white room, free of ideas or cues or words of any kind. She was not even worried, not at first; she only felt curious, as if she were an observer. There were no images or connections to help her make sense of or evaluate whether what Noreen had said could possibly be true.*

*Slowly a question formed. What month was it? she wondered, with just the slightest sense of urgency. She could see the large bank of classroom windows before her. She looked down at the football field below. There was only half a foot of snow. It was November. Yes. It must be. November.*

*Ursula smiled then, saying, "Whew! For a minute, you scared me, Noreen." She felt relieved, absolutely confident. "It's still months away."*

*There had been no smile in return. Noreen had hesitated, her face incredulous. It was a look Ursula recognized; she had seen it all too often lately on Andreas's face. But while he was always certain Ursula just wasn't paying attention, Noreen clearly thought she was dealing with someone who was off her rocker, senile.*

*"Ursula. It's February. February 2nd, Groundhog Day. You couldn't forget that?" She shook her head, then stared down into Ursula's eyes. "Wee Willie called for an early spring this morning."*

*Wee Willie? Oh, the wretched new groundhog. Ursula felt suddenly hyper-aware; she needed to play along if she wanted to avoid a scene. After only the slightest pause, she said easily, "Of course, I know that." Some part of her grateful that she was getting good at this type of thing. Lying was a new skill for her. She had always been proud of her directness, her honesty, but she was learning to distract people from her mistakes. "Who could forget the dizzying heights of North American meteorological prognostication?" she laughed, patting Noreen on the shoulder, but inside she was terrified. It couldn't be February: it was November.*

Only it wasn't.

Ursula lay there and remembered mistake after mistake she'd made all day after that. She forgot to collect the parental slips for the field trip until Lacey Stewart came up to turn hers in, and then, even after Ursula had gathered the rest, she misplaced them. They simply vanished amidst the piles of papers on her workbench. She wrote the wrong homework assignment on the board. She forgot to administer the unit quiz, and then, fifteen minutes before class ended, when the students reminded her, she set them to work on it, but forgot to take in their papers when the bell rang. It was hopeless, she was hopeless. The more she tried to concentrate, the more distracted she became.

She tried to argue it away. The research she'd done indicated that she was only suffering from Mild Cognitive Impairment, not full-blown dementia. There were things she could do to fend off the decline. She worked her mind hard, every single day. She had revamped all her lesson plans. For the past few years, she'd been writing her book, too; it was slow going, but her research kept her mind agile. She still spoke three languages fluently. She didn't have Alzheimer's. She couldn't. Still, the most terrifying thing, the fact that no one seemed capable of understanding, was that she never knew when or why her mind would go blank.

And then she remembered what had happened that morning.

A herd of moose had been there in the centre of the racetrack when she'd arrived at school that day. No wonder she'd forgotten what month it was—the enormous beasts had thrown her off kilter. It was the only thing that made sense. Moose travelled most in November, their rutting season. She spotted them first thing as she pulled into the teachers' parking lot. She saw only two at first, then three more a little further away. Five shaggy-dark great beasts, more like a dream than reality. For a moment her mind had refused to define what she saw; at first, she'd thought that the horses were out again.

Joe Reichert, the old farmer who used to live on the outskirts of town, never bothered to mend his rail fence; it was not unusual to see one or two half-wild horses grazing on the football field or out munching on the front lawn. Even after he sold the place and moved to Alberta, the new owners were no better. But it had only taken a second to realize that these were no horses. She was still haunted by the huge heads lifting as she'd driven by. The bull's gigantic rack, his long glance at her, so casual and unhurried. No need to demonstrate *his* dominance. The cows surveyed Ursula with quiet indifference and found her harmless. Now that was something she could hope for: let her forgetting be harmless.

She was suddenly aware of Andreas, snoring beside her. Careful not to waken him, she gently pulled a section of the duvet free, swaddled herself like a caterpillar in a leaf, and drifted off to sleep.

The next evening, they were seated at the dining room table, the setting sun streaming in through the wall of glass in the living room. Ursula fidgeted and ate very little. Finally, she took her napkin off her lap and set it beside her plate, turning to face Andreas directly.

She wanted to approach him in the old language, hoping that would help her reach the part he kept so proudly locked away. His family didn't believe in illness, didn't understand what it was like to lose a loved one, let alone part of yourself. She would spell out her feelings; for once he would have to understand. Her Baseldytsch was still good, the cadence and intonation robust and natural, even after nearly forty years in Canada. For that, she thanked Babbe, who had made time to call her every single day. Even when he was hardly well enough to speak, he always made time to listen.

As relaxed and nonchalant as Andreas had been yesterday after the appointment, even he must realize that they had every reason in the world to be worried now. Empathy was not his strong suit—she'd always known that—but even sympathy would do. She had cooked one of his favourite meals, yet when the time came to talk, she couldn't think of where to begin. She watched helplessly as the man who was supposed to share her heart sliced efficiently into his veal cutlet and swirled his fork-skewered Brussels sprouts in the special nutmeg sauce, the one she'd made tonight to remind him that she cared about him.

She would start slowly, with small talk. She was trying to think of something to say when there was a loud ping. He pulled out his phone, texted the mysterious intruder, and put the device back into his pocket. She braced herself and smiled as warmly as she could. "So, how are things going at the Distance Education Unit? Did you get your contract for the spring online courses yet?"

Andreas stopped chewing. He looked at her for a second, then lowered his eyes back to his plate and said, "Why do you ask?" He speared another Brussels sprout and lifted his fork to his mouth.

"Oh, no reason. It's been a long time since you've talked about your work, that's all."

He said nothing. That was normal—he was chewing vigorously—but Ursula wondered if he was eating with such conviction just to keep her at bay.

Unwilling to give up, she asked, "How is the veal? That sauce is thicker than usual, don't you think?"

He didn't reply.

"Andreas?" she tried again.

At last he said, "Hmm?"

"The sauce? Is it too thick?"

He speared another Brussels sprout, lifted it to his mouth, chewed appraisingly, and swallowed. His eyes met hers for a moment as he said, "No, it's fine."

He helped himself to another piece of veal, his mind clearly anywhere else but with her. She knew her fears were not the sort he would ever want to dwell on. On the other hand, she had to hand it to him. He was conveying his point, his lack of emotional support, as effectively as anyone could, in the way that he always did, without having to say what he thought. She felt more alone than ever.

Without another word, she rose, carried her dishes into the kitchen, and loaded them into the dishwasher. When she came back to the table, he smiled, stood up, thanked her, squeezed her shoulder, and went to sit down with his tablet in his easy chair in the living room.

He turned on the TV and flipped channels, watching the news, *Ice Pilots*, and some documentary, all at the same time. Numbly, she carried his plate and the rest of the dishes out to the kitchen. By the time she was through cleaning up, he was engrossed in an old Arnold Schwarzenegger movie. He didn't even bother to call goodnight as she walked through the living room and went up the stairs to their bedroom.

The rest of the week passed in a blur, but when the alarm went off at 8:00 a.m. on Saturday, she knew what she'd see: Andreas had already left. He'd been up before dawn, doing whatever he did these days. After her usual morning yoga routine, Ursula dressed quickly in a pair of jeans and a long-sleeved work shirt and went downstairs to fix herself a cappuccino. She was leaning against the counter, eating her granola, when the doorbell rang. It was a man in a uniform, carrying boxes.

Half an hour later she was out on the front deck, catching her breath. She stood with her left hand flat on the doorframe, her right hand resting on top of the last three boxes that the UPS van had dropped off. From the ones she had already opened downstairs, she knew immediately that the contents wouldn't fit their décor. They were good quality, of course, but antiques were not their style; Andreas was so fastidious about clutter, so fond of his precious mid-century chic. But she couldn't just donate her father's last things to the thrift shop. Her sister Kathrin had been kind to hold onto them for as long as she had. Ursula had another reason not to go through them yet; she knew that every reminder would intensify her pain. There had been so much to dispose of: dishes, furniture, towels, knickknacks, all things his three children, approaching old age themselves, didn't need. None of the grandchildren needed anything either; they each had their own households already. Thank goodness Babbe had appointed Norbert the executor. She was glad he had not chosen her, the eldest—the eldest living child. No. She was not going to think of that now; it was too distressing. Norbert was a businessman, and although he had about as much imagination as a snowball in January, patience, honesty, and predictability were qualities that stood him in good stead with the Swiss legal system.

For the moment, Babbe's things would be safe in the spare room, out of the way in the basement. She wasn't hiding them; she was simply not ready to think about them yet. When she had carried down the last of the boxes, she stacked them tidily, climbed the stairs, and stopped to catch her breath. She had to blink as she ascended the dark stairwell, the morning sun sloping into the kitchen. It had been such a dark winter. But before she had time to admire the rare sight that Andreas had taken to calling "that bright orb in the sky," she felt a sharp pain like an ice pick, again and again, on the top left side of her head.

Ursula reached up and pressed her fingers to the sore spot, rubbed back and forth; pianissimo and forte, it made no difference. Pianist's hands, her mother called them, pianist's hands and a temperament to match. No. She must stop. No good ever came from arguing with the dead. She moved her hands to the back of her neck, massaged her shoulders.

Mechanically, she emptied the dishwasher and refilled it, tidying the counters and sinks. As she cleaned, she looked out at the uninspiring black-capped chickadees and various types of sparrows hopping around on the ground below the bird feeder, shades of brown and white—so unlike the ones she had loved as a child, all those years ago in Basel. That first winter, when she realized that common birds, unremarkable birds, were all they'd likely attract in Humboldt, she'd bought a book, looked up the different species, taught herself to see their subtle marks and their shading. Dimly she remembered that there were even some birds that forgot in order to remember. Goldfinches? American goldfinches, that was it. To remember where they'd cached their seeds for winter, goldfinches had to purge their mating tune each fall and relearn it every spring.

Why couldn't she free up some much-needed brain space? Or maybe she already had; her mating call seemed to have been still for a long time, as was Andreas's. She had been startled to feel that longing for him in the doctor's office, and again later that night, at the restaurant. But the urges had passed quickly enough. She looked out at the clear plastic feeder suspended from its tall wooden post. Squirrel-proof, allegedly. So much for the fancy bag of seed, its pictures of red cardinals and blue jays and other colourful birds. Did anything ever turn out as promised?

Andreas was no doubt home now, upstairs in his office, his attention riveted to his iPad or his computer. Why did he always think that anything new must be better? After all these years, he was still a mystery to her, now more than ever. Most of the time she had no idea what was going on in that head of his. He could be a spy, a philanderer. Just for a moment she felt that odd jolt of curiosity again. Where *did* he go in the mornings? Was this some new adaptation to his insomnia? Or was he up to something—and if so, with whom? She trusted him, of course, but he was so darned friendly with strangers, such a bloody Prince Charming. He had seemed distracted for weeks, and now, with her dementia diagnosed, why wouldn't he feel entitled to seek comfort in the arms of some alluring young colleague, someone who could be his intellectual equal?

Through the window, she could see their cat Adam slinking under the trees near the post, back and forth, forth and back, checking out all the angles, preparing to launch himself at the feeder. He tried. Repeatedly. He failed. Predictably. At last, he hunkered down beneath a tall blue spruce, thrashed his tail a bit, then simply skulked away. The unattainable birds lit peacefully and fed. Even the damned cat was a realist. Why work yourself up about what could not be changed?

She was so tired of thinking, thinking, thinking—she couldn't stop imagining the long decline to come; she could see it, like some especially vivid video loop. She rubbed the spot on her head, but that only intensified the pain. Only an hour had passed since she'd finished her morning yoga. She tried so hard just to quiet her monkey mind, squirrel brain, whatever you wanted to call it, but she could not. Her mind always went back to her problems.

And yet, after all the mix-ups, all the confusion she felt, everything in the doctor's office, still she knew she had to prove Dr. Paul wrong. If she just tried harder, somehow she would remember not to forget. She couldn't have dementia. True, she didn't remember his exact words, but he had recommended she retire, pronto, and join that self-help group. And if he was right, no one would believe it wasn't her fault; the gossips in coffee row would surmise that she was playing sick on purpose, trying to recapture her wandering husband's attention. You could be sure that they knew where Andreas was going every morning.

Her hands moved to her neck and she massaged the taut muscles forcefully, as hard as she could. She rotated each shoulder, desperate to relax, to break the force of the migraine. She reached into the kitchen cabinet for a glass and her pill bottle, frowned at the noise overhead. Andreas was pacing again. He often walked around in his study, said it helped him think. She filled her glass with water and swallowed the two tablets in a single gulp.

He was irritated about something, probably something that had nothing to do with her, but that was the mystery; he was a master of the opaque. Last night, making one last-ditch effort to draw him into conversation, she'd made him a cappuccino and delivered it to him as he flipped channels. He'd taken it happily enough, smiling into her eyes with that heart-stopping look of his. Then, after only a sip, he had winced, got up, and poured the whole cup down the drain, smiling as if he still expected to charm her breath away. So now her coffee wasn't good enough for him? For a moment she felt as though she couldn't breathe, but it had nothing to do with romance. She held her tongue. She kept the peace.

Whatever mystery Andreas was hiding, for the medication to take effect she needed to lie down, she needed darkness, and she needed it now. She set her glass in the dishwasher, headed through the living room, and slipped upstairs to her bed.

# 8

Andreas stood at the living room window, watching the road out front. Mia's moving day at last: she would be here at any moment. Within minutes the U-Haul wheeled onto their street. As he went to the entrance to pull the pins from the hinges and lean the door against the wall, he called out to alert the high school students Ursula had recruited to help unload the truck. They were gathered around the dining-room table, drinking coffee, munching their way through the tray of doughnuts he'd bought at the bakery. As usual, Ursula was rushing around, fussing, making sure no one freed the yowling cat from the bedroom where she had him corralled.

Andreas went back to the door, watching Mia back up the driveway. As he waited, he spotted a hapless robin who had decided not to go south for the winter, sitting there all puffed up and sunning herself on a waving limb, ragged and restless in the lone Schubert chokecherry tree on the front lawn. He looked curiously at the tree itself: it had buds—had had them since fall, trees always did—but these were different somehow, too plump for February. He watched his daughter just miss the gatepost and muttered, "Mia. Don't drive like a girl. Pay attention."

He looked around, glad no one had heard him. There was no point in upsetting Ursula. And finally Mia was here, really here, safe and sound. It was going to be a bit of a challenge. She was going to need an adjustment period, certainly, being back in the old town, and he was not so naïve as to imagine everything would be simple with three adults sharing a house. His father always said that the Chinese symbol for war was two women living under the same roof. But Ursula loved her daughter, he knew she did, and the extra help around the house would be great for her. He thought about all the things they could do again, picnic excursions and weekend trips to the lake and late nights reminiscing around the campfire.

And Mia could be counted on to share his views; she knew—as Ursula once had—how important it was to maintain standards. No one in Humboldt had anything quite like their yard. They had made it a showpiece, the shrubs and flowers elegant, the orchard a thing to be proud of, even the shade lush with fashionable hostas and periwinkle. Ursula had traded the good old Humboldt clay beneath their garden to the local potter, who had let them pick out a fine set of dishes. But in the past year or so, Ursula had lost interest in gardening, as she had in so many other necessary elements of life: cooking and sex and housecleaning. She'd begun to favour that natural look that Canadians went for, thatches of tall Japanese irises and bland yellow daylilies or smelly Shasta daisies. She abandoned their rose garden, claiming the winters were too cold. She left clumps of delphiniums without dividing them or digging out ones that didn't thrive, and she let the tall stems dry instead of pruning them back for a second flourish. The casual observer might not see how the whole place had gone to seed, but that was precisely the shame of it—once upon a time, everything Ursula did had to be perfect.

She needed a project to focus on; that was Ursula's trouble. Mia would surely help motivate her mother, make things nice again. They would bring in new plants, new roses, hardy ones that would thrive in the sun on the south side of the house. And where the grass was thin and bedraggled beneath the now-mature trees, they could plant groundcovers and feathery bright astilbes. They would buy black cast-iron planters and fill them with luminous waxy red or pink begonias and lime-coloured vines and tall spikes. Setting the place to rights again would relieve Ursula's hypochondria. Order and routine calmed the mind and healed the body. And though he did not want to dwell on the possibility, straightening things up would be good for resale if events unfolded at the university in the way he feared they just might.

# 9

Mia finished stacking the last of her heavy boxes in the garage and went through the side door to see what her parents were up to. As she entered the hallway, she called, "Mamme? Dad? Where are you?" It was nearly seven o'clock. She was starving. Surely supper would be ready before long.

She was not disappointed. The familiar delicious odours spoke to her immediately, long before she reached the dining room. Mamme had gone all out. After the students had left and while Mia was arranging her boxes, her mother must have cleared off the dining-room table and set up the raclette grill. She could hear the food sizzling, could smell the rich mushrooms browning, the spicy peppers and onions and asparagus, the soft cheese bubbling in the trays below. Ah, Mamme. She always did things right.

But it was her father's voice that answered from the kitchen. "Go and see if anything needs turning, please, Sweetheart." She went through to the dining room and found the raclette grill cooking away in the centre of the table, which was set with wine glasses and the family's best plates. Their places were marked by the spring green linen napkins she'd made all those years ago for Home Ec class, each one neatly ironed and folded, their tidy dark hand-embroidered initials beneath the forks to designate who would sit where. The wine stood waiting: pinot gris, her mother's favourite. Everything was ready.

When she returned to the kitchen her father was looking odd yet somehow strangely determined, wearing a striped red-and-white apron and pulling a rack out of the oven with thick silicone mitts. He poked a small skewer into one of the foil-wrapped potatoes. Satisfied, he turned the heat off, pushed the rack back in, and shut the oven door.

"But where's Mamme?" she asked. "And when did you become so domestic?"

"Hey! Your father is a liberated man," he smiled, taking off his oven mitts and waving them at her with his right hand. "Would your mother tolerate anything else? Why don't you go and call her? She's finishing some marking upstairs in her study."

Mia nodded and set off across the house. As she passed through the open living room, she admired the new black Scandi woodstove in the centre of the far wall. So little else had changed. The familiar furniture suited the house, though it hadn't been rearranged since her childhood.

When she reached the bottom of the stairs, she called, "Mamme? Supper's ready. Dad sent me to call you."

No reply. She tried again. "Mamme?"

There wasn't a sound from upstairs.

Mia's legs ached from all the bending and lifting she'd done these last few days. With only her next-door neighbour's help with the bed and the sofa, she had loaded the truck herself, carried her entire household down the stairs from her apartment on the third floor last night, and this morning she had been out on the road by six a.m. for the eight-hour drive.

She walked stiffly up the stairs at first but sped up as her muscles warmed. When she reached the top landing, she turned to the right, where the door to her mother's study was ajar. She could see Mamme leaning over her marking, but something was odd. She was talking to someone.

"No, I can't wait, not with something like this." She sounded so stern. Mia felt sorry for the student she knew must be on the other end of the line. She pushed the door open wider, and saw her mother from the back, seated at the desk. Her head propped up on one elbow, she had her right hand at her ear. She seemed to be listening, but there was no phone in sight. And Mamme, with her scorn for new technology, was the last person Mia could picture using a wireless headset.

Mia didn't know what to do. Why would she be talking to herself? Did Dad know she did that? When she had thought her mother was on the phone, she had intended to catch her eye, gesture for her to come, pretend to fork food into her mouth from an imaginary plate on her palm. Should she interrupt her? Introduce herself to her mother's invisible friend?

Instead, she cleared her throat, and Mamme startled, sitting up straight and swivelling her desk chair around. She seemed confused and turned away again immediately, putting her hand back to the side of her face as she said quietly, "That's for sure."

Mia's heart constricted. She ached to see her mother like that. She had been sure Dad was exaggerating the strangeness of Mamme's recent behaviour. He didn't believe in illness. If she'd had malaria, for God's sake, he still wouldn't have believed she was sick. No one could deny that this was odd, even for Mamme.

Mia decided to act as normal as possible. "Come downstairs, Mamme. Dad has supper almost ready. Raclette! You can finish your marking later—"

Her mother said, "Noon would work."

What in the world did that mean, *noon*? Work for what? But Mia was even more surprised when her mother stood and obediently followed her out to the landing. Had she actually abandoned an exam booklet in the middle of marking? Mia stopped and wrapped both arms around her mother's shoulders. She could feel how tense Mamme was, how rigidly she was holding herself. Mia hugged harder, and, after a split second, Mamme wrapped her left arm around her daughter's waist and squeezed back firmly.

"Alright, Mia," she said, releasing herself. "Thank you. The cheese must be melted by now—we'd better get to the table before your father gets cross again."

*Cross? Again?* Mia wondered but said nothing. What on earth was wrong with Mamme?

# 10

When the two women walked into the dining room, arm in arm, Ursula saw that Andreas was pouring her favourite wine, not the fendant du Valais he favoured. She smiled. *So he must still care,* she thought. A voice inside corrected her: *He must still care about giving the impression that he cares.*

Where had that come from? Ursula shook her head. He was making an effort, after all. Leaving Mia with Andreas to fuss with cooking the vegetables and the mushrooms on the little grill, she went to the kitchen to fetch the Kirsch and the liqueur glasses.

When she was safely away from their oh-so-watchful eyes, she pulled her iPhone and Bluetooth earpiece from her pocket and slipped them safely into her purse. At least Mia hadn't guessed what she'd been doing. And now that Kathy had made her an appointment with the new holistic doctor, she could try to relax tonight. Andreas always thought teaching school was so much easier than teaching university. He'd wax poetic about the time off, the short days. She used to correct him, but it no longer seemed worth the effort. No wonder she was confused; she was exhausted.

She opened the refrigerator and checked the crispers to make sure that he had brought out all the vegetables she'd bought for the occasion. Andreas was quite a snob about raclette, a purist. He didn't care for peppers or asparagus, just cheese and potatoes and plenty of wine. Ursula opened the wall oven, quickly withdrew three large potatoes, and put them into a stoneware bowl, popping the rack back in to keep the rest hot until needed. Setting the bowl down on the counter, she opened the liquor cupboard and took out the liqueur and three small glasses. She needed to hurry: the vegetables would be mush if they were overdone, and the cheese would burn or turn dry and tough.

She could hear Mia and Andreas bantering loudly about sports. Both Andreas and Mia were excellent skaters, but only boys had been allowed to join the local hockey team when Mia was young. She had had to be content with figure skating; that was what girls did then, at least in Humboldt. Ursula could hardly wait to tell her what she'd heard yesterday.

"The curling league is looking for new members. It's a perfect opportunity to connect—well, reconnect—with the community."

Mia said nothing as she passed her father some more cheese.

Fearing that her excellent idea was not being well received, Ursula couldn't stop herself from adding, "Maybe you'll meet somebody."

At that, Mia grimaced and said, "I'm sure I'll meet *somebody*, Mamme. Probably a lot of somebodies."

Ursula wished she had held her tongue; her idea had come out wrong. She hadn't meant it as a reproach; when would Mia have found time to build a relationship? And Ursula certainly had not meant that she needed a man to define herself. What an idiotic thing to imply. But now that Mia was stuck up here again, they had to make the best of it. All of her classmates had married by twenty-four or -five. They each had a string of kids. Most had divorced or moved away, or both. What could be worse for a girl who wanted to live in New York or Vancouver than spending her thirties as a nursemaid in a one-horse town, watching her increasingly demanding, increasingly senile mother all the time, trying to make sure she didn't wander away or burn the house down while making a cup of tea? With Andreas's love of technology, they would likely snap a GPS bracelet on her and keep her in lockdown, until finally she'd be so far gone she would only be able to sit in a chair all day, needing someone to clean her after they took her to the toilet—or, Ursula cringed, changed her diapers. It was too much to bear. And it would be so much worse for Mia.

As if he could hear her thoughts, Andreas rose silently and went to the kitchen. Ursula wondered what he was doing, but he simply came back and passed around second potatoes. Ursula handed the heavy bowl to Mia, who took one, peeled the foil back, and cut it open. Taking a little tray out from under the grill, she spooned the soft cheese over the potato and added the juicy mushrooms and peppers and asparagus spears. Andreas refilled the pans with more cheese and slid them back under the grill.

Ursula reached for her wine glass and took a healthy swallow. "You have to understand, Mia. We want you to find something to do up here, something fun. The last thing we want is to hold you back. We know how lonely Humboldt can be." She took a long drink. Mia said nothing. Ursula tried to will herself to stop talking.

Andreas, now loading the grill with more veggies, appeared not to notice how awkwardly Ursula was acting, but he did object, laughing, "Hey! Speak for yourself," as he rested his hand on her forearm. "Just because we're not as young as we once were doesn't mean we'll hold her back. We're cool, we're happening, aren't we?" He adjusted his retro glasses and struck a pose, stroking a long imaginary hipster beard and fitting on an invisible toque. He pretended to hold a roach between two fingers and puffed.

Mia and Ursula couldn't stop themselves from laughing at this performance.

"Well. As my father always said, *life sends us the troubles we most need and least expect.* And we can hope. Though I hope you don't start smoking dope," Ursula finished, turning to Andreas and wagging her finger.

The two laughed, but looked at one another, puzzled, almost as if they didn't know what troubles she was talking about. Ursula smiled. She felt happy for once. Let them figure it out. No one could blame her for rambling. They must be worried, too, about themselves, the changes to their lifestyle. The dementia would be bad for her but so much worse for them: she, at least, would be oblivious.

As if they had rehearsed it, Mia and Andreas raised their glasses together: "To hope!" And she raised hers, too, and they clinked their glasses together. Soon Andreas had refilled the potato bowl, and they all helped themselves to more. An hour and a half later, they polished off the last trays of bubbling cheese and the hot vegetables. The meal was completed with a sense of ease and comfort that quite surprised her, and she thought about that night at the Station Place. Oddly, since the diagnosis, she'd smiled more deeply and laughed more often than ever she thought she could again.

# 11

As she lay in bed, Mia looked around the bedroom. It was not the one she'd had as a child; that was Dad's study now. It was weird being at home again. Everything felt so familiar, yet so different. Her parents seemed like strangers to her. Not working should feel like a holiday, yet somehow it was more like she was grounded, stuck in the house, all her friends someplace else, no one around to distract her from the mind-numbing pace of small-town life. If she was bored and listless already, Christ Jesus, what was she going to do with herself? It might take months to find another job. Double Jesus. If she was going to fight off this depression, Mia knew she was on her own. She was going to have to put her back into it, even if that meant going out alone. Despite her clumsy way of tackling the topic at dinner, Mamme was right. She needed to meet people, build a network, and find some new ideas if ever she was going to stomp her way out of this swamp.

And if it came to that, how hard could it be to learn to curl? Everybody in Humboldt did it. She liked bowling, that much she knew. She'd won a junior league trophy, playing Saturday afternoons in high school. One of her school friends had had a brand-new driver's license and an old Datsun and had ferried eight kids to the bowling alley in Humboldt and back every weekend. They had been jammed into that old tin can like anchovies, but they knew better than to tell their parents that, and everything had been fine. No one ever got hurt, even when it was forty below and the windshield froze up on the inside from their breath and they drove off the road on the way to deliver Annie back to Bruno. A passing farmer had gone home, gotten his tractor out, hauled them out of the ditch, and sent them safely on their way. She'd had to straddle the gearshift and scrape the windshield clear on the inside so her friend could see out as he drove them all home. Her parents had never seemed to worry. And if they had, what else was there to do in Humboldt?

Sleepily, she thought maybe Mamme was right. Was that the reason why she'd had to move home again: there was someone she had to meet? That thought made her so indignant her eyes popped open again. Where in the cesspool of her mind did that unholy crap come from?

She was almost asleep when another strange thought passed through her mind: maybe it was a story that only she could tell that was waiting for her. Now *that* kind of capital-D Destiny she could believe in. She really was so tired. With that, she breathed in the fragrance of her mother's lavender-scented sheets and drifted off to sleep.

# 12

It was Sunday night, and once again, Andreas was wide awake. Damn it, this was now a pattern. He'd given up coffee, foregoing his beloved after-supper cappuccino even when Ursula fixed it for him. He'd started meditating; he'd counted tens of thousands of sheep. He tossed and turned, tossed and turned. As always, Ursula was snoring, his prim little wife sawing wood in a way that would embarrass a drunken lumberjack. He turned on the white-noise app on his phone, listened to its heavy drizzle pattering through a forest of leaves. He lay there trying to slow his own breathing, pretending that her snores were thunder off in the distance.

He turned off the app and looked at the time. It was already one-thirty a.m., and he hadn't been to sleep yet. In three and a half hours he had to get up for his run. His mother used to complain about his father's racket, and he'd always been so sure, so damned certain, that his dainty little Ursula would never be a problem. Well, he had been wrong. And now the bloody cat was snoring, too.

Damn it. After another half an hour of desperately trying different positions—pillow over his head, blankets and pillow over his head, hands over his ears—he was furious and exhausted. He shook her shoulder. "Ursula. Wake up. You're snoring."

"Huh? What's wrong?" She opened her eyes just a smidgen.

"You're snoring. Roll over onto your side."

"Hmmph! I'm not…" Her eyes squeezed shut, and, in seconds, she was snoring again.

He picked his iPhone back up; it lit at his touch. He checked the news, then wished he had not. The prairie economy was still in a downturn, the price of oil hovering at barely thirty-five dollars a barrel. Provincial cutbacks were hitting hard at post-secondary, as always, and the universities in Saskatoon and Regina were up in arms. There was nothing reported about distance courses or sessional postings specifically, but he knew that the bean-counters in administration were always looking for ways to cut. Every university had its own financial worries now. And what would he tell Ursula if he lost more web courses from the DEU? That was twenty grand a year, and he'd been counting on it. They had some money saved for retirement, but he'd planned to phase out his in-person classes, teach online until seventy. What if Steven were right?

Andreas put his phone back on the night table. There was no point in getting all worked up again. So many rumours were flying, all of them negative. He would just have to pray—figuratively speaking, of course—that the union would prevail in negotiations, and the whole problem would fail to materialize. Surely the university couldn't pride itself on its top-employer awards and then reassign his courses to faculty members. It wasn't Sears, for God's sake. They weren't going out of business. One thing was for certain: he was going to be exhausted if he didn't get some sleep soon. He turned the pattering rain app back on, pulled his share of the covers from Ursula, and tried again to stop thinking. Finally, he drifted off.

An hour later, Andreas was lying on his back, his eyes open again. Ursula was fast asleep at his side. Adam slept just as soundly, a curl of gray fluff at the foot of the bed. Andreas rolled over, punched his pillow, and tried to find a more restful position. Balance in life meant balance in sleep. What was the matter? It was ridiculous. Health was a matter of training. Like the mind, the body could be trained to behave in completely predictable ways, so long as one was persistent. But now, after that silly dream, here it was—he reached over to check his phone on the night table—three forty-nine a.m. And he was awake again. Wide awake.

He lay there in the glow of the phone. Dreams were just the mind's way of purging the events of the day. He massaged his jaws. Damn. It had all seemed more than real: pretty bloody spectacular.

It had happened ten years ago in Humboldt. Horn blaring, the huge truck blasted up Main Street towards the junction with Highway 5. Ambling jaywalkers leapt to the safety of the sidewalks; people gathered, hands fluttering, pointing or seizing one another's sleeves. No one guessed that at that very last moment, just before the big rig seemed about to hurtle straight into heavy traffic, the driver would crank the steering wheel hard, as fast as he could. What an enormous time it took that trailer to jackknife. The hitch swung over oh-so-slowly, and the great truck tipped gently, gently, tilted still so slowly, until it was quite flat over on its side, and then ever-so-lightly, the whole rig slid, and slid, blowing clean through the foot-thick brick of the Petro-Canada gas station, so casually, ever-so-gently erupting in such thick plumes, sprays of ochre and gray and white confetti. And finally, when the dust had cleared, the entire south side of the store was gone, nothing but rubble. Folks ran from the nearby shops, the whole scene ending with the slow applause of bricks dropping one by one, with little flourishes of thick yellow dust. Just as in the actual event, in the dream he and Ursula had been right in the middle of all the chaos—but not like this. And why dream now of a wreck that had happened all those years ago?

*Andreas was checking out rototillers at the hardware store and Ursula was holding two types of trowel when the horn started to blow. After the runaway hurtled past, dream-Ursula stepped briskly onto the pavement, facing down the street after the truck as it started to flip. In her hands, she held an enormous deep-pink umbrella popped open in front of her. That couldn't be right; Ursula hated attention. But she just stood there calmly, protecting the crowd, debris bouncing off the bright undulating silk, the whole town shielded and saved by his little wife, of all people.*

*Everyone said that driver must have horseshoes, yet no one said a word about Ursula's performance. She just gave the umbrella a little shake, folded it, and stepped back inside the hardware store, went to the till, and returned the magic thing as if it were a pair of rubber galoshes that didn't quite fit, after all.*

Unlike most dreams, this one felt real, indeed because so much of it had been. The actual incident had occurred at two-forty p.m., not yet a quarter-to-three, or most of the old-timers would have been in the Prairie Perk next door for their afternoon coffee break. It was a miracle the truck hadn't slid right into the gas pumps. In the explosion, more than coffee row would have been wiped out. For God's sake, there was a school across the street. That luck, that sensational luck, was the town's claim to fame, long after the walls had been matched and patched. So why would he be dreaming of Ursula as some sort of saviour?

If anything, *he* was the hero. He had shielded *her* from talk, the chatter of the panopticon, especially since her troubles had started. It wasn't until four months ago that he'd first noticed she was not herself. She had forgotten a few appointments, and he'd stepped right in to help. He watched her calendar, texted her reminders. When she missed paying the utility and credit card bills, he'd taken over the finances, started picking up the dry-cleaning. And in doing all this, he had said not one single word of reproach to her. She was so proud of their life together, their sensible choices, the fine efficiency with which she had always conquered every task.

To tell the truth, he'd half wondered if Ursula was right, if she could have Alzheimer's...But Dr. Paul had been clear. Ursula was absolutely fine. More and more often these days, he found himself longing for the grand retirement they'd once planned. It had all seemed so real. He would give up his traipsing all over the province, just teach online to keep a little money flowing. They would start new hobbies, reinvent themselves. He could build a canoe, take up Japanese wood-joinery, make artisanal bread. They could travel, really travel, in Europe again. They'd keep old age at bay with Sudoku and plenty of books and foreign films. Navel-gazing was for neurotics, Ursula knew that. She had told him to stop saying it often enough.

So why now, now that Ursula had been cleared by the doctor, why this new species of anxiety? If there was nothing wrong with *her*, perhaps something was wrong with *them*. Andreas was afraid that even if he could get his wife to speak *with* him, instead of *at* him, they might both discover that all the lovely possibilities of their lives—of their married life—had withered and blown away. But he could never say a word about that, not to Ursula, and certainly not to anyone else, no siree.

He checked his phone again: four-fifty-nine. He shut off the alarm. He wanted so much to huddle under the warm blankets again. This useless retrospection—this was the problem. Health was a commitment. The doctor had warned him, if he did not start getting regular exercise... He gently folded back the covers, quietly swung his legs over the bed, set them on the floor without a sound, and stood up cautiously.

He went down the stairs quietly and into the kitchen. As he sipped the hit of espresso he had decided to allow himself, he looked out the east window at the thermometer. Only -24 this morning: positively balmy for February in Humboldt. He assumed the position, one foot far in front of the other. He did his stretches, reversed his legs, stretched again. No point in risking an injury. He put on his jacket and laced up his runners, strode quickly through the darkened enclosed porch, and went out, his breath a bright cloud under the back light. He swung the gate closed quietly as he went through and started to run, the night above him clear and shining with stars.

It was odd how you could go along, perfectly happy for such a long time, and then, out of nowhere, suddenly you could see your life from some new perspective, andHA the whole struggle looked meaningless. Ursula could cling to her odd New-Age beliefs, but *this* life was the only shot you got, he knew. And despite his efforts to correct her, still she had succeeded in filling Mia with a strain of the same delusion. He adjusted his stride to turn the corner, avoiding a big patch of ice. At least Ursula didn't go to church. And she never asked him to read her books anymore. All that time she had put into channeling positive energy. He used to tease her that he lost *his* mind a long time ago, that day they met. He remembered how sweet, how innocent she had looked when she'd tripped at his feet —*the trip of a lifetime,* they'd joked together ever afterwards—that blushing horrified face beneath her Liza Minelli mop of hair.

He puffed harder as he crossed the street and ran up the next street. At least she hadn't woken up today. The last thing he wanted was to wake Ursula, who hadn't even realized that he'd started running every morning, rain or snow or shine or sleet. He could have been a God-damned American postman for all she cared. Mia, on the other hand, had spotted his new kicks on the porch right away.

"Hey, Dad, what's with the Lunarepics?"

He'd smiled sheepishly. "I ordered them online."

"A fashion statement? Out to impress the townies? Or are you leading a double life?"

"Hardly. When would I have time for that?" He'd put his arm around her shoulders in a quick hug. "I've started running in the mornings. It's not a big deal."

"You, Dad, exercise? That's extraordinary. Of course it's a big deal. Good for you. At your age, staying fit requires a serious commitment. But you're still pretty young for an old man," she'd said, hugging him back.

"Let's not make a thing of it, okay? I haven't told your mother, not until I'm sure it's going to last. You know how she—"

"No problemo, Dad. I get it. Mum's the word."

In a few minutes he had reached the first intersection. As the weatherman had predicted, a high-pressure system had moved in, and the air was brutal. He jogged stiffly, his breath bright with crystals under the streetlights, as he waited for the signal to change. He sprinted down the residential street in the direction that seemed to promise the least traffic, wary of feeding gossip. He knew how news travelled. His new fitness regime would seem peculiar here in ways that it wouldn't in an urban locale, where plenty of people, even sixtyish men, routinely ran for exercise. But in a small town, things were different. What farmer or tradesman ever needed—or wanted—to add to his work, invent ways to burn calories? To avoid attracting attention, Andreas made sure he ran the Godforsaken streets in a variable pattern, under cover of darkness.

Rural Saskatchewanians were even worse for gossip than the Swiss, and that was saying something. In Basel, everybody always had an opinion. The Swiss had rules, serious rules, meant to be followed. Everything was regulated, and his mother said it had only gotten worse since he and Ursula had left: there were actually laws now that insisted you had to keep your guinea pigs in pairs, for Christ's sake;

if one died, you had to buy or rent a companion. No lonely rodent hearts there, not with animal rights such a thing now. And no washing cars on Sunday or hanging out laundry or flushing a toilet after eleven p.m. People had better measure up or be prepared to hear about it. Nothing stopped Swiss tongues: not strangers, and certainly not the passive-aggressive Canadian pseudo-politeness that people used here to punish deviants. The one good thing about living in Humboldt was that the government didn't try to legislate every little aspect of life.

This morning, after only two weeks of running, Andreas's knees were sore, his back hurt, and the pain in his right side was starting to strain his breathing. He knew he shouldn't drink so much; at least, that was what the doctor had told him. But Andreas hadn't wanted to worry anyone. Ursula would have been sure to notice if he turned down the glass of wine they always had with dinner, or the kirsch or schnapps they often nursed through the evening. And who could go to sleep without some brandy to go with the chocolate?

Still, he regretted his wicked ways, at least at this particular moment. The familiar sensations had set in as soon as he started running. The pain latched onto his head. He was nauseated, a burning sensation in his throat and stomach. Just a slight hangover, no doubt, and what kind of a man would give up his run for a thing like that? A dead man, that's who. The doctor had been clear. He had to change his ways, or he wouldn't have time to be sorry; he would have a *cardiovascular event,* or whatever the hell they called it now. That pot belly that Mia and Ursula so liked to tease him about, saying he looked like a mosquito who had swallowed an olive, was just one of the signs. He forced himself to keep running, but the faster he ran, the worse he felt; the faster his blood pumped, the more pain. Humboldt was hardly the place he had planned to grow old; he had always intended to move to a city as soon as Mia was grown. No wonder he was almost sick and Ursula refused to believe she wasn't losing her mind. What were they doing still living here, for Christ's sake?

The pain shifted its grip, took hold even more fiercely. Andreas knew he needed to steer his thoughts back to sunny pastures. Things weren't that bad. This past week he had discovered he *liked* watching the town come to life in the mornings. Out here, none of it seemed real—not the trouble at the university, nor Ursula's moods, nor even his own inability to calm himself. He picked up his pace, passed down another street, another. At least you couldn't get lost in a place this size. He was passing the Ukrainian Catholic Church of All Saints, no less, its otherworldly silver domes perched proudly above white stucco walls, the whole thing gleaming in the trio of floodlights some patron had installed at the front corners of the church. The Ukrainian flock was still a going concern in Humboldt. He could just make out a black figure, backlit through the tall windows, moving in the shadows at the rear of the building. So the good father was an early riser, too. No shortage of sinners, then, even in a town like this.

At this time of year, the sun wouldn't rise for two more hours, but already he could see shop lights starting to come on down the street. The baker at the Danish Oven would have been on duty since three a.m. The gas station and its convenience store opened at six—he could see the fluorescent light in their sign stutter and hold. And the shift must have changed at the hospital, judging by the headlights streaming down the highway.

Now *those* people had stressful jobs. Ursula never missed a beat if it related to her, but she was pretty clueless about other people's lives and feelings. She'd never asked about the meds he was taking, and he certainly wasn't going to volunteer that information. Fortunately, Ursula was completely preoccupied with herself these days. He wasn't keeping secrets, not really. There was nothing she could do, in any case. It was all on him.

He had no one to commiserate with, not about his health, his marriage, or his worries about his teaching. Since he'd lost the contracts for Yorkton and his online course this term, and the doctor had told him to manage his stress, he stayed in his office most of the time, pretended to be working from home. Thank goodness for Muenster and Prince Albert—at least he still had those contracts. As far as Ursula was concerned, he was still teaching his web courses. For all she knew, his students were still spread around the province. True, things would be a little better now that Mia was home. He would enjoy having a friendly presence in the house, but he didn't expect her to carry his worries. She had to get out there again and figure out a way to make a real life for herself, the sooner the better. As he rounded the corner, the wind caught him, and he realized he was cold. He clapped his black gloves together hard and fast as he ran, trying to thaw out his fingers. There was a reason they called the lining *thin*. A person needed God-damned *thick*sulate out here, with the temperature often 30 below in the morning.

He glanced at his phone. It was time to head back. Glancing down the street in both directions, he jogged against the light to cross and ran up the long street that led towards home.

# 13

Mia pushed back the patterned duvet, sat up, settled her feet into her slippers, and went to the bathroom to wash. Who was that ghost in the mirror? She took her hairbrush and swept her long blonde hair back from her face. Without makeup, she looked pale, puffy. She longed to crawl back into bed and pull the covers over her head. But this was now a No-Moping Zone, she knew that. She kicked off her slippers, stripped off her pajamas, turned the shower on, and waited for the water to warm. Ten minutes later, when she toweled herself dry, she felt renewed, refreshed, resilient. She brushed her wet hair back taut into a ponytail, wrapped the towel tightly around her body, and returned to her room. From the closet she selected a pair of jeans and a long-sleeved t-shirt. She slipped her feet back into her slippers and climbed the stairs to the kitchen.

The room was dark except for the single bulb Mamme always left on over the stove. There were sounds coming from the upstairs bathroom; someone was already up, rustling around. Good. She flicked on the lights overhead and filled the kettle, switching it on. She retrieved a medium-sized pot from the cupboard, measured the steel-cut oats, the boiling water, and a pinch of salt into the pot, and turned on the burner. In half a minute, the bubbles were rising. She stirred the porridge with a wooden spoon and lowered the gas. As she surveyed the fridge, the thickening mass heaved and sighed, and she stirred it from time to time in between taking out the cream container, a plastic clamshell of strawberries, three oranges, and a tub of Greek yogurt. She carried the fruit to the sink, rinsed it thoroughly, and patted the berries dry. What on earth she could write about, especially up here? They would crucify her (or her parents) if she wrote anything political. For all its NDP years, Saskatchewan was Conservative country now, but she was used to that; it had been that way for years now—and Alberta was worse, if possible. There had been only that one election when Alberta's NDP had taken a majority—with a woman leader, no less. That had been really newsworthy, astonishing. But what kind of change could happen in government in only four years? The United Conservatives had won the next round. That was hardly news—it was kismet. People got what they voted for.

Maybe she should wander over to the public library later, check out the public notice board, see if there was anything happening around town. She sliced the berries into a glass serving bowl, stirred the thick oatmeal, and turned off the heat. If only finding direction in life were as simple as getting breakfast. She skinned the oranges in long wavy peels, removing the strands of pith and separating the fruit into segments, swirling them into the thick yogurt with two spoonsful of honey. Setting out the good crystal sugar bowl with dark Demerara sugar, she filled the matching creamer and set both in the centre of the table. At last, she spooned the porridge into three of the good bowls, the bands of glaze layered dark and white and spring green, and took them to the dining-room table, setting them beside the real silver spoons on the linen napkins. There. The colours, the textures—everything beautiful.

Flowers, that's what was missing. She moved the vase of yellow tulips and grape hyacinths from the kitchen windowsill to the centre of the table and went to the bottom of the stairs, calling, "Mamme? Dad? Breakfast's getting cold. Come and get it!"

# 14

The clock-radio had gone off an hour ago, its horrible beeping intruding on Ursula's dreams. For a moment she had lain there stunned, wondering why Andreas hadn't shut the thing off. When she reached over to shake him, of course his place was empty. Why did he never wake her when he got up? He knew she hated the sound that old relic made. She hoisted herself up on one elbow, stretched over to the table on his side of the bed, swatted at the switch. She rolled over, threw back the duvet, and set her feet into her blue slippers. Hurrying around the bedroom, she was half-aware of the new "prairie sky" paint she had chosen for its calming hue. She certainly didn't feel calm. She was not even certain that Andreas liked it, although he had rolled it on without complaint only a month before.

She did her yoga, showered, and dressed as quickly as she could. By then Mia was calling something about breakfast. When Ursula reached the bottom of the staircase, her eyes widened as she took in the waiting table. "Mia! You shouldn't have gone to all this trouble."

Mia shook her head, ponytail waving. "No trouble,

Mamme. I needed to fix my own food, anyway. Isn't Dad coming down?"

"Your father must still be out running, I guess." Ursula seated herself, helping herself to three spoons of sugar for her porridge and a moat of cream. She set the sugar bowl and creamer next to Mia.

"You know about that?" Mia paused, scooping a spoonful of yogurt into her bowl. "He wasn't trying to hide anything—"

Ursula smiled warmly and patted Mia's hand. The girl was so ready to try to make peace between them these days—they had to be careful she didn't end up in the middle. "I didn't say he was, Mia. The first few times, I didn't know what to think; he was gone before the regular alarm. But when I saw his new running shoes out in the porch, I put two and two together. I'm not that far gone."

"Far gone?" Mia looked at her phone. "He *is* later than usual. I'm sure everything is okay. Maybe he met someone and went for coffee."

"He could be spying for the Chinese, for all I know," Ursula smiled, shaking her head. "He never says a word about what he's doing or why, just sets his alarm for five a.m., slips from the bedroom before I'm really awake. After all these years enslaved by his iPad and the sofa and the television, he must be exhausted. The things men do."

Mia shook her head. "I'm glad that he's taking his health seriously. You should be, too."

"Well, it just seems so odd, out of the blue, without a word about why. Your father can be so secretive."

"I wouldn't say that. He's pretty open-minded. And since when are *you* so tough on him? You two have always been like a pair of lovestruck teenagers. Really, you embarrassed me throughout my entire childhood and adolescence, the way you hold hands and kiss in public. You never keep secrets."

Ursula wanted to say that though she couldn't say why, things were different now. She wished Mia would mind her own business, but she couldn't hurt her by saying that, so she held her tongue. After a few moments of silence, Mia must have decided it was time to change the topic.

"So, how's school these days? Is this year's crop of students coming along?"

"Well, they're quiet souls. Noreen told me that, at the last dance they held, they all wore headphones and danced without a band or a DJ." Ursula shook her head.

"That must have looked pretty surreal."

"So Noreen said. And whenever they have any time to spare, they rarely talk to one another; they just pull out their phones. Gen Z, they call them; they're a new phenomenon. Not sure if the Z stands for asleep, you know, zzzzzz? But they're cheerful and polite, when you can get them to talk. Some of them are catching on in chemistry, but the new math is really making it hard for them to understand the equations."

"It always does, doesn't it? When isn't there some new math to worry about? That must give you and Dad something to talk about?"

Ursula spooned up every drop of porridge and cream and helped herself to yogurt and fruit. "You would think so," she said cautiously.

Mia sat in silence as her mother ate. After a while she said, "Dad still isn't home. I hope he's okay?"

"I'm sure he's fine. He probably met someone, and they're talking their heads off."

Mia pointed at the clock on the wall behind her mother. "And speaking of talking, you'd better get going, Mamme, or they'll have to teach the class without you."

Ursula looked over and gasped. It was ten minutes to 8:00. "Goodness, you're right. Thank you, *Schätzli*, for this lovely start to the day." Quickly she rose, kissing Mia's forehead. "I hope the rest of your day is equally productive and happy."

Gathering her bags and books, she hurried off to the garage.

# 15

By the time Andreas came in from his run, Mia had cleared the dirty dishes away and was just putting the food in the fridge.

"Hey!" she scolded. "You missed my gourmet breakfast."

"Well, I certainly didn't mean to do that. Fix your old man up with some leftovers?"

"Just this once," she said, with a mocking frown.

He gave her a quick hug and bent to kiss her cheek. She pushed him away, joking. While he went up to shower, she nuked his porridge in the microwave, set it on a tray with a spoon and the cream and sugar. She retrieved the bowl of fruit and yogurt, made him a cup of cappuccino, and took it all upstairs to his office so he could start work while he ate. As she passed the bathroom, she could hear him still singing in the shower, so she knocked on the door, saying, "Food's up!"

"Great! Thanks, Sweetheart," he called. "Leave it on my desk, please. I'll be out in a minute."

She went downstairs and finished straightening up the kitchen, wondering what to do next. She'd only been home for a few days, and apparently, if you could judge by Mamme's odd tone and Dad's strange behaviour, it was a good thing she was here. Things were decidedly off-kilter. She felt a twinge of guilt, but for the life of her she didn't know why. It wasn't like Mamme to be critical of Dad. The two of them had always been unified, like some impenetrable brick wall. There had never been any kind of tension here before. But then, this was the first time she'd had to move home, and it felt as if she were thirteen years old again, marooned, all her friends away for the summer, despising the thought of school but longing for something—anything—to break the monotony. It was *so* isolated here. She missed Zoë and Alison, her crew from Calgary. Should she take a job of some sort, maybe work in the gas station or the grocery store? That might be better than nothing; at least she would be around people again.

She shook her head as she straightened the dish towels—things must pretty damned drastic if *that* kind of career suicide appealed to her. She drummed her fingers on the counter, making a plan for the day. After she finished the kitchen, she would scrub the bathrooms and make a grocery list. She had purposefully ignored the bacon in the refrigerator; she was so tired of meat already, after last night's roast, the sequel to Mamme's dense luncheon meatloaf. If she left it to them, they'd serve steak for breakfast. The only way to control that was to do more of the shopping and cooking. God, she missed having a place of her own. She had to take charge of this narrative or lose every bit of freedom she'd fought for.

What was it Zoë had said when Alison questioned the wisdom of Mia's retreat to the frozen North? "Please. She is a grown woman, embarking on life in a new direction."

Maybe she should have it tattooed on her forehead or get cards printed to help her remember. There was a reason for all this; there had to be. She bustled around the kitchen, sweeping the floor. Look at all that fur—when had Mamme swept last? That wasn't like her, to leave things a mess. She strode into the living room. Maybe this was what Dad had been rattling on about: the clutter, the mysterious changes Mamme was going through. She got out the vacuum cleaner, worked thoroughly around the room, and emptied the canister into the garbage, which was full too.

Huh. Maybe helping out *was* her purpose, at least for now. Mamme and Dad had changed very little in the house over the years; surely it was time for a refresh. True, the gray sofa she'd grown up with had been recovered in good caliente-coloured linen. With its retro lines, it looked new and trendy, even hip. The place used to look like a show home, though Mamme, especially, could not care less about fashion. No moody deep teal or glamorous black-plum lacquer here. The woman was pure Swiss—she worshipped the gods of order. The walls were crisp and white, and everything looked fresh except for the original accent wall with the diagonal cedar panelling. But when Mia had mentioned it, they'd made it clear that they had no intention of renovating. Her parents were as loyal to their things as they were to one another.

Mamme had argued, "Doesn't rustic go well with modern? Shiplap is just painted wood panelling, and that goes with black metal—they do it everywhere now. Don't you like the new woodstove?" she'd asked, defensively. And Mia hadn't bothered to explain; she'd just let it go. Now she ran her hand lightly along the cedar and found her fingers chalky with dust. What *was* going on? The vacuum was still out, so she fetched a chair to stand on and got right to it.

There. That was better.

But it was enough to make her look more closely. She walked around the living room; the tops of her framed photos were dusty, too. She was working on them when her father came down, carrying the tray with his breakfast things. He smiled at her. "Would you like a cappuccino, Mia? Let me fix you one."

"Thanks, Dad. You shouldn't have to wait on me." She wiped her hands on a rag and tightened her ponytail. "But, since you're asking, I guess, sure, I'd love one. A big spoonful of sugar, please? I just want to finish this."

He disappeared back into the kitchen. By the time he returned bearing pastries and her coffee, Mia had rearranged all the chairs and was about to lift the sofa. He set down the tray in the dining room, and together they repositioned the couch across from the wall of glass that looked over the front yard. They moved the coffee table into position.

"There!" she said. "The room looks new again."

Her father grinned as he looked around, and said, "Sure does—a total reboot. Except for that eyesore."

He pointed at the bookshelf that had once been as neat as a library. Mia hadn't even noticed the odd collection over there beside the stairs. As she read the spines, though, it was plain it could only be Mamme pursuing her interests with some kind of fortune-teller's abandon: not only ecology, but also sustainable architecture, geo-engineering, and mass extinction, a good many of the books in Hochdeutsch.

Andreas cleared his throat and said, "If only your mother would get fired up about cleaning—but you know our Mamme likes her things just so—" Right then his cell phone rang. He glanced at the screen, smiled, and said, "Excuse me for a moment—I have to take this. I shouldn't be too—" He patted Mia on the shoulder and took the call, making his way up the stairs to his study, talking as he walked. "Yes, that's what Steven said, but, as we agreed, we can't let them back us into—"

Mia smiled, and reached for the top row of the bookcase. At first, she just lifted the horizontal stacks that were perched on the front of the shelves, dusting as she worked, but when she looked more closely, it was clear that the books were in no particular order. She took the piles down and turned to the rows behind. Even the shelved books seemed to have no rhythm at all. She would need to empty the shelves, re-organize the entire collection.

Time sped by as she sorted and ordered by topic, then author, then year; it was creative, this kind of recalibration. She was in the zone. Some books held loose paper scraps, brittle and yellowed. Why would Mamme keep all that clutter? Marie Kondo would have had a heart attack. She grimaced and dropped the slips to the floor. No wonder Mamme was out of sorts.

As she worked, she found herself humming. Her father was right; overcoming adversity really was like surviving winter—you had to endure, but once things started to melt, green shoots would start to sprout, and bloom after bloom would follow. And at least while she was helping her parents, she didn't have to worry about what to write.

# 16

Andreas leaned back in his office chair, staring out the window but seeing nothing. If Steven's intel was right, Arts and Science might be looking to save money by cutting more sessionals' hours, leaving faculty to handle all students, no, *clients,* themselves, online. And the sessionals had been complaining for years that most *clients* shied away from the kind of mentoring that would help them. The resulting low grades reflected badly on the teacher, and, when administrators were looking for scapegoats, remaining sessional positions would be cut—and that would mean financial ruin not just for him, but for a whole class of academic workers.

With all this extra time, what was he supposed to do? Research? He'd never had time to do much of that, the one thing that might have allowed him to get a faculty position. But it was certainly too late now. He shook his head. As if faculty were going to want to cope with first-year students anyway, who couldn't remember the simplest algebraic equations, couldn't solve a thing without their calculators, let alone do calculus. Were high school teachers teaching anything in the classroom?

Not for the first time, he envied Ursula. It took her no time at all to prepare lessons; she had generous numbers of holidays and professional days—and the entire summer to herself. And when she was working, her day had well-defined limits.

Even with his reduced load, there was no outside of work. Panicked students wrote at all hours of the day and night. Ursula had prep time and spares and was free to leave any time after her last class was dismissed, although of course she never did. No, he could just imagine her, puttering around in her empty classroom, making posters and putting up arts-and-craftsy corkboard displays, popping down to gossip with the other teachers. She had peers, comrades, community. Lately, when at last she deigned to come home, she would set sail at 5:00 p.m., expecting him to have supper cooked and on the table by the time she had changed out of her teaching clothes.

Of course, she had no idea about what he was going through: he had shielded her from all his problems. The last thing he wanted was to worry her, even if the lost contracts might be just the tip of the fucking iceberg. If only, just for once, they could really talk, as they used to do before she'd become so preoccupied with her imaginary condition. If only Ursula could understand how very lucky she was to have gotten out of the academic life when the getting was good.

He shook his head. There was no point in dwelling on choices made so long ago. He turned to his computer and opened his email: only seven new messages in the last hour. He turned to stare out the window again. What was he going to cook for supper? They should have a nice meal, something to celebrate Mia's hard work.

# 17

As Ursula hurried through the parking lot at school, she couldn't escape the irony: now, thanks to relaxing so leisurely over Mia's fine breakfast in an attempt to get away from her worries, she was going to be late for class. She strode through the almost-empty hallways. But as her mind tried to conjure the lesson she was going to teach, a strange thought, a convoy of strange thoughts, flew by so fast they didn't register, and that same blank feeling tried to take hold of her.

Startled, she pushed the sensation aside. She slipped between the tall young people jostling and talking at the back of her class. The room was noisy with the rattle of stools and students setting out books and laptops. She went to the closet, slipped off her jacket and boots, pulled on her lab coat and pumps, straightened her skirt, adjusted her scarf, and walked to her place at the front workbench.

Clearing her throat loudly, she smiled as firmly as she could. The students settled. The room fell silent and she took attendance. "Please open your books to Chapter 11," she said, and began to teach, writing formulas and working solutions on the whiteboard.

Maybe it was the breakfast; maybe the extra time she had spent on her lesson plans was paying off. For whatever reason, at last she was in the zone again. The details, the concepts, everything fell into place as she worked through the equations. It was exhilarating. She could still command the material. But when her classes were finally over, on the short drive home, there was a moose, this one by the side of the road. A young cow, legs folded, head tucked into one knee as if she were resting. No blood, no sign of injury, just a tall white stake planted beside her to alert the road crew to stop and pick her up. Ursula thought she should take a photo to show Andreas, the beast looked so odd, so unnaturally natural. Six moose she'd seen this month, yet not one photo to prove it. She had tried to snap a shot of the herd on Groundhog Day, but by the time she had hunted around in her purse, located her iPhone, and aimed it, the field was empty. They had vanished, the whole lot of them, and she was alone again. No wonder she'd been so startled, so preoccupied, when Noreen had interrogated her. Anyone would think she'd imagined the whole thing.

Ten minutes later, Ursula pulled into the garage, tired, hungry, ready for a nice supper with her loving family and a chance to rest afterwards, maybe put up her feet or do a little reading. She opened the door from the garage into the house, climbed the stairs, and poked her head into the kitchen, calling through the open door, "Andreas? Mia? Hello!"

"In here!" Mia's voice carried pleasantly from somewhere not too far away.

Ursula could smell something cooking; someone had made supper already. That was a treat. She took off her boots and set them neatly on the boot rack, then pulled off her cozy fuchsia jacket and hung it up.

Mia was wedging the last volumes back onto the bookshelves when Ursula entered the living room.

For a moment, Ursula felt completely disoriented. This wasn't her house; everything was changed. Even the furniture had been rearranged. What had happened to her bookcase, the books she'd stacked so carefully by their related ideas, her research? And why was Mia standing there grinning, smudges of dust on her forehead and cheeks, a pile of filthy green cloths lying on the floor?

Before Ursula could even gather her thoughts to speak, Mia crossed the room and hugged her. "So, how does it look, Mamme? You'll have no trouble finding things now."

Ursula couldn't say a word. She dragged her gaze from the bookcase to stare at her daughter's face. Those shining gray eyes, just like her father's, so proud and hopeful and utterly—what was the phrase Andreas always used?—*without malice aforethought*. Ursula couldn't find a single thing to say. She couldn't let Mia know what she'd done. All that time, gone. Her entire project, all her research, gone, gone, impossible to replicate. Ursula tried to conceal her rising panic.

She stared at each shelf on the immaculate bookcase.

"It was quite the challenge, but, since you were at work and I wasn't, I thought I might as well make myself useful. At first, I only planned to rearrange the chairs and the sofa, just to freshen the room, give things a reboot. But when Dad pointed out the rat's nest over here, I knew I had to help. It's taken all day to straighten things out, but at least now you can find your books again."

"*Mia*," Ursula said. "What did you do? Where are my bookmarks?"

"What bookmarks?" Mia looked puzzled.

Ursula hesitated. "Those slips of paper, my notes?"

"Oh, those tattered things?" Mia wrinkled her nose. "I threw them out. I couldn't make sense of them."

Ursula was speechless. All the priceless connections, the page numbers, the ideas she wanted to quote. Every bit of correlation gone. She swallowed hard, ran her hand through her short hair.

"Doesn't it look great?" Mia wiped her hands on a clean cloth, took off her hair elastic, smoothed back her ponytail, and wrapped it in place.

"Well—yes, it does *look*—but Mia, what did your father say?" Ursula was peering around the room as if he were hiding somewhere behind the newly reconfigured furniture.

Mia frowned. "He helped with the couch, but after that, he was in his office, working. He knew I was cleaning; he encouraged me. We wanted to surprise you."

"Well." She swallowed hard. "You have certainly succeeded in doing that." Ursula stepped over to the bookshelf, tracing the neat row of spines, trying helplessly to recognize authors, titles, anything at all.

But there was nothing. Not one idea. No clue at all. She was in that white room, the walls curving away and away.

As if from a distance, she heard Mia say proudly, "You had them piled in such random clumps; I couldn't discern any pattern or rhythm at all. They're in perfect order now. It's the system I learned when I worked at the library in high school." She paused, then continued firmly. "You can find anything now—anyone could."

Just then Andreas ran down the stairs and strode across the room, smiling as if nothing were wrong. He settled his arm around Ursula's shoulders and gave her a squeeze.

"So, Sweetheart, what do you think?"

Ursula's eyes turned up to his. She looked straight at him for a moment, her eyes locked on his, then swivelled back to face Mia.

"That was very kind of you, Mia. You've worked so hard. Is supper almost ready? I just need to speak with your father for a moment—" She slipped out from under his arm. "Please." She looked at him again, nodding her head sideways towards the kitchen.

# 18

Andreas lifted his eyebrows but continued to smile. Ursula said nothing as she turned. He shrugged at Mia, fell in behind his wife, as always, and followed her through the doorway.

She closed the door behind him with an ominous click.

So she was going to play it that way. As casually as he could, he reached into the cupboard and took down three wineglasses, then pulled out the corkscrew. He knew he had to keep his cool. "So, what's up?"

She spoke softly, her tone urgent. "Andreas. Don't play the innocent with me." Her voice rose slightly. "You know perfectly well what's up. Why did you think I left my work that way? I had a system—theme by theme, book by book. Pages marked. Why in the name of God would you let her destroy all that?"

"Let her? Destroy all what?" He glanced blandly over his shoulder at her as he opened the wine. "I didn't *let* her do anything. She had already started cleaning when I came in; she was well underway. And what's the big deal? I hardly think—"

She lowered her voice, hissing, "You hardly think? *You* of all people are always thinking. You of all people know I can't remember names or connections after I set a book down—given my condition, you know how impossible it will be for me to work on my book now. It was all—"

Andreas grimaced as he opened a drawer. "Your condition? What condition is this?"

"What condition—you know very well what I'm talking about! My entire project is lost. She says you told her to clean it. How could you do this to me?"

Turning, he said mildly: "What are you talking about? Sweetheart, I love you. Look, the doctor was right. You clearly need a break." He replaced the bottle opener in the drawer and poured the wine. "We discussed this. He said you might be going a little crazy with all the stress. And I say again, honestly, what's the big deal?" Still smiling, he held out a glass of wine.

"You must be joking!" She waved his hand away.

He lowered his voice and set the glass on the counter, frowning. Now she really was being unreasonable. "Should Mia have to ask permission to do your housework? You're not going to make a fuss, after she's worked all day for you—" His words came more quickly. He hissed, "Do you want her to hear you? You should be grateful. She's put your blessed books in an order anyone can use—"

"*Anyone* doesn't need to use them! I do!"

"Ursula. You're missing the point. All you need to know is the topic and the author's name. You're a brilliant woman; surely you can manage that—"

She hissed back, her voice rising, "That's precisely the point. I can't! You know I can't. That's what I'm saying. You heard the doctor. You of all people should know exactly what people with MCI can't do. If things were a mess, they were the way I needed them to be. Now I'll never be able to find a thing."

Andreas's voice rose involuntarily as he braced himself against the counter. "For Christ's sake! You don't have MCI! If you'd come home after class, give yourself a fucking bit of rest, you'd have no trouble remembering anything." He slammed his palm on the counter. "Or maybe you could act like a grownup just once! For your daughter? Christ Jesus!"

"So this is my fault? You're never on my side. Nothing I do ever fits into your perfect schemes. And I don't blame Mia: I blame you! You were here! She says you encouraged her. Why in the name of God would you let anyone touch my things? This is personal!"

"Personal? Vacuuming is personal to you? And what *side* are you talking about? Whatever you're insinuating, Mia is *not* 'anyone,' for Christ's sake. And for your information, I did not *let* her do it. I was about to warn her away from your precious system when the phone rang. Is it my fault, too, that the university expects me to do my job occasionally? It's hardly my fault that you left your things in such Christly disarray. All I did was point out the dust—"

The door opened quietly.

Mia was shaking her head, ponytail waving, her face flushed. "Mamme! You've got to believe me. I was so sure you'd be pleased. I only wanted to help, then one thing led to another. You can't know how sorry I am—"

"And she is pleased, or will be, when she has time to think about it. Give her a few minutes to take in the new effect. Never one for surprises, our Mamme," Andreas smiled grimly. He walked over and put his arm around Mia's shoulders. "Your mother's just tired, Sweetheart. She's had a long day."

He held Mia, and, with his other arm, reached out to draw Ursula towards them. She accepted the gesture silently but without protest. He looked down into Mia's face, and then her mother's. "Let's have some supper, okay? It's almost ready. I'll fry up these lamb chops, glaze the carrots and sauté the spinach, and we'll have our meal." He nodded at the oven. "See? The potatoes are starting to brown—everything will be ready in fifteen minutes."

Ursula put her arms around Mia, saying, "Sweetheart. I wasn't upset at *you*. I know how much work you did. I was surprised that your father—"

Andreas stiffened, but Ursula just smiled and reached over to touch Mia's arm. "Thank you for trying to help. It must have been like cleaning the Augean stables."

Andreas felt himself relax. "There, what do I always say? Our Mamme just needs a little time to come around."

Ursula's face looked as if it would shatter, she was smiling so hard. "Yes, that's what *you* always say. I'll just go change my clothes before dinner." She hugged Mia again and left without another word.

At least that had gone better than he had expected. Andreas wondered what he would have done if Ursula had really decided to make a fuss, but here they were—the whole scene had taken less than ten minutes.

"That didn't happen. And if it did, it wasn't that bad," he recited. "And if it was, it wasn't my fault."

Mia came back from the dining room. "Who are you talking to?"

"Oh, no-one, Sweetheart. Just a joke your mother and I share."

He started to hum as he turned back to set the chops frying. Things were looking up already. As the lamb sizzled, he washed the spinach, patted it dry, and tossed it into the hot butter.

# 19

Ursula hurried through the main floor, stopping abruptly when she reached the bookcase. Her mind was scanning, searching, seeking for names, titles, correlations. Nothing. Not one blessed thing. She felt hopeless: all that work, her entire web of connections, completely and utterly lost.

When at last she started reluctantly up the stairs, she couldn't stop herself from glancing back. In the dining room, Mia was spreading a white tablecloth on the table. Ursula could hear the chops sizzling. Andreas was at the stove, now singing opera. Mia walked into the kitchen and stood behind her father, saying something Ursula couldn't hear. The two laughed, and Mia gave her father a little shove.

Ursula stood there, numb, longing to share the harmony between them.

Andreas carried a covered casserole into the dining room and set it on a trivet. Mia followed him, balancing a basket of buns and the napkins on her left arm and carrying a stack of plates and cutlery with her right. Just for a moment she glanced at her mother, but then Andreas said something in a low voice, and she turned towards him again. They walked away and back into the kitchen.

Desperate, Ursula turned and went up the stairs. The very last thing she wanted to do was to hurt Mia. She knew who was at fault: it was Saint Andreas and his all-consuming concern for appearances. Not so many years ago, when Mia was growing up, she herself had been frantic to keep things in order, but that was different. They were all adults now. Who cared if things got a bit dusty? No one else ever used her books. No, it was the same old problem, just a different iteration. His impossible standards, the ones she never had been able to meet.

She'd need time, if she was ever going to salvage her project; at least he had that right. But the books were only a symptom. What was she going to do with all this fury, this endless rage? Ursula was forced to acknowledge the thought that had first come to her in the neurologist's office: surely Andreas had stopped loving her. Or maybe he never had.

She walked into their bedroom, opened the closet, and the answer stood before her: her suitcase. She could extricate herself, once and for all. She felt a tantalizing sense of relief, just out of reach. It would be so easy, so very easy, finally just to leave him behind, leave him and his enormous sense of superiority.

She could be free, freer than free.

She worked quickly, stashing socks and stockings and underwear in the suitcase, layering t-shirts and sweaters and skirts and blouses on top of jeans. She would take what she needed for now. If she wanted to, she could come back for the rest of her things later, when he was out.

She heard Mia's voice calling, "Mamme! Supper's ready," and suddenly she remembered.

Mia. She sat down hard on the edge of the bed. Now that was a problem, one she had no idea how to solve. She couldn't do this to Mia. She couldn't make her think she had broken their marriage.

Whatever had changed with Andreas, it had nothing to do with Mia. How long had Ursula felt this resentment? The tension between them had been building ever since she had started losing her memory; she could remember that well enough. He'd stopped listening to her. Most days they rarely spoke, let alone fought. She cursed under her breath. Why had she shielded their daughter? Just this morning, Mia had complained that they were too demonstrative in public; it was embarrassing, she'd said. How could she know that that was all behind them now? If Ursula left Andreas, Mia would surely think it was all her fault. She'd never believe that at the best of times they simply ignored one another. Ursula bent her head and covered her face with her hands.

Andreas was calling her now, too, from the bottom of the stairs. His precious lamb chops were getting cold. Could she not have a single minute to herself? She reached over and pushed her clothes down hard, zipped the suitcase up quickly, and stashed it in the back of the closet.

The next time she needed a go-bag, she'd be ready.

# 20

Mia was anxious. Surprised by the confrontation tonight and her parents' ridiculous little spat, she knew it was time to get out of the house and give them some time alone, at least for the evening. There was the bar in the Pioneer Hotel. If she went out for a while, they could talk, or, more importantly, have a chance to listen to one another. She certainly wasn't going to side with one of them. She wasn't some disinterested third-party judge here to rule over their squabbles.

For all Dad's charm, his constant questions about travel and projects abroad indicated that he expected her stay at home to be a short one. He wanted her to re-establish herself in her field, and he had said as much. And her mother was so distracted, so distant, so worried about whatever it was that she wouldn't say—and now, these cracks in their marriage, the accusations about Dad's shortcomings? Mia's head hurt.

She pulled on her jeans and a thick pair of socks. A gray t-shirt, a loose deep-red merino sweater—it was always better to layer. She went into the bathroom and washed her face. She did her makeup, gave her hair a quick brush, used the straightening iron to tame the frizz into gentle waves, and she was ready to go. She looked in the mirror. Her eyes looked different; even she could see that. Could that look be confidence, arrived at last? Or maybe just defiance? She turned out the bathroom light and walked upstairs.

She could see her father sitting in his easy chair, but she didn't go over to kiss him goodbye. Let him wonder, she thought. She was a grown-up; she was entitled to as much privacy as anyone else. Mamme was nowhere to be seen. And if her parents knew where she was going, they would wait up to find out whom she'd met. They never stopped believing that Mr. Right would descend from the Heavens at some completely unexpected moment to rescue her, as Dad had done for Mamme. Well, there weren't going to be any Greek gods or sprained ankles tonight.

She was in the enclosed porch, pulling on her boots, when she changed her mind. They would probably just phone or text her, and wouldn't that look sweet at the bar, her parents checking in. She yelled back through the house, "Don't wait up. I'm going out for a while. Expect me when you see me."

And then, without listening for any reply, she was gone.

The next evening, it was apparent that her parents had not used her absence to work things through. Dinner was still tense. After Mamme had noisily cleared the supper dishes from the table, Mia was determined to end their nonsense. She'd get them talking, come hell or high water. She brought out her laptop and sat her parents down on the sofa, showing them the gorgeous photos she'd taken while she was travelling and living away. Quiet at first, soon they started to join in. They loved the images she'd taken in Montreal and Québec City the best. The old cities were almost European. But the architectural shots, the abstracts, excited them too, as they were vivid and fresh, absolutely stunning. Mia knew she had a remarkable eye. That was one thing the family shared: they all had great taste. Even Mamme seemed to be enjoying herself. They talked about Mia's work, all the freelance projects she'd done. She told them about her frustration with the system, how difficult it was, the politics of not-what-you-know-but-who-you-know, the old buddy-boy system. The opportunities she had had to pass up because she couldn't do unpaid internships in places like Toronto or New York City. The baby-boomer dinosaurs who never seemed to leave their jobs, and, like all millennials, she still had student loans sucking her dry, years and years after graduation.

At last Mia left them sipping their nightcaps and walked over to Mamme's collection. She retrieved a book that had appeared as if by coincidence the afternoon she had been cleaning. It was one she had bought herself when first it came out, but then, with her books still boxed up from her move from Calgary, she hadn't had time to even think about retrieving her own copy. "Appearing again right here," she said, "right now—it has to mean something."

"It means your mother was interested in it, too," Dad said. "That she shares your taste is simply a matter of experience, not some kind of sign."

Mia said nothing. There was no point in arguing with him. He was never going to see signs the way she and Mamme did.

He took the book and read the title out loud: *Franklin's Lost Ship: The Discovery of the H.M.S. Erebus.* He flipped a few pages, scanned the text on the dust jacket, and handed it back to Mia. "It's always been an important topic to you, for sure, Sweetheart," he said. "But what can you do with it? There are so many books already out or in the works. I saw one on Amazon the other day by Michael Palin—if it's reached the travel god, the subject must be pretty mainstream by now."

A little hurt, Mia refused to give ground. Mamme leaned over the coffee table, opened the book to a two-page photo spread, and put on her glasses to read the fine print. The image was not of the ancient wreck, but of the new 3-D model made using multi-beam sonar.

Ursula frowned a bit as she looked at Andreas and said, "There are plenty of riddles left to solve. I bought it because it fits my research: like Franklin, we don't know the consequences of our technology, won't know them, until it's too late. The ships that are now such sought-after fossils were absolutely cutting edge in their time. It's so ironic."

Mia nodded. "*Cutting edge* might not be quite the right words—if they'd been able to cut themselves free from the ice, they wouldn't have perished. But it's even more ironic that it took the latest in twenty-first century gear to find the *Erebus*. And theories change with every new discovery. When I was in school, researchers thought the crew had died from the lead used to solder their cans of food—the new tinned food that was supposed to keep them safe for years. Anthropologists believed that the last survivors tried eating the dead, whose bodies were full of lead, and it only poisoned them faster. Now even that idea's being disputed. Some brave new voyage! All those men, slowly dying, one after another. Without knowing what the crew was thinking, without a personal point of view, the whole disaster is still one giant mystery."

# 21

A spread of etchings caught Ursula's eye as Mia paged through, stopping here and there: PORTRAITS OF CAPTAIN SIR JOHN FRANKLIN AND HIS CREW. The faces, the uniforms—all looked so familiar. She knew she'd *seen* them before, not here—in some place she couldn't identify. She recalled those exact faces, not sitting prim in these portraits, but working, out on the white snow, pulling the ship—was it déjà vu? No matter how she tried, she couldn't place where she'd seen them. Her mind kept spinning and clicking like a slide-projector, to no avail. The ill-fated expedition, the faces of the dead, were hardly things she wanted to dwell on. All those fine young men lost, forever. Of course, the horror of the history made the topic so interesting to Mia, and to everyone else.

Their daughter had always loved to be frightened, even as a young child. Ursula often wished that she had shielded Mia from Andreas's fascination with politics and historical accounts. Other mothers had their refrigerators papered with drawings of flowers and unicorns and rainbows, or speedboats and cottages at the lake, or ponies romping through flower-strewn meadows. But in Grade Four, the year Mia started social studies, she became fascinated by catastrophes in general, and the Franklin Expedition in particular. She brought home drawings of dying sailors with skeletal ships behind them wedged in sheets of ice, tremendous icebergs looming above, Inuit watching from dog sleds. Although she never tired of the subject, eventually she expanded her artistic talents to include mushroom clouds over Japan, the glowing landscapes of Chernobyl, ragged images of devastated clearcut rainforests, the past, present, and future blended together in the most foreboding ways.

While Ursula prayed that Mia would find happier thoughts as she grew older, their daughter continued to insist that one day she would see these places for herself, especially the North. Ursula was undeniably relieved when Mia reached high school and started to take an interest in boys. But in university, journalism became her passion. With the wreck of the *Erebus* discovered in 2014, and later the *Terror*, its mast aptly poking through what the Inuit had named Terror Bay, Ursula told herself that the story had broken, there would be no point in going up there now. Poor timing, Ursula thought, bad luck, from a bad-luck story itself. And though she was relieved, she was ashamed of herself, too: she knew all too well what it cost to give up a dream.

She made herself pay attention as Mia flipped through the pages, pointing out items of interest to her parents. Before they realized it, it was eleven p.m., and Andreas was yawning. They were all so tired; they hugged one another and headed off to bed. In half an hour the house was silent. Andreas and Adam were snoring away, but for once, Ursula just lay there, lost in thought, Andreas's Amazon rainstorm pattering away on his phone. At last, exhausted, she drifted into a restless sleep.

At 3:00 a.m., Ursula woke suddenly, feeling free at last,

as never she had before. It was astonishing, such an odd dream, so peculiar and vivid.

*She had been in the Viktoria-Gewächshaus at the University of Basel, the dome-shaped Botanical Garden, with its lush tropical foliage and rippling pool of water. Suddenly she was up high on a cliff, seabirds swooping above, soaring beside and beneath her. She gazed past the leather sandals on her feet. The canopy below rustled in the breeze, thick and green and lush. Enormous glossy leaves danced in wind and light and shadow, a living carpet beckoning her. The dark rubber-tree leaves and radiant fronds of the palms she knew and could not name— everything was waving, the trills and caws of monkeys and toucans rising all around her.*

*A fast stream, a river, split the view below. There was a landing, a docked vessel, a wooden ship with enormous sails, and men on deck wearing what appeared to be navy pea coats. She shifted her focus and counted a dozen sailors busy on the snow-white beach below. Some were hauling hard on taut ropes, trying to pull the vessel along. She recognized those men. The ship was frozen in—in the jungle. How could that be? She lifted her gaze momentarily, taking in all those birds, and when she looked back, the human figures looked microscopic, a colony of insects. She stood and inhaled what felt like her first breath of freedom, until, satisfied at last, she turned from the cliff and started to walk away.*

*What happened next wasn't planned; it was instinct. She whirled and ran back three long strides to the edge. Her arms stretched out as far as possible, and she flew, not one bit afraid, each of her senses lit with euphoria, her whole being bright with pleasure. All those hard years of common sense, of doing the right thing, of weighing goals, agonizing over strategies and outcomes—how incredible it felt just to give in, to renounce every renunciation, all responsibility left behind her on the cliff.*

*She was free.*

*She glided down through the air, not a nearly-old woman falling out of the sky but a raptor at ease in its element, shifting direction to the tilt of intention, riding the currents—but as she flew nearer to the tops of the trees, she could make out the shock on the faces on the beach as they turned up towards her—and she watched the men below stop, alarmed to see her fall. For once, she was not afraid.*

*So this was hope. When had she last known such a thing? It was glorious, an exquisite feeling. She would feel this way forever. She watched the great leaves come closer and closer—*

*And then she remembered.*

*There was karma here, such bad karma. Mia, Andreas, her students. This was a terrible mistake. If she died this way, the best she could hope for would be to be born again as someone, something, else. More likely, she'd have to relive it all, the misery of this life, over and over again. Or worse, yes, likely much worse, three hundred thousand lifetimes of suffering just to pay for this oh-so-precious moment of choice. What right had she to give up, she and her first- world problems?*

*And then she felt herself cleave away. She watched as her own body continued to fall and fall and fall, saw herself hit the waves and lose her breath, felt the gigantic splash, the pure panic of her feathered limbs flailing, as all the froth and swirl sucked her down. At the same time, she—another Ursula—remained safe back on top of the cliff. She could feel herself standing there as she looked down at that other self, the drowning hope dying.*

She gasped with relief, felt the cold air on her legs. She was awake, alive.

Andreas was beside her, snoring, tightly bundled in all the covers. She wrestled her share from him, wrapped herself up, and slipped quietly back to sleep.

# 22

Andreas came home early from his run, eager to put his new plan into action. He quietly took off his runners and neatly hung his jacket up in the enclosed porch. As he opened the door and walked into the kitchen, he wondered where everyone was. Surely it was late for Ursula still to be asleep? There was no sign of her. Maybe she had gone to work early? The kitchen looked pristine, untouched. And where was Mia? He'd heard her in the bathroom when he left. She must have gone back to bed; she'd done that the last few mornings, and it was time he put a stop to it. A young person like her needed purpose, and pronto.

He brewed the one cappuccino he allowed himself daily and took a sip of it, wincing. He still hated it unsweetened, but the doctor had been clear. Fat was not the only thing you had to watch out for; sugar was a demon, too. He cradled the mug to warm his hands. If the bookshelf fiasco on Monday had meant anything, Mia was going to turn into an unpaid housekeeper, and then her career would really be over. Almost since the day she'd arrived, she'd been playing maid. She fixed their breakfast, cleaned the house, did the shopping. When she wasn't doing household chores, she was back in bed, napping at all hours of the day. Her research and her writing were at a complete standstill. He knew she had to use her skills and seek out new connections: use 'em or lose 'em, that was the way that game was played. And certainly she needed to stop maundering on about old Franklin and his crew.

What would it take to for her to find a real story, something she could sink her teeth into? And her photography, what about that? She needed a topic, friends, exercise, and—most of all—plenty of time and space to herself. They could set up an office for her, encourage her to bring out all her papers and notebooks. She could research online at first, and then he'd persuade Ursula that they should fund her travel this time, let her go wherever she wanted to really suss things out. An office would get Mia going, keep her busy, and help show Ursula that he meant to make amends to her, too, for failing to protect her research. Once Mia had a project, she'd have no reason to meddle with her mother's things, she'd lose interest in cleaning, and the house would revert to whatever state Ursula desired. He could live with a little dust; these last few years had taught him that. And then, when they could all do their own thing, everybody could just chill out, relax. There would be no more ridiculous fuss.

He climbed the stairs quietly, cautiously opening the door. Ursula was still sleeping, her face open and innocent, a look he had not seen in a long, long time. She looked almost free. She must have recovered from her despair, that funk she'd been in for months now. He gathered his clothes quietly, slipped down the stairs and into the main-floor bathroom, shut the door as soundlessly as he could, and turned on the light.

Jesus. Was he ever going to get used to seeing that old gray man in the mirror? Christ, he was such a relic—okay, a relic in better shape than he'd been for many years, but a relic all the same. He undressed and turned on the water, reaching into the shower to test it. When it was nice and hot, he stepped in. The relief was unbelievable. There was nothing like a long shower after a hard run. He began to hum, softly.

# 23

The morning light glinted gracefully through the winter trees, filtered long through the canopy of branches. She had to admit it: Dad had been right. Having her things set up in a space of her own really was going to be nice. As a child, Mia had always been afraid of basements, but she knew from her various stints as a tenant that you could get used to any space if the price was right and the proportions were good. The best thing was that the spare room, the one that her father had finally persuaded her to use as a study, had a window that faced east into the backyard.

The view was backlit now by the rising sun. When she stood, she could see out at ground level, past her Grade-One spruce tree and into what Dad now called Mamme's Meadow. There were some photos on the wall that Mamme had taken last summer, and *meadow* was definitely the word, the fuzzy ornamental grasses sprinkled with daisies and clumps of wild-looking sprays of dried flowers waving in drifts between the fruit trees. Everything was bolstered with snow now, but the effect of the early-morning light entering the room was breathtaking. She was reminded of something, but she couldn't say what at first. And then it came to her: Jasper, that was it. They used to take hikes when they stayed in the little cabins at Miette Hot Springs. She remembered when she was six and her parents had taken her there. When they had said the name of the resort, "Miette," she'd thought it meant "Little Mia." Her parents had laughed, of course; they all laughed together. And after that there had been no decision at all: the hot springs were their favourite family destination.

She was glad her father had persisted after all. She had been annoyed, at first, when he insisted that she needed a study. Perhaps he thought she wasn't working hard enough. Even he had to recognize that all the cooking and cleaning she was doing was helpful. What did he think she had to write about, anyway, that would satisfy him? But when she went down and looked at the room, she could see for herself immediately that the place was in chaos. Dad was just being polite, too polite to ask for her help. Her parents despised clutter, yet the room was filled with old stuff that nobody could want. When her father joined her downstairs, the two set right to work, talking and joking as they carried out the boxes full of old clothes and odds and ends that were piled in the room.

"Honestly," Dad said. "Your mother must have purged the attic to find all this old stuff."

"Maybe this will make up for what I did to her bookcase. Maybe if she sees I'm trying to get back to work—"

"None of that, now. I told your mother you needed a study, and she's right on board with the plan. You're not still thinking about her books? Because I'm not, and I'm sure your mother has forgotten all about it. Better at forgetting, better at forgiving, right? Let's take the old stationary bike upstairs, too. It can go to the thrift store with the rest."

Mia remembered the year Dad had bought that bike for Mamme at a Boxing Day sale, a year ago. He swore she'd never used it, not even once. "When I want to ride a bicycle," she had told him, "I will do so outdoors, thank you very much." Mia winced to hear her mother's words, worried that Dad had felt hurt, but he never said a thing about it. She supposed that that was what love was like: you accepted people as they were and simply refused to take offense.

After they had emptied the room and cleaned it, they spent the rest of the morning moving in Mia's belongings. When she excavated her shelving unit from the garage, her father whistled. It was quite the set, with its live-edged boards, the ones she had bought from a furniture maker who was going out of business and moving to Toronto, hoping to have better luck there, just as she was falling in love with West Coast life four years ago. At the time, she couldn't see why anyone would leave: Vancouver was fabulous. Soon enough, though, she had learned that the city was fabulous only for those who were independently wealthy, or were busy laundering money for organized crime, or who some-how managed to find high-paying work in their fields. For the penniless and out-of-work, the place couldn't be more Dickensian. Mia felt like a street urchin, peering in at the good life through nose-smudged glass. What did it matter if the night life was amazing when the only work you could find was freelance, and to live on that you had to take a second job as a waitress in a tiny pizza place in the toughest part of town?

At least that was behind her now. Dad helped set up her desk, its heavy glass top resting on sawhorses and a small steel filing cabinet. She loved the industrial look. All she had to do was unload her books, set up her laptop, et voilà! She would be back in business. Her father had gone upstairs to make lunch, and Mia looked around the new room. It was fine. She gazed out the window and dreamed of Miette. The sun went under a cloud, and the sudden chill made her shiver. None of this was going to mean a damned thing if she didn't find something to write about. She shook off the thought and went back to work.

She was filling her bookshelves when she had the odd sensation that someone was watching her. She turned. A large snowshoe hare, up on its haunches, was peering in through the window. As she watched, it hopped away through the trees. Dad called, "Lunch is ready," so she went upstairs and carried down the tray with their mugs and sandwiches while he brought two folding chairs.

When they entered the room, the wind had picked up, the waving branches outside making the walls seem dark, shaking with shadows.

Dad turned on the light overhead and whistled. "Not bad for a morning's work, eh, Mia?"

"Not bad at all. But we still have to get that all that stuff to the thrift store."

"Don't worry. I'll drop it off this afternoon, on my way to the university. My working from home seems to have raised a few red flags, judging by that frantic phone call from Steven the other day. If I don't put in an appearance soon, they're going to think I've abandoned the committee."

After their meal, Mia helped Andreas move the bike and the boxes onto the truck. The workers at the thrift store would help him unload, so she went back downstairs to settle in. She bent to take out a few of her old notebooks and paged through to see if any leads she'd once had could be reanimated. The political stuff was out of date, of course, but there were lots of notes about mass migration, mass extinction, and climate change that were even more relevant now than they had been. If only she had known how prescient she'd been—it would have been great to have a story like that ready to run now.

She lost track of the time, and before she'd made it through more than half-a-dozen notebooks, she heard the garage door open. Her father was home already. He went up to his study when he came in, so she stayed put, persevering. The sun was shining from the doorway to the west when she looked at her watch: Mamme would be home before she knew it. Mia's plan was to get supper started, and she needed groceries for that. Her father had done the evening meals lately. She could come back to her notes tomorrow. Surely one of these old mysteries would speak to her, if indeed there was anything there to find, and in the meantime, she could ruminate over what she'd already seen.

She went upstairs and dressed to go outside. Sunshine usually meant a high-pressure weather system, so it was bound to be cold out there. She texted her father to say she was going out for a bit, but she'd be back in time to make supper. He was to leave everything to her. The last week had been awkward, but everything was going her way today. She made her way to her car, which was parked out on the street; gave it a few moments to warm up; then drove across town to Sobeys grocery store. She wanted to prepare the delicious roasted-flour soup, *mehlsuppe*, that her mother had always loved. It was a family favourite, one of the classics—a dish from Basel, right out of their childhood and into hers. She hadn't had it for years. She wanted to surprise them, to show them how much she appreciated all the help.

There was very little traffic, and within minutes she had pulled into the parking lot. She got out of her car and crossed to the entrance, stomping her feet a bit before entering the store. She took a plastic basket from beside the door and briskly walked up and down the aisles, hurriedly scanning the signs hanging above. First, she went down the produce aisles to find some fruit for dessert, something healthy—grapes and cantaloupe, and, because they were on special, two pints of fresh raspberries. Probably from Chile at this time of the year; with deforestation and all the miles they'd travelled, they were an environmental disaster, but either someone was going to buy them or they'd go to waste. Next, she went down the soup aisle for beef stock.

As she passed the coffee display, she picked up a bag of the Kicking Horse dark-roast beans that they all loved.

*Let's see*, she muttered to herself, *we need more butter—and cheese.* She walked over to the dairy cooler. *Here we are. Butter, check. Gruyère, Gruyère—where are you?* Armstrong, Black Diamond, Kraft—even something holey called "Swiss," but clearly not what she needed. She turned to the deli counter and smiled at the generous display. Sorting through the blocks of wrapped Gruyère, she noted it was imported. Good. She compared the pieces and chose the largest one; she wanted plenty for leftovers. All of a sudden, she was aware of someone watching her. She looked down the aisle. There was a tall guy, mid-thirties or so, not six feet away. Nicely built, dark brown hair. He smiled, looking a bit embarrassed as she met his gaze. *Kinda hot*, she thought. She felt foolish, checking him out in the grocery store. But from the smile on his face, he didn't seem to mind. In fact, there was something familiar about him. She walked back to the refrigerator, selected a carton of cream for Mamme's coffee, and told herself she was being ridiculous. When he spoke, she almost jumped out of her skin.

"Finding everything you need?"

Mia blushed and turned. "I think so, thanks." She looked at him as she shut the glass door.

He was smiling, but not in a creepy way. His brown eyes were friendly yet piercing. "I hope you don't mind me saying so, but you look so familiar. I think I saw you at the bar the other night. You grew up around here, right?"

"About a million years ago. And you—I remember you, too. You're—?"

"Ryan, Ryan Thomson. And you're Mia, right, Mia Koehl-Niederhauser? Or you used to be?"

"Still am. But that's amazing—Ryan, how are you? What're you doing these days?"

"I'm home, helping my parents out on the farm for the next few months. Dad had a hip replacement, needs someone to take care of things for a while. It will be a change for me. I'm an archaeologist now. Just landed a contract in Rocky Mountain House for the fall."

"Congrats! I've just moved home, too, but from Calgary. I'm a journalist." Why in the world had she told him that? Now she was going to have to explain what she was doing up here. She had to get out of there before she made a total ass of herself. "Well, it's so nice to see you. I wish I weren't in such a hurry right now. I have to get home to make supper—"

"Sure, of course. Hey, do you like curling? Come by the arena if you have time next Wednesday night. We can have a beer and catch up."

"Ah, that old trick—get the newbies drunk?"

"No, seriously, it'll be fun. You'll love it, and I want to hear what you've been up to. See you there."

She smiled and nodded at him and moved on, wondering what she could tell him. He seemed friendly enough, though, and it had been nice to see him. She still felt mildly silly but was pleased at the prospect of seeing him again.

The young girl at the till had a hard time remembering the codes for the raspberries and cantaloupe. She tried and tried again, then finally asked for help from the cashier on the next aisle. By the time Mia had paid, it was a quarter to four. She wanted to buy wine but decided against it. The whole plan would be for nought if she didn't make it home before Mamme arrived. In any case, her parents always kept plenty of wine. The hard part, as Dad always said, was finding something you really liked.

# 24

As she left her classroom to go to her appointment with the holistic doctor—or miracle man, Ursula thought wryly—the town's noon siren was just beginning its wail. She found herself almost swept down the hall and through the school doors with the swarm of students. She crossed the parking lot to her car, got in, drove downtown, then turned onto a side street. She had no trouble finding the office, since she'd scouted the location on Monday on her way home from work. She had also written the date and time in her planner *and* programmed a reminder on her phone. She wasn't going to mess up, not this time.

The doctor was set up in the old brick building that had once housed the most expensive plumber in Humboldt. When the potash mine had come to the region, new construction had boomed, and in his prosperity, the plumber had moved two streets over into a prime location on Main Street itself. In actual fact, Dr. Chernov was not a medical doctor at all, but a homeopath. She'd never been to one before, but Kathy, her hairstylist, swore the man had cured her when no one else could. Kathy had tried a range of treatments for her irritable bowel syndrome—all kinds of diets—gluten-free, probiotic, even strictly vegan. Nothing had worked, not even the trendy new FODMAP. Dr. Chernov had set her right in less than a month. Her disorder stemmed from an old emotional trauma, he said, and once they dealt with that, the symptoms simply went away. Now Kathy took her young family to him for everything. When he'd been in Saskatoon, his practice had been so busy he had closed it to new patients, but now, moving into semi-retirement up here, he'd agreed to see Ursula as a special favour to Kathy. That was all very well, but the little Ursula knew about homeopaths made her more than a bit nervous. They had such peculiar ideas, she'd heard.

Still, she had to do something. She parked her Honda on the next street over so that no one would guess where she was going. The day was brisk, the sun was shining, and the brief walk got her blood pumping. When she entered the waiting room, she was surprised. Such strange décor for a doctor's office: the walls were cinderblock painted glossy white, with bargain-store giclée canvas prints of sailing ships and closeups of arcane marine instruments dotted with droplets of water that shone like tiny convex mirrors. The reading selection was eclectic, too, to say the least; the bookshelf was packed tight with *Reader's Digest* condensed novels and children's storybooks and paperback thrillers. On the end table lay a storybook of Noah's Ark with pop-up animals in battered-looking pairs. She seated herself gingerly in one of the ratty metal folding chairs and checked her emails on her phone.

Ten minutes later, when the door to the waiting room opened, a balding man in an open-necked checked shirt and a short lab coat stood in the doorway and called her name. When she rose, he smiled and handed her a clipboard with a sheaf of papers to fill out. Kathy had warned her he'd want to take a detailed history, but as she flipped through the pages, she couldn't believe all the minutiae that were required. She forced herself to calm down and read the instructions; those, at least, were clear enough.

Circle all the regions of the body affected by pain. List all physical and mental illnesses for two, preferably three generations. Were her parents and siblings still living? If not, give cause of death—and age. Grandparents? Great-grandparents? Cousins? Aunts and uncles? Great-aunts and great-uncles? Pregnancies? Living children? Stillbirths? Miscarriages? Heart attacks? Strokes? Diabetes? Cancer? Suicide? Other? List medications and supplements in detail: times, strengths, frequency. How long had she been taking them? What surgeries had she had, starting from infancy? At what ages? Successful or not? What childhood illnesses and when? Complications?

As Ursula read, she loosened the gray knitted scarf at her throat. The place was blasting hot. How could she answer all those questions, even if she knew such details, which she did not? Her mother had died so suddenly; she had hardly thought to leave her children a complete medical history. The doctor was still standing near the ancient reception desk at the front of the waiting room, shuffling papers in a file cabinet. Ursula faked a cough, and then, when he didn't turn toward her, she gave up and simply said, "Dr. Chernov? You'll have to forgive me. I have another class to teach at two. I won't have time to fill out all of these forms."

He turned to face her, his expression untroubled. "Of course," he said. "I understand. Is there someone at home who could help you? You can take the forms with you and bring them when you come next time."

Ursula's face flushed. So Kathy couldn't keep her mouth shut? Ursula had warned her that she wanted him to be unbiased, to find something that could be fixed. She didn't want him to start with assumptions—

"This is just our first meeting. It will only take a few minutes, Mrs. Koehl-Niederhauser. May I call you Ursula? If you would come this way, please?"

"Yes, of course. But I am in quite a hurry—" She straightened her back as she rose, standing as tall as she could. Since he simply kept walking, the effect was lost. In the end, she found herself rushing to catch up as he strode down the narrow hallway.

He led her into a small room with a heavy metal desk. A dusty laptop sat to one side, and there was another filing cabinet, this one narrow and olive green, in the corner behind his desk. He offered her a folding metal chair and went behind the desk to sit on a tattered version with a vinyl seat. He asked a few questions, jotting down the partial answers she supplied on a notepad. At last he flipped back through the pages he had written, his eyes scanning back and forth between different sections.

He looked up and asked, "How long have you had a sweet tooth?"

"I beg your pardon? What did Kathy say—?"

"Kathy didn't tell me anything. But it's clear you've been having trouble with your memory."

Ursula grimaced. She thought of the fine Swiss chocolate she ate in the middle of the night when she couldn't sleep, or after school, for a pick-me-up. She thought of the rich cakes she craved, the thick rice custard or maple-syrup-drenched waffles she and Andreas and Mia liked to have with sweet whipped cream and bottled cherries. "What makes you ask that?"

"Well, it's quite simple. You were overwhelmed by the details I asked for, even before you read the questions. Then there is the family history of strokes that you've outlined. One of the most common forms of dementia is vascular, where a series of mini-strokes gradually impairs function."

"Who said I have dementia? And what does that have to do with a sweet tooth?"

"We see a lot of addiction to sugar in those with the symptoms of dementia. People know the connection between strokes and high blood pressure, but they don't realize that too much starch and sugar raise triglycerides, and that can lead to strokes. And another sugar-driven condition—metabolic syndrome—is linked to a form of dementia: Alzheimer's. Plenty of researchers, even traditional medical doctors, are starting to admit what we have said for years: dementia may be caused by chronic high blood sugar. Some call it Type III Diabetes."

Standing up quickly and walking over to the filing cabinet behind his desk, he opened the top drawer, rifled through, and within a moment or two pulled a photocopy out of a file. He jabbed his index finger at the title before handing it to her.

She took the article and skimmed the first page.

"Yes," he said, as if she had spoken aloud. "It does sound crazy. But lack of exercise and too many carbohydrates are at the root of many illnesses, and now researchers suggest that insulin resistance and insulin deficiency, metabolic syndrome," he paused, gesturing with his hands as if to caress a big belly, "is part of the larger picture for dementia."

"Metabolic syndrome?"

"Patients have at least three of the following: high blood pressure, high fasting blood sugar, high triglycerides or LDL cholesterol, low HDL cholesterol, and too much fat around the waist. Most people these days take no steps to remove that danger. Metabolic syndrome can lead to diabetes, heart disease, and stroke. And now we think it may lead to Alzheimer's."

"But if Kathy didn't tell you, why would you think I have dementia? I'm too young to have Alzheimer's!"

"It would be early onset, yes, if you do have it. And early-onset Alzheimer's is genetic, so we would expect at least one of your parents to have had it. It may be too soon to tell. What did your neurologist recommend?"

She was about to protest that her mother had died in a car accident, so no one could know what her cognitive powers would have been like as she aged. But his last question threw her off that track.

"What makes you think I've seen a neurologist?" She put her palms flat on the doctor's desk and pushed herself up to stand. "Kathy must have told you that."

Dr. Chernov waved his hand at her, gestured for her to be seated.

"Kathy did not speak to me about your symptoms or their treatment. I've had lots of practice observing people, and most patients won't go to a homeopath until they've exhausted the government's healthcare system. Patients seek me out when they've had news they don't want to hear. It was an educated guess, a bit of a magic trick. So, what did he say? Or was it she? I don't read minds, you know." He gave her a broad smile.

Ursula did not smile back. "He, Dr. Paul, took a detailed history, ordered bloodwork, a full physical, cognitive testing, the whole battery you would expect. I can't recall word for word what he said. I was worn out by the time he met with us to review the results; he talked about mild cognitive impairment, MCI. He put me on the waitlist for an MRI, but since the case is hardly an emergency, he warned us it will likely be months before they call me in. I've been frantic—"

"MCI? That's a common problem with aging. Why would that upset you?"

"It's the first rung to dementia—"

"No, no, not at all. It's not inevitable, at least not in the way we think of it. Often, with chelation, or other de-toxification regimes—but we can talk about that later, after we confirm the diagnosis." He leaned forward. "Look. You're a professional, a scientist. You comprehend medical terminology. And you've been able to remember and understand a lot for someone with a poor memory. What makes you believe you have MCI?"

"It's useless, I can't remember things. I get so muddled."

"For instance?"

"I have a brilliant idea one moment and the next second it's gone. This happens over and over. I'll be talking to someone, and I can't wait for them to stop so that I can get my thoughts out. I interrupt, but then I can't even remember what I was going to say. And when I tried to start preparing our income taxes the other night, I couldn't hold two four-digit figures in my head long enough to add them, not even with a calculator. I spent hours and hours and got almost nothing done."

She shook her head, withdrew a crumpled tissue from her pocket. She blew her nose, her voice bewildered and soft. "I love math. I'm a teacher; I'm supposed to know what I'm doing, for Heaven's sake!" She shook her head. "I've always worked with figures and formulas. Go ahead, ask me what I ate for breakfast. I can't remember. I can't remember what I can't remember."

"Give me a specific example."

"One day last month, I went outside to shovel snow and forgot to turn the stove off. My husband came out of his study and found the house full of smoke, the dozen eggs I meant to hard-boil burned to briquettes. He was livid. The bottom of the aluminum pot actually stuck to the burner when he lifted it, just peeled off like a sheet of tin foil. I could have burned down the house, and yet when I went outside, I didn't even have the sense, not an inkling, that I was forgetting anything. That's what terrifies me: I have no failsafe at all, no interior nudges, no intuition. Someday I'll have an accident, and someone will die. Even my husband knows that."

"And?"

She shook her head. It was too awful, too ridiculous to say.

"Ursula? What is it? What makes you forget?"

"It's so random. I just can't remember. I'm an idiot." Bewildered, she shook her head. "It's impossible."

"No. You are not an idiot, that much is for certain. You had no trouble remembering or narrating the story of your alleged memory lapse, either. If you were cognitively impaired, that would not be possible." He smiled. "I'm going to need to see your test results. It's unlikely Dr. Paul will share them with me, so we'll do our own. Will you put yourself through the wringer again? We'll have to wait and see what he finds on the MRI. But I'll redo the others, the cognitive series and the bloodwork."

Ursula looked at her phone, checking the date as well as the time.

"Is that really necessary? And now that I've done them already, won't I know the answers? Honestly, tests never show a thing wrong with me—they never do. All of my tests are always normal. Even when I was pregnant, the tests were negative, and yet we have a perfectly healthy adult daughter." She paused, unsure. "I'll have to think about it and get back to you in a few days."

# 25

When Andreas emerged from his study to fetch himself another cup of something hot, he was greeted by a delicious odour wafting up the stairs. That had to be flour roasting in butter. Mia must be back. But she was talking with someone; who was with her? He glanced at his phone; it was only four-thirty. Ursula wouldn't be home for another hour. That was odd. The next moment it became clear: it *was* Ursula, and she was shouting. Andreas took the stairs two at a time and ran through the living room.

In the doorway he could see Mia, wearing her mother's striped apron, her long hair pulled back in a single braid, standing in front of the stove, stirring something in the Dutch oven with a wooden spoon. On the cutting board there was a pile of sliced onions, ready to be cooked after the flour had roasted. She should have been the picture of domestic bliss.

But beside her Ursula was shouting and gesticulating. She glared up at him furiously as he entered the room. "Are you two trying to drive me *insane*? First my books, now my things—"

"What are you talking about, Ursula? What things?"

"My father's things! Those boxes you so casually gave away. The ones you didn't even offer to help me with. Don't pretend you didn't know—you purposely stayed in your office while I struggled to carry them all down to the storeroom. I heard you pacing upstairs, waiting for me to finish—"

"When was this?" Andreas crossed his arms across his chest.

"Don't play the fool—you know you heard me— Saturday morning, the week before Mia moved home."

"Ursula, you're imagining things. I did no such thing." He almost said, "That didn't happen," but he could see she was in no mood for a joke. "I don't know anything about this. And if you needed my help, why on earth didn't you ask?"

"Your help? When would you have deigned to give me your help?" She raised her finger and jabbed at his chest. "Those were my things, my irreplaceable things! The last mementoes I had of my father. How on earth did you *think* I would feel?"

Mia emptied the flour into a bowl to cool, melted the butter and added the onions, her face more distressed than ever. She shook her head, her left hand smoothing tears from her eyes. She stared into the pot, then hesitantly glanced up at her mother. "Mamme, I'm so sorry. I was so sure you knew about the study. How could we know you wanted those things? It just looked like old stuff you'd never use—"

Andreas tried to take charge. "Ursula! Get a hold of yourself! This was my idea. I told you I was going to give Mia the spare room, don't you remember? We discussed it—"

"*We discussed it?*" She mimicked him, her voice squeaky with rage. "*We discussed this, we discussed that.*" Her face looked as though she was about to explode. "*You know* I can't stand that expression. And we certainly did *not* discuss this. I would never have agreed to it. You said no such thing."

"But Darling! We talked about it last night, as we were getting ready for bed. Honestly, don't you remember?" He reached out, put his hands on her shoulders.

She shook them off and paused for a moment. Then she said, "I remember no such thing. But that's what I've been saying for months—I don't remember! I can't remember anything."

"No, no, no. No. You are not going to make this about you, not this time. We cleared out the room for Mia. She needs a space to work."

Ursula paused for a second, nodded, and spoke. "Of course Mia needs a place to work. You did say that much, and I agreed. But why put her down there in the cold? I assumed you would set her up upstairs with you, in your office—her old bedroom, I might add. You have lots of room. Mia hates basements! There are spiders down there! It's bad enough she has to sleep on the lower level. And why would you give her the one room that was full of my things?"

She turned back to her daughter. "Mia, I'm not saying this is your fault. But surely you see you can't just give other people's things away? You can't gang up on me—"

Mia looked up at Andreas, her eyes full of tears.

He put his arm around Ursula's shoulders. "Darling. This is not a conspiracy, just a miscommunication. We discussed it, we did, before we went to sleep last night. I told you I was going to help Mia set up an office. You told me to go ahead. I said I wanted Mia to have a space as soon as possible, and you just nodded and went to sleep. Can't you see this isn't easy for her, being stuck back here in the old folks' home? And we didn't mean to upset you; we saved you the trouble of having to clean out the spare room."

She pushed away hard, wrenched herself from his grasp. "Saved me? You *saved* me? By throwing away my irreplaceable things. How could you? This is personal!"

"Oh, no. Not that again! Ursula, two days ago *vacuuming* was personal. What isn't personal to you? Enlighten me." He snorted, folding his arms tightly.

She reached up and pushed his chest with both hands, so hard that he had to stumble back a small step. "Yes, precisely! Why *would* you upset me *again*? I'll tell you why. You have no regard for my work, my research, or my feelings—"

"Research? What research? What are you talking about? You're not making sense." He took a breath, tried to measure his words. "Ursula. Let's not make this bigger than it is. We can simply go and get the boxes back from the Good Neighbour store. It's only been a few hours. They won't have unpacked them. Come with me. You can round up whatever you've lost. If we have to buy it back, no problem. It won't hurt us to make a donation."

"You wouldn't be so calm if they were *your* things—"

"Mamme, we're sorry. You can't imagine how sorry we are. Just let Dad fix this. Go with him now, before anything is unpacked. I'll finish the soup, and we can eat as soon as you get back. Maybe you're hungry."

"I am not hungry—I'm ANGRY! I can't remember when I've felt so—"

She looked like a bonfire that had been doused with kerosene. She strode to the cupboard, reached in, and seized one of their precious dinner plates, looking as fresh as when they were new. She took it in both hands. Andreas grew white with shock as he realized what she was going to do. And she smashed it, as hard as she could, on the lip of the black granite countertop.

Dust and shards flew everywhere, and then there was silence. The three just stood there, stunned. At last, Andreas walked over to Ursula. He shook his head, ran his hand along the edge of the counter to see if it was chipped: by some miracle it was not. He whistled, shook his head in complete disbelief as he turned to her. "Christ, Ursula, what are you thinking? Our irreplaceable set—"

Ursula stood completely still, her back straight, her head as high as could be. She didn't even turn to face Andreas. "I haven't touched a thing that belongs to you. This set is mine, and I'll smash every blessed piece if I want to. I dug the clay. I made the deal with the potter. I picked out the pattern." He tried to put his arms around her, but she moved away. "Go. For God's sake just leave me alone. Clearly you don't care a thing about me anymore."

# 26

Ursula turned quickly back to the cupboard, but before she could reach in for another plate, Andreas stepped in front of her, leaned purposefully against the counter, and crossed his arms. She shouldered her way around him, tried to cut in from behind. She went to reach into the cupboard again, but he was too quick. Seizing her hands, he held them and pulled her into the middle of the kitchen. Some part of her observed how passionate he seemed, yet she couldn't believe he still felt such a thing for her.

"Ursula! For God's sake, listen to me," he said, wrapping first one arm and then the other tightly around her. She tried to kick him. He dodged, and she missed. She tried to kick him again. "Listen," he said, with a little laugh. "Cut it out! Mia and I will go to the store and get your things. Hey! Stop it! This is not what you want—you'll see—"

She didn't plan it. It just happened. Some pure primal urge awoke in her, some part of her she had always been able to suppress before. She couldn't stop herself, barely believed what she was doing, either. She looked straight up into his face and spat at him.

Immediately Andreas dropped his arms, his face flushed, contorted, a caricature. He might have been made of stone. Everything slowed down again, as it had when she'd smashed the plate. She followed his movements one by one, as if she didn't know him. She had time to think, "I spat that smile off his charming face," as if she were some kind of an observer watching some ridiculous farce. She had never felt so—so—? What did she feel? Relieved? Vindicated?

Alone. She felt alone, absolutely alone.

She stood still, watched him pull a paper towel from the roll, wet it, wipe the spit from his cheek, and toss the crumpled paper into the stainless-steel trashcan. The room was completely silent except for the pot still sizzling on the stove. Without a single word, Andreas left the room. She heard him cross the dining room and the living room, walk up the stairs, each step putting more distance—and less hope of forgiveness—between them. He would go to his study, she knew. As all her rage died, she found herself standing in the centre of the kitchen with poor Mia, the precious plate in pieces, dust and shards of pottery littering the countertop and floor. The exquisite set, irreplaceable, the one that had anchored every family meal they'd ever had, absolutely, irretrievably ruined.

Mia stood there, staring at the stove. She had stopped stirring some time ago, and the odour of charred onions and burned flour was overpowering. The room was hot, and the Gruyère she had grated was a limp haystack on the cutting board. Ursula went over to open the kitchen window. She could see one of the robins trying to get seed out of the feeder. Instead of looking plump and cheery, the bird appeared thin, ridiculous, feeble. Like she was. There weren't supposed to be robins here at the end of February. And the feeder was set up for winter birds. Smaller birds.

God, she thought. Had they ever had a fight in front of Mia before? Ursula couldn't remember a single time. Filled with shame and regret, she writhed inside. What on earth had possessed her? And how, now, was she ever going to fix what she'd done?

She went over to Mia, who was scraping the burned mess into the garbage, digging at the bottom of the Dutch oven with a wooden spoon and scraping away the stubborn bits of onion. Ursula gently took the pot from her, went to the sink and set it down there, running a stream of hot water. She felt herself move like an automaton. She squirted in dish soap, turned off the tap, and reached down into the pot drawer, drawing out another large pot. She added butter, stirred carefully as it bubbled.

She knew she had to say something. But what could one say after such a performance? Even if she could say, *I'm so sorry, Mia, Sweetheart. I don't know what came over me. I've done foolish things before, but never anything like this. I'm an idiot—I'm so sorry you had to see all this—this craziness*, would even that sort of apology make any difference? Wouldn't she just sound even more pathetic?

So she said nothing, just stirred and got out an onion. As she started to slice, her eyes stung, but she refused to cry. Mia glanced at her sideways, saying, "Mamme, what are you doing? I couldn't eat a thing, certainly not the soup I was going to surprise you with. What on earth is the matter with you? I'm going upstairs to see if Dad is okay, and if you care about anything, you should come, too."

Ursula shook her head. "He won't want to see me yet. I'll make the soup and then at least if anybody is hungry, we'll have something to eat." She watched her knife go slice slice slice through the onion as if someone else were wielding it.

Ursula could hear every footfall as Mia walked out of the kitchen, went slowly through the dining room, picked up speed through the living room, and ran up the stairs.

By the time Ursula could hear them talking at Andreas's study door, she had softened the onion, and was ready to add the flour that Mia had roasted. "Honestly, what are you doing?" she asked herself. "How could anyone be hungry?" But for God-knew-what reason, she couldn't stop. She had to make things right.

As she stirred and added the broth, wine, and seasoning, she tried to untangle the afternoon, the questions and fears she'd felt during her visit to Dr. Chernov, the ones that had plagued her all through the long classes afterwards while she was teaching. She'd come home right after school, looking for comfort, planning to start to go through Babbe's boxes. How could that have been a coincidence? Had it been fate that Andreas had chosen today to remove them? When she found her space invaded, her father's presence erased, for a minute she thought she had actually lost her mind. If only they had asked, she would have moved the things herself, gladly. But that was no excuse. God only knew why she had done it, how she had pounced on Mia, and then, for God's sake, Andreas. Where in the world was this unstoppable rage coming from?

What had Dr. Chernov warned her about? He'd told her to watch out for something, just as she'd left, but now she couldn't remember what. "That's one of the symptoms," he'd said. She tried to think, but nothing came. She wasn't in the white room, not this time, though. She clung to her sense of purpose, worked on, methodically stirring the soup, finally putting the pot out in the enclosed back porch to cool. At last she went upstairs; she was ready to apologize. But as she reached Andreas's study, the two voices fell silent. When she knocked on the closed door, no one replied.

One thing was certain. If she had any doubt about whether she needed to see Dr. Chernov again, there was absolutely no question now.

# 27

For the first time he could remember, Andreas slept on the sofa in his study that night. It was rock hard, damned cold leather, with the bloody button tufts that Ursula had talked him into. He missed his bed. Their bed. If he'd felt up to joking, he would have said he missed it sorely. And when morning came, he was so tired he almost decided to skip his run, just this once. But he knew that was a slippery slope: skipping his run today would make it that much harder to talk himself back into it tomorrow. As he lay there, trying to persuade himself that he had to take care of himself—no bloody way anyone else was going to do that—the events of the last few weeks rose before him.

He was a patient man—he knew that about himself—but even he had limits. Jesus H. Christ. What in God's name had gotten into Ursula? He knew she was still in a panic about her memory, despite the doctor's reassurances. And then there was her bloody book project; he shouldn't have mocked her so-called research. But if whatever she was writing was so important to her, why in the world had she just abandoned her academic career all those years ago?

Having summers off, for God's sake—wasn't that better than having to teach twelve months a year, as he did? He wished he had known those boxes were her father's things. Of course she was upset, and he was sorry. But if the stuff was so Goddamned precious, why hadn't she gone through it, brought it out, set it on display? What was it doing still boxed up, lying around down there, a year and more after the funeral? Who kept bedrooms full of stuff like that? Hoarders, that's who. People who weren't right in the head. Maybe she was right about that, too. Something sure as hell was wrong with her.

He realized that none of this was calming him down. He heaved himself off the couch, put his running clothes on, went downstairs, did a few stretches, pulled on his jacket and toque, and laced up his runners. He grimaced, noting that it felt good to prove he had the discipline to push himself. That, at least, might stop him from spitting back at her, if she ever had the nerve to do it again. He opened the back door, stepped out into the cold, and the wind took the door, slamming it shut behind him. Or maybe he should simply take off, leave her for good. That would show her. What a relief that would be.

He thought about it as he ran. He was oh-so-tempted. But there was Mia to think about. He could hardly abandon her, not when her mother seemed to be coming unglued. And where would he go, anyway? *Marriage*, he muttered, as he ran down the sidewalk, already panting, *is a true meeting of the minds. And if you believe that fucking bullshit, you'll believe anything.*

Within minutes he was at the main road. He stuck to his shortest route, which was also the darkest. Why did they never replace those streetlight bulbs? All the frustration of the last few weeks had made him faster and stronger, given him more endurance. Maybe that's what Ursula needed: some good hard exercise, a way to blow off some steam. Something sure as hell had to happen; things couldn't continue the way they were. As he jogged in place at the traffic light, he knew he'd have to call Dr. Paul, tell him what was going on, and get his thoughts on the picture. Surely nothing the man had said had prepared him for eruptions like this. It made no sense. A year or two ago, his wife had been a perfectly normal high school teacher. If it wasn't dementia, why these tantrums, this unprecedented rage—what in hell could it be?

# 28

Ursula was exhausted. For the first time in their marriage, Andreas hadn't come to bed. She kept hearing what her mother-in-law had told her all those years ago. She could still see the old woman's strong, calm face, the serene waves of her white hair. Andreas was her eldest son. At the time Ursula had thought she was ancient, though Silke then would have been more than ten years younger than Ursula was now.

They had been staying at his parents' home, and the two women had returned from shopping to find Andreas out with two of his brothers. While they waited, his mother tried on the mid-length blue dress she had bought for the wedding. Ursula sat on the sofa, half watching, looking through family photo albums. Silke must have sensed that Ursula was feeling out of place, having trouble adjusting to the Niederhauser family's noise and chaos. It did seem that someone was always shouting, usually two or three at a time. A house with four sons was seldom quiet.

Silke had asked Ursula how things were going. "All brides are nervous, aren't they? Not having any daughters,

I wouldn't know. And my own wedding was so quiet, I can't imagine I was very nervous. I'm hardly the type," she smiled. "But you do look unsettled. This is all new to you."

Ursula confessed that she had a headache. Silke nodded.

"That's to be expected," she said. "The boys are pretty loud, especially when they're all together. But in our family, noise is nothing to worry about. As long as they're yelling, every quarrel can be worked through. But if one of them becomes so angry that he says nothing, now *that's* a cause for concern."

"Concern? About what?" Ursula looked up nervously.

"For us, silence means rage, absolute fury. There's nothing a person can do but wait it out, try to make amends, and that's not easy, not at all. I've only seen my husband silent once in all our years of marriage, and I never care to repeat that experience. It's much easier to avoid such problems than it is to mend them."

It was not a warning that a young bride forgets. Yet not once in all these years—not until now—had Ursula discovered whether her mother-in-law had been telling the truth. She and Andreas disagreed now and then, but he never yelled and seldom even raised his voice. He liked to hear himself talk—especially to strangers, but even with her he was keen to share his opinions. If he really was done talking, as he seemed to be at last, if she had finally reached that dreaded shore, what in the world was she going to do? She lay awake for hours, thinking. He hadn't even come in to get his pajamas. She could hear him tossing and turning in his study.

At last, she was so tired, so worried, she couldn't help herself. She fell asleep.

*She was being chased up and down the hills of Basel by a man whose face she couldn't recognize. She was being slotted into a locker—no, a bookshelf—squeezed so tight she couldn't breathe, all of her words stripped from her. She was as flat and brittle as a dinner plate. Andreas was smashing her against the countertop, again and again, and she was chewing nails and spitting rust all over the room.*

She woke up disturbed, then drifted back into a restless sleep.

*A group of draft horses were lined up along a fence overlooking the highway. They stood there, so still, so gentle, a row of enormous bays, their coats deep red, the thick strands of black hair in their manes and tails lifting slightly in the breeze. They had feathers, too. That was what the farmers called the long white hair that draped down their pasterns over their hooves. Clydesdales, that was the breed. They stood there, looking out, eight across. They could free themselves, push down the fence, pop the staples off the old gray rotting posts, if only they all took that single first step forward together. Instead, they just stood there, captives. Silent, calm, steadfast as fate. Ursula wasn't sure why she felt such tremendous longing.*

*The scene shifted, and six of the eight walked down onto the ice of the dugout. For a moment everything was still. There was a cracking sound, slow at first, and suddenly the ice gave way, faster and faster, cracks racing in all directions. The six horses went through, first one foot and then the others, all the terrified beasts thrashing and wheeling and snorting and squealing, all of them flailing and trying to shy their way to safety across the fractured jagged ice and up the steep dirt slope of the dugout. It was impossible. One went down into the black water, and the widening hole enveloped the next one, and the next, and the next, until every horse was bobbing up and down between the pans of ice in the freezing water, whinnying desperately, heads thrashing. Ursula was in agony as she watched them struggle. There was nothing she could do. All too soon, everything slowed, grew quieter. One by one, horse by horse, each head disappeared under the surface, until, once again, all was still.*

*When she looked up the hill, there was a moose, a bull with an enormous rack, standing at the top, watching. As the terrifying sounds quieted, as the dying horses went under at last, the ice froze over top of them, the dugout surface frayed with rough white seams. The moose paused, made his way down, and walked out into the middle of the same plateau that had just swallowed the horses. He stood there a long moment, turned, clambered easily up the side of the dugout, and disappeared across the field past where the last two horses stood, noses to withers. They made no sign when he passed, which was odd. Horses are terrified of moose, Ursula knew that, but all she could see were the last two horses, seemingly calm, dreaming as they looked out over the hillside again.*

At six a.m., Ursula awakened with a start. She hurried to get up and dress; something inside kept saying, "He's gone. Gone, gone, gone. He's been gone so long—" The words turned into a song that stuck in her head. Her father used to call it an earworm: she couldn't get rid of the words or the terrible fear they brought her. She went downstairs, bustled about for a minute, made sure the kitchen was perfectly tidy, and prayed for Andreas to come back from his run. She needed to see him. She had to apologize.

Her mind raced through this possibility and that. Maybe he wouldn't come in if he could see her. She went into the darkened living room, sat down in her chair, and waited. And waited and waited. At last, there was no denying it: he wasn't coming. Maybe he wouldn't ever come back. Not while she was there. Weary and sick at heart, she forced herself to walk to the porch, put on her boots, pull on her jacket, arrange her scarf and books and bags, lock the door, and trudge through to the garage. Her car started easily. Usually she turned on the seat warmer; it was a nice luxury during a winter in Humboldt, but today she didn't care, not one bit. Let her frozen bum stay numb.

As she pulled up to the first stoplight, waiting to drive across the highway, she thought she must be losing her mind. Andreas was running towards her down the side-walk. In the same moment someone, something stepped out and attempted to cross in the glare of a semi-trailer's lights. There was no mistaking the large ears, the hesitant grace, the shapely corona of light, and then the silhouette crumpled flat. Thick flickers of steam drifted upwards in the headlights, the water in the warm blood rising as vapour off the frozen highway.

# 29

Mia was dreaming.

*She was in the murderer's house, the one working for the Americans. Was it one of Putin's men, the one who had organized the troll farms to help elect the American president? She didn't know how she knew this, but dreams were like that—you knew things without knowing how. Everyone was curious to see the place. She and Dad strode up the path and entered through the back door, and before she knew it there were clusters of professional people, accountants and teachers, lawyers and office administrators, all standing around sipping Perrier or champagne, glasses full of bubbles, their conversation a wave of low murmurs, the women standing there in their black or gray skirts and discreet ivory blouses, the men dressed in running gear, of all things, all of them strangers gathered in the day-dark of the empty townhouse. She didn't know what to make of it, so she slipped between the groups and made her way into the kitchen. She ran a glass of tap water and sipped it, trying to think, but before she knew it, she was sitting on the murderer's warm gray felt* couch. *There were throw pillows, navy and tangerine and white, splashy mid-century geometrics, two of them plumped up in one corner.*

*Suddenly she awakened, and the room was empty. She was lying on the sofa, head resting on a fine velvet cushion, her knees slightly raised under a light heather-gray throw that someone had stretched over her to keep the chill off. A white ceramic lamp touched with brass glowed on the table by her head, though she didn't remember turning it on, and the room looked cozy, somehow, in the soft halo of light.*

*It didn't look like the murderer's house anymore; it looked like home, and she relaxed, found herself at ease. Suddenly, the RCMP were there, arresting everyone. What the uninvited guests hadn't guessed was that the murderer was already in prison, and of course the police knew that; they had seen the lamplight in the window and knew that the intruders must have broken in.*

Mia woke up, feeling odd, strangely guilty. What had she done? But how could this weird dream *not* mean that her mother's reaction was her fault? The message was clear— *the lights were on, there was nobody home*—but the light wouldn't have been on if she hadn't left it on, illuminated the situation. Feeling anxious, she rolled over in bed and reached for her phone. It was only six a.m. She pushed herself up and leaned back against the soft padded head-board for a moment, trying to understand what she was feeling, this piercing helpless guilt. Try as she might, she couldn't say why she felt that way or how she could cure it. After five long minutes, she still had no idea what it could mean. She was being ridiculous: as Dad always said, *navel-gazing is for neurotics.* You couldn't let things get to you. And when Mia had been a surly teenager, moping, Mamme had always insisted, *Do something, anything. The cure is in the effort.* She had to get up. It was just a dream, after all.

*The day is still young,* the voice in her head seemed to taunt.

She lay in bed, listening. She heard her father go downstairs, make a racket, and slam the outside door. Just fifteen minutes later, Mamme's alarm went. Mia could hear her as she hurried around before making her way to the main floor. Dad's departure was not unusual, except for the noise; he was generally out the door before her mother came downstairs. He'd be gone an hour or two, and then, by the time he came back, Mia would have his breakfast ready, and they could drink their first cup of coffee of the day together. But today Mamme didn't leave. Mia heard her bustling around in the kitchen for a minute, and then she was silent—so silent that Mia wondered if she had left—until suddenly, long after Dad should have been home, she finally heard her mother close the door behind her. Her behaviour was really unusual, bordering on bizarre. She was going to be late for school. She couldn't even have had breakfast, but Mia was in no mood to care.

What was she going to do? *Stay the hell out of it, that's what*, she muttered.

Her father came in the back door not too long after Mamme finally left, but he didn't call for Mia, just went to have his shower and then went out again. By the time Mia dared to go to the kitchen, the house was deserted and still.

The kitchen was immaculate, as neat as could be. As if that were what mattered. Mamme had washed the burned pot, cleaned up all the utensils, and stored the ridiculous soup she had insisted on making all by herself last night. Mia really had to hand it to her mother: her need for cleanliness must be bred in the bone, as much a part of her genetic code as her stubbornness. Such things would never change: at least she could be sure of that. Mia set the coffee to brew, made herself some toast, buttered it, and spread it thickly with her mother's good homemade apricot jam.

Last night, after the explosion, Dad had made Mia promise she wouldn't give up her brand-new study. He was emphatic: moving out would only make her mother feel worse. She would be ashamed of herself already. He assured her that what she really wanted were her Babbe's things, not some storage room. He promised Mia he'd go to the thrift store as soon as it opened and retrieve all the boxes. He said he'd leave the stuff where Mamme would find it when she came home and that would probably settle everything down. She'd have to admit he was trying.

But Mia wasn't holding her breath waiting for Mamme to apologize; the whole ridiculous scene had seemed too well-scripted, like reality TV. People never went postal because of one little thing; there was always a pattern of escalation. She'd been away too long, maybe, after all; she had missed the signs. She took her coffee and toast and went to stand by the kitchen window. Out to the east, the sun was rising between the trees. The clear sky, pale yellow and blue, promised another glorious day. She had to admit she had been terrified last night. She had never seen anything like it, not in all the time she'd lived at home. Her parents still held hands in public, didn't they? For God's sake, they acted like teenagers. It was embarrassing how kissy-kissy they were, or used to be.

They'd always done everything together—cooking, cleaning, shopping—and they never so much as raised their voices at one another. She tried to beam positive energy towards her mother, hoping that would defuse her negativity, her incredible rage. But for someone who thought of herself as an old soul, Mamme was packing a fuck-load of self-pity these days. She'd have accrued some serious karma for her bad behaviour. What in Christ's name was going on?

Mia filled the sink with hot water, squirted in some soap, washed her breakfast plate, rinsed it, put it in the dishrack to dry; washed her mug, set that in too, and drained the sink. She squeezed out the dish cloth, wiped up the toast crumbs and a small splat of jam. As she rinsed the cloth and hung it over the faucet to dry, she looked carefully at the counter. If you knew where to look, you could just see two faint scuff marks about four inches apart where the thick ring on the bottom on the plate had struck the granite lip, but the black stone itself hadn't chipped. She ran her hand along it: still almost perfect, smooth and cold, like her mother's heart. The woman was so, so lucky to have Dad, all the care he took of her.

She went to the bathroom and looked in the mirror. What a wreck. Her hair was driving her crazy. She loosened it, ran her fingers through the waves, then shook her head. Nope—loose, it looked like a rat's nest. She picked up her hairbrush and brushed her hair vigorously, pulled it back again, tighter, and twisted it all into a chignon. Nothing like a bun to make yourself feel businesslike. She needed to start on her own work; that research wasn't going to do itself.

She walked back to the kitchen and poured another cup of coffee. Maybe it was a day for new beginnings. She would take the stuff unsweetened. She took a sip, grimaced, and added a generous splash of milk, stirred, then took the cup to her study. As she sat down at her desk, the morning sun streamed through the branches outside and into the room, patterns of light and dark dancing around her shadow on the wall. She turned on her desk lamp and started to dig through her notebooks.

# 30

Ursula thought a deer had been hit, yet she was equally sure she'd seen Andreas running just before the cloud of vapour rose and obscured the scene. She could not put away the thought that he had been right there, too. What if it had been him? His blood, hitting the freezing pavement? She couldn't reason away the waves of terror that flooded over her. What if she had had her chance to make things right last night and utterly failed? Maybe even the universe was tired of her, would ensure there were no second chances for her to make amends. If only she had gone to his study to apologize right away instead of making the wretched soup. What if he were lying there dead now, or injured, crumpled and bleeding to death?

She drove back and circled past the accident site to make sure he was all right, but there was no body at all, no deer and no Andreas. She drove through their narrow alley, past their kitchen, around the block and through the intersection, over and over, each time scanning the area intently. There was a dark patch on the highway, but no body. Relieved, she squeezed the steering wheel with both hands.

He wasn't there. He wasn't hurt, he wasn't a flailing horse in her dream. It had been a nightmare, nothing more—not a premonition.

As she drove away, she was filled with fear again. The intersection was deserted. She circled back by their house once more through the alley. She was driving past for the third time when she saw him through the kitchen window, talking on his phone.

At first, she was so grateful, she almost cried. Thank God—he was alive. But then she was furious. To whom was he talking—the woman he was meeting with when he went for these supposed runs? He was gone so long today, there was no way he was out on the hills for all that time. Not alone. Andreas had never paid the slightest attention to his health—or to hers. *Health is a matter of willpower,* he'd said so often that she could reproduce his exact tone and inflection. Why on earth would anyone start running at sixty-five years old?

She looked at the clock on the dashboard. She was late; her prep period was nearly over. Reluctantly, she drove to the school, parked her car, walked through the parking lot and into the building. She strode to the staff washroom and stared at the stranger in the mirror. She looked fine: a bit bright in the eyes, perhaps, but straight-backed, composed. No matter how stressed she was, no one would ever question her posture; that was one of the advantages of being petite. From her childhood on, her mother had always taught her to stand as tall as she could. It helped people to notice you. She took off her ski jacket, fluffed her hair, arranged her scarf, gathered her bag and her coat, and strode out the door, down the hall to her lab, a fake smile firmly fixed on her face.

When she reached the classroom, it was empty. Praise the universe. She hung up her jacket, changed out of her boots, took down her lab coat from the hook behind the door, slipped it on, went to the board, and started writing notes and equations. By the time the noisy Grade Elevens filed in for Chem 20 a few minutes later, there was no hint that anything in her world was amiss. The period passed quickly enough, as did the one that followed. But at noon she firmly closed the door behind the last student.

She went back to her desk and placed the call. Ten minutes later she was still on hold. As she waited, she tried to calm herself. She reviewed in detail everything that had happened in the past few weeks. She slowed her breathing. Maybe the strange dreams had been trying to warn her: if you were on thin ice, panic would kill you. But it was hard to wait—even tolerating the good doctor's muzak was a challenge. She'd expected soft, meditative tinkling Asian tones or some stunning Russian orchestral. Instead, she was forced to listen over and over to the torment of Shania Twain's "Gonna Get Higher," a seamlessly orgasmic loop that Ursula, who had never felt lower, found almost impossible to tolerate.

What choice did she have? Whatever the cost of the new tests, whatever the trouble, she needed to know what was happening to her. She felt more and more desperate as the minutes dragged by. Would Andreas leave her? She was lost, so ashamed of herself. Why on earth had she spat at him? She could feel loss and emptiness flood every part of her. Her anguish was real, physical. And then it struck her.

Would Andreas or Mia remember, and, if so, would they even care?

It was one year and two months to the day since Babbe had died.

# 31

Andreas stomped the snow off his running shoes as he entered the porch, pulled off his gloves, and blew hard to warm his stiff fingers. This might be the warmest winter on record, but the weather up here was still unbelievably cold. Christ. It had been such a strange year. He remembered a winter years ago when they'd had a blizzard every blessed Monday in March. This morning he had had to stop and wait, hiding, when he saw Ursula driving away from the house and then circling back. At last, she was gone. Thank God. The coast was clear.

He took off his jacket and toque, hung them in the porch, slipped off his runners, set them in place on the rack, and stepped into the kitchen. He stopped himself from stamping his cold feet. Mia wasn't up yet. She must still be sleeping. Good. At least he could protect *her*—and her rights. He moved quietly. He needed time to unwind from his run, think about what to do. It was clear that something had to happen; things couldn't continue like this. Ursula's outburst last night had taken things to a new level. As plain as frost on a windowpane, the woman needed a psychiatrist.

Could one specialist refer her to another? Ursula had always been highly strung. So much had been happening in the world that could upset her, too. There was the crazy-ass stress of not knowing what the Canadian governments (municipal, provincial, or federal) would do, let alone the Chinese, the Russians, or the bloody U.S. President. Half of all Americans and Canadians seemed to accept that "alternative facts" could be true, while others were riled up in the streets, marching. There were protests about Russians and racists, and, all the while, Iran and North Korea literally had their hands on the nukes. And yet all Ursula seemed to worry about was how to teach chemistry to teenagers dreaming of video games. Such a waste of a brilliant mind. No wonder she was losing it.

Should he get in touch with the school this morning, or talk to a lawyer first? If he couldn't get those contracts back, damnit, they would need her income—and her benefits. Yes, there was always the pittance that he could draw from CPP, but that was so much less than what he'd been making a year ago. He pulled out his phone and searched "liability," "burn-out," and "aggression." The wi-fi was frigging slow again— must be another storm over Newfoundland. Why some genius had decided that Newfoundland, of all places, was a good place to situate the gateway of a satellite, he could not imagine. While he waited for the search to load, he ground some of the expensive Kicking Horse beans. He knew he had been cheating, allowing himself too much coffee lately, but today was hardly the day to scrimp on comfort.

No one answered Dr. Paul's phone, so he left a detailed message on voicemail and fixed himself a double shot of espresso. He'd been avoiding caffeine since his insomnia had started, in case it was spoiling his sleep, but that was precisely the problem: he hadn't slept, so he needed *something* to keep him on track this morning. There was so much that needed doing. He went to stir in some sugar, thought better of it, and sipped it black. He stared out the window. He thought he saw Ursula's car going down the alley. He must be seeing things, must be more stressed than he knew. He put his phone back in his pocket and ran his hand through his hair. He turned the kitchen light off so that he could see out the window. That really did look like Ursula's Honda. Why would she be going past now? Was he paranoid, too? He shook his head, walked quietly through the hallway, and went to shower and change; he might as well be at the thrift store when it opened. There was nothing more important than that, at least to Ursula, which meant no one else was going to have any Goddamned peace unless he retrieved her things. He showered quickly, dressed, and set off.

Thank goodness his luck had held. The staff hadn't even opened the boxes, and he had no trouble at all in identifying them, clearly marked with her sister Kathrin's beautiful script. He texted Mia to reassure her that he had the goods, then packed them into his vehicle and drove home. At last, he unloaded the boxes and went up to his study to start the day's work. Around four-thirty, the doctor's office returned his call.

The nurse informed him that Dr. Paul was surprised to hear about Ursula's outburst, and that it was impossible to know the cause. Aggression was one of the symptoms of dementia, but that was usually a late-stage symptom, and certainly other conditions could cause stress. Having an adult child move home might require some readjustment. Andreas protested that this was completely out of the ordinary—his wife had never acted like this before— but the nurse just repeated Dr. Paul's suggestion: Ursula should retire or take a leave. If there were a problem, such as advanced Alzheimer's or a tumour, it would show up on the MRI. She was on the waiting list, but it would be another two months at least—more likely five or six. For any future problems, they should contact their family doctor.

Andreas worked his hand through his hair again. Advanced Alzheimer's? Dr. Paul had ruled that out, hadn't he? But a tumour. He'd never even considered the possibility of a tumour.

# 32

If she was going to survive the family drama, Mia knew she would have to get busy. She was unpacking and shelving her books in her office when a volume she'd bought years ago caught her eye: *Frozen in Time*, Beattie and Geiger's book about the Franklin Expedition. The front cover bloomed with the fearsome image of dead young John Torrington, gone for one hundred and thirty years yet looking almost fresh, as if he had shuffled off this mortal coil a mere month or two before. The image was gruesome, yes, but the photo had such presence. Mia had never felt more of a sense of destiny. She had to find out more, no matter what her parents said.

With the latest in technology, all those men were sure they were prepared for every kind of danger—proof, Mia thought, of what Dad always said: *irony is not dead.* You never knew what would get you, even when you thought you had prepared for every possible calamity. Like Mamme going ballistic—twice—in the first month she was home. Mia pushed the thought away, refusing to think about it any further. Yes, she had decided to clean, but tackling the bookshelf had been Dad's idea, not hers. He should have known Mamme would want her things left alone, the old bastard, and still he hadn't warned her. Well, in any case, Dad was right about her getting back to work. What she needed now was to find herself a story, any story. That was a fact. But where to start? She fetched herself another cup of coffee and set to work. By mid-morning, her office was organized, she had reviewed her notebooks and done her prep work, and she was in the car and headed for the one place she might find help.

"The Franklin Expedition?" the boy at the circulation desk echoed.

"You know, the nineteenth-century explorers from Britain, the ones who tried to find the Northwest Passage? No survivors—all hands lost?" Mia was in a hurry. She wanted to be home in time to have lunch with Dad, just to make sure he ate something, and it didn't help that this kid had no idea what she was talking about. "Could you ask the librarian, please?"

"I am the librarian right now, ma'am," he replied. "At your service."

Mia forced herself to smile and remain calm, though kids were not her strong suit, especially in the morning. What was he, fifteen? God, she was getting lots of practice in keeping her patience. Could she have been this clue-less when she worked here, all those summers ago? "Well, the computers won't load, so I can't access your catalogue. Could you help me find something?"

"I'll do my best," he said stiffly.

"I just need to know what call letters to start with. The expedition took place in the late 1840s. Did you not study Franklin in school? There was a big discovery in 2014; the team of researchers found the HMS *Erebus,* and later, its sister ship, the *Terror.* It would be in your Canadian history section."

"HMS?"

"Yes, Her Majesty's Ship. Franklin's ships. Searchers believed that the *Terror* had been crushed, ground to bits by the ice. Finding it safe and whole and resting neatly on the seafloor was a real win."

"The *Terror*? Does this have something to do with the French Revolution?"

"No, no, not at all. I guess social studies isn't compulsory anymore, eh? But you've heard of the Northwest Passage? There are ships going through now all the time near the place where Franklin's ships were frozen in solid for three full years."

He looked suspicious. "There's a section on global warming, but that's pure bunk, ma'am. I mean, really. Look at the weather we had this February and March. It was never that cold for so long, not in all my dad's lifetime. At least now the President cancelled all that money they were going to waste on that deal in Paris—"

"You mean the American President? The Paris Accord?" There was clearly no way to convert him, so she simply said, "I don't think the books I need will be in that section. But you never know. Let's have a look. When will your supervisor be in?"

"Mrs. Richards only comes in at 11:00, ma'am. We're a small staff right now; I'm the only student. It's a quiet place to study when I'm done my work," he said. She saw him close the game on his phone as he came around the counter and led her to a display in the corner of the library.

As she looked around, she could see why Mamme was convinced that the students and town folk didn't believe the science. The display was worse than sparse—it was skeletal. There were a couple of behemoths by Naomi Klein, a VHS copy of Al Gore's ancient video *An Inconvenient Truth,* and a few books by David Suzuki and friends. She picked up *The Sacred Balance.* Both it and his *Green Guide* looked pristine. According to the cards in the back, neither had ever been taken out. When she glanced through the latter, she saw someone had scrawled, "Who Gives a Shit?" in red felt pen right across a two-page spread. *Somebody had better give a shit pretty soon,* she thought, but she knew she had to pick her battles. Reporting the damage to the young clerk would do more harm than good: if they saw it had been vandalised, the book would be removed from circulation. She snapped it shut and set it back in its holder on the table.

The branch computers were still refusing to cooperate. As she walked briskly through the aisles, she soon discovered the Canadian history section, right where it had been when she had worked summers at the library all those years ago. She pulled out her notebook and flipped to the last page, where she had scrawled a list of some titles from her research. She traced the rows, spied one of the books she wanted, way up top, above her head. She grimaced. As though it were some fundamental law of nature, whatever book she wanted was always absolutely on the top of the stacks, no matter what library she was in. Why did she have to be short, like Mamme, when Dad was so tall? Suddenly she laughed at herself. Such first-world problems. All she was looking for was a lead or two—and who knew whether she would find that today or in a month. Or a year. The books she was looking for weren't new by any means. She pulled over the round metal library stool, climbed up on it, and reached up top, running the titles with her right index finger. Quickly she saw something. The volume was wedged in, and as she tried to pull it out, the book beside it launched itself at her: Beattie's *Frozen in Time*, the same one she'd found at home. *What about that, huh, Dad? Just another coincidence?* But this time there was something else. As she got down to pick up and reshelve the book, she found another item had fallen down too, but it wasn't really a book at all—it was about ninety pages or so, a soft-backed beige pamphlet entitled *Lieut. John Irving, R.N., of H.M.S. Terror, A Memorial Sketch with Letters.*

Inside the cover was a small paper plaque: "Donated by the Thomson family, Humboldt, Saskatchewan, 1984, in honour of John's birth." If she remembered correctly, Ryan Thomson's oldest brother was named John. Huh. Kind of a jerk at school, if she remembered him right. Always putting Ryan down. She flipped through the pages. At the front there was a note about the text being out of print, so it had been retyped, and copies made for family, as some sort of heirloom. Even when Mia was little, she'd heard the stories that surrounded the Thomsons. They were a big deal in Humboldt, one of the few families of settlers that wasn't German—birthed their offspring in a sod shack on the home quarter, as tough and rugged as they came. And they were adventurers, as Dad always said.

Pretty fascinating people. Mia flipped quickly through the pages, pausing here and there at the illustrations. In the back there was a large family tree that folded out to four pages, tracing back to 1836. Right at the bottom, there was the line that linked their famous many-times-great-great-uncle John through his brother, Lewis, all the way down to the present-day Thomson brothers: John, Stephen, Robert, and Ryan. Ryan had been in her grade at school—she blushed for a minute, remembering their meeting in the grocery store. They'd hung out as kids, at least until they reached high school. If Ryan was home helping out on the farm, she wondered what had happened to those older brothers—all out living the life fantastic in Vancouver or Toronto or Montreal, she was pretty sure. That was where those explorer types always went nowadays.

Mia had been both exhilarated and devastated when the *Erebus* was found five years ago, but there hadn't been much media attention, hardly any television work. Once, she would have sworn she would help solve the mystery of what happened to the crew, all those well-provisioned, relentless sailors. But, as her mother had pointed out, Mia would be miserable up North: she hated the cold, and although she was a strong swimmer, the discovery of Franklin's ships had not seemed imminent enough to persuade her to learn how to dive. And surely by now, most of the questions about the condition of the ship and why its crew had abandoned it would be under investigation by archaeologists, not journalists. Still, this book on Irving might give her another angle. No archaic instrument or dinner service could really reveal what the journey had been like through the eyes of the crew. Irving's letters, his testimony, would help her make links to what the archaeologists uncovered, show the voyage from the intimate perspective of one of the officers himself, a man setting off on life in a new direction—like she was. Mia shivered. Still, analyzing his final words, the ones carried home to Scotland by the last ship to see the crew alive, could help put some flesh on the old bones. And the pamphlet was an unassuming little volume, so far overlooked. Like the Suzuki, it had never even been taken out. She stood on the library stool again to check the top shelf one last time, craning to see if any more books had fallen behind, but there were none. This one would have to do.

Flipping through, she approached the circulation desk, where the boy was apparently now deep in *Clash of Clans*. She coughed twice to show that she was waiting, but he just smiled. Well, she could afford to wait a minute. She had found the book she was meant to. When at last he was ready, the young clerk began her application to reactivate her library account. She paid the three dollars and answered his questions as pleasantly as she could, and at last he solemnly scanned the book and passed her the card. At least now she had something new to think about, something of her own. She would lose herself in Lt. Irving's letters home to Scotland and in online research online and would let her parents work out whatever the hell they were really fighting about.

She was curious, though, just for a minute. Surely the rift went deeper than books and boxes. It wasn't like Mamme to be so needy, so sensitive. Well, Mia would give her folks some privacy. She'd hide herself in her new office, read, and fill notebooks with ideas. She couldn't wait to get started. As she passed through the foyer of the library, she stopped for a moment to scan the bulletin board. She found it the best way to take the pulse of the town, to see if anything interesting was happening. People posted all kinds of personal shit on that board.

*Homemade Pierogis for Sale, $5.00/dozen.*

*Vintage car rally, Saturday, May 18.*

*AA Meeting, 7:30 p.m., Yoga, Saturdays, 9:00 a.m., the United Church basement.*

*Ginger kittens to good homes, reasonable price, ready for pickup.*

She paused at the last notice. She'd never been able to resist kittens but, moving around as she had, always living in apartments, pets had never been an option. The poster had a photo of four adorable apricot tabbies, all chewing on one another, blue-eyed and innocent. She'd always wanted an orange cat. Maybe she needed a new little friend of her own. She considered the idea for a moment, then shook her head. Now was hardly the time to do something that would tie her down. What about the North?

When she went through the scanner before she reached the door, the machine beeped loudly at her. Frustrated, she returned to the circulation desk. The young Lochinvar had failed to check her prize out properly. She waited while he made the necessary correction and handed her the book.

On her way out, she passed by the bulletin board again. There they were, those adorable rascals. A sign, she thought. There had to be a reason she saw the notice again. Quickly she tore off a slip with the phone number. She'd be following the universe, thank you very much. And from now on, her parents could do their own damned thing. She'd be busy.

# 33

Ursula wiped her hands on the red-and-white towel, hung it on the oven handle, and took off her apron. She leaned against the counter for a moment, gazing out the window into the darkness. She didn't know what to do. She hadn't been able to think of a thing to say to Andreas or Mia as they silently devoured—no, she corrected herself; that word might imply enjoyment—as they hastily consumed the fried pork chops and green beans and baked potatoes she had prepared for supper. The two of them left without a word of thanks, so Ursula had cleared the table, as usual, and tidied the kitchen. She could hardly go and sit in the living room with Andreas now, pretending that nothing was wrong; besides, she could hear the squealing car chases and loud explosions in the action film he must be watching. Stallone or Schwarzenegger, she wondered absently. Aside from his poor mother, who had kept endlessly busy with housework, Andreas had grown up in a family of all men, developing tastes that were entirely different from Ursula's. At least he wouldn't blame her for that; she was sure he didn't even know that it was partly his choice in television that had driven her to start researching in the evenings. She wished Mia had stayed to help with the dishes so they could have talked, maybe smoothed things over, but Mia had finished her meal and left the table without even excusing herself, taking the stairs two at a time down to her study.

Ursula asked herself what she was going to do with the long evening ahead. She was grateful that Andreas had returned her boxes yesterday. She'd made sure she was pleasant about that, even though he had deposited them in the laundry room, of all places. She knew she should at least look at them, sort through one or two, maybe find the courage to try to thank him again before he went to bed. She took one last look around the kitchen, moved some steaks (Andreas's favourite) from the freezer to the refrigerator to thaw for tomorrow, and started down the stairs.

As she passed Mia's study, she hesitated, tempted to knock on the door, but she knew that Mia was angry with her and would never take her side. She was her father's girl, no doubt about that. Ursula turned and trudged down the hall to the laundry room, turning on the lights. Through the open door she could see the boxes stacked in the corner. If the spring melt flooded in through the window they were piled below, they would be the first things ruined. But she wasn't going to dwell on that now. She was in the wrong this time, and it was hardly surprising if he wanted her to hurt.

Taking a deep breath, she went over to the boxes. Several held books; maybe Babbe had left a letter or a journal, some connection to him, anything that would take away her isolation from everyone and everything. She opened box after box, flipped through novels and histories, biographies and medical texts, but there were no letters, nothing personal. But when she pulled out the last book, there it was: a framed photo of the blossoms on her tree. She had sent it to Babbe all those years ago as a sign that miracles could happen, were happening, for her on this side of the ocean.

How had she forgotten that? For a moment she felt like crying, remembering how he, at least, had always cherished her dreams. She would hang it here, in her little domain, to remember him by.

She repacked the boxes, piled them again, and moved on to the next stack. From Kathrin's notation, she could see that the top one held her doll collection. That she knew by heart; her parents had brought home a lovely doll for her each time they travelled. But as she opened the flaps and lifted the tissue paper, she found something sparkly, a necklace twined around the glass cloche that protected the first doll, the pianist. She reached in and untangled it, drew it free, and held it up for closer inspection.

There it was, the *A* embossed on a tiny silver petal beside a small engraved cross. Especially tonight, the cross seemed stern, sorrowful, forbidding, and she tried not to look at it. Instead, she watched the letter swing and glitter beside it on the chain that suspended the two, remembering how it had looked around her mother's still-smooth neck when Mamme had leaned down to kiss Ursula on the forehead. Every night the almost-heart would dangle near, and always, Ursula would knot her fingers so that she would not reach up to seize it, this first-last memory of the sister she had never known, Annelis.

Her parents never spoke of their loss. When little Norbert was born, Ursula had overheard the babysitter gossiping with their neighbour about Ursula's elder sister, Annelis, the image of Mamme, tiny hands with determined fingers stretching for the piano keys, ever stretching, aiming at perfection, a natural performer. And how one dreadful day, Mamme and Babbe had each thought Annelis was with the other—by the time the searchers found the little boots near the flooded river, it was too late. As she'd listened to the two women tut-tutting, Ursula knew right then that she must make herself love the piano, too. She would never let her mother hurt that way again.

Just remembering, Ursula couldn't breathe. She slipped the chain into her pocket, set the tissue paper back in place, and left the half-opened box on the table beside the clothes dryer, her heart like a bird trapped under glass. She turned the lights off as she left the room, climbed the stairs, and found her way to the privacy of her bed. She comforted herself as best she could. At least, sleeping alone, she didn't have to hide this new-old pain from Andreas. As always, he would be absolutely unaware of anyone's problems but his own.

# 34

Sleeping in the study was even worse the second night. Andreas had drifted off soon after turning in but was startled out of his dreams at two thirty-four a.m., of all the Christ-forsaken moments, and was still wide awake when his alarm went off at five. He shut it off and for a long minute he just lay there cursing silently. What was the use? He might as well get up, face the frigging day, and get ready for his run. Why in hell couldn't he sleep anymore? He pushed himself up on one elbow, untangled his legs from the flimsy throw blanket he'd liberated from the living room, and swung his feet to the floor. As he tried to stand, he stumbled. His left foot was asleep; well, hallelujah, at least some part of him was getting its beauty rest after all. He shook his left leg silently, wiggled his toes, then forced himself to settle down, move slowly, walk deliberately, quietly. Silence was essential to this operation. The last thing he needed was to confront an angry Ursula. He'd slept in his terry bathrobe for some sort of warmth, over top of the pajamas he had finally rescued when she was downstairs. Grimly, he tightened the belt and walked across the room. He picked up his running clothes from the back of the chair where he'd draped them yesterday morning, padded quietly down the stairs, and slipped into the main-floor bathroom.

He washed his face half-heartedly and patted it dry. He'd shave later—maybe. Yes, he was slacking, but he just didn't give a frick about anything today. The freaking couch was so hard and cold, but he was damned if he'd go to Ursula and ask for a blessed blanket, pretty please; no, that would nourish the little demon's belief that she was in control, so he simply made do and shivered. He couldn't remember being so Christforsaken angry before.

The worst of it was, the damned woman was right. There *was* something wrong with her, as she had been insisting, a problem with her brain—but it wasn't dementia. No, siree. It was her all-consuming need to micromanage every blessed detail that related to every bloody person she came in contact with, and him most of all. He pulled on his clothes, wondering when he had ever felt this kind of rage before. Was there nothing he could control these days?

Dressed at last, he went into the kitchen. He knew better than to skip his stretches, though his heart certainly wasn't in them. He leaned down one side and then the other, sliding his hand along his thigh and calf, stretching hard to touch the floor. Look at the way she'd reacted when he'd returned her bloody boxes. He'd felt apprehensive enough, terrified of another fucking scene; he knew he had been taking a chance, refusing to return her things to what was now Mia's study. He lunged forward with his right knee bent, his left leg dropping almost to the floor. He repeated the move ten times, then reversed. Ursula had acted as if he were the most wonderful man in the world. "Thank you, Andreas," she said, when he told her that her things were in the laundry room. "That's perfect," she purred, as if she hadn't put them all through that incredible shit-show the day before. Who *was* this woman and what did she want from him? He reversed legs again, did his stretches, and stepped quickly into the back porch. He put on his runners and tied them, looped a scarf around his neck, pulled on his jacket, gathered his toque and gloves, and slipped quietly out the back door and through the gate. Before he knew it, he was running down the hill.

The air was harsh. Frost collected on his stubbled chin as the fog of his breath touched it. He knew it was really too cold to run, but Christ, he needed the exercise to work out some of this frustration. The bloody stoplight was against him and he paused out of habit, pushing the button and impatiently jogging in place. Muttering, "Screw this!" he ran across the street despite the red hand signal. As he was taking the corner in front of the Ukrainian Catholic Church, his right foot skidded out from under him. His left ankle folded over and he fell awkwardly, hitting the back of his head. He lay dazed at first, looking up at the streetlights, feeling the burn of the cold from the frozen sidewalk.

Christ. Such a rookie mistake. At least no one had seen him; there were no cars coming, no lights down the street. He lifted his hand and touched the back of his head gingerly. Nothing abnormal, nothing broken, just some swelling. He lifted his leg carefully, bent his knee, and felt for his ankle. His head ached, his foot throbbed, and his thoughts raced. For a moment he just lay there, wondering how in the world he was going to get up. "Jesus Christ."

He was attempting to kneel when a strange voice behind him said, "Need a hand?"

Andreas looked back, embarrassed as all hell. "No, thanks—I'm almost up. Thanks, anyway. I just surprised myself, that's all. Any fool could see that patch of ice—I wasn't paying attention, I guess." Andreas struggled to heave himself to his feet and brushed himself off, keeping most of his weight on his good leg. The coatless stranger was all in black. He must be the priest Andreas had seen through the windows at the back of the church most mornings. Andreas hated to discuss religion at the best of times and right then he was busy cursing himself. His leg was going to be a problem after all. He couldn't finish his run. He was an idiot. Why hadn't he looked where he was going? He had sprained his right ankle in September a year and a half ago, playing basketball at that faculty event, and now he'd hurt his good left one. Ursula, just back from Europe at the time, had seemed oblivious to his pain. Three months of physio were needed to get the swelling to subside, and the joint had never felt right again, not entirely. It was his Achilles' heel, he used to joke, back when he still tried to make Ursula laugh. Now, for Christ's sake, he'd have two weak spots. But he wasn't going to tell a stranger all that, certainly not some priest.

"Looks like you could use a moment to sit down and rest. I just put the coffee on. Come inside and have a cup?"

"Thanks, Father, no. I have to get back home to start work—"

"Work? It's only five-forty-five. Come on, just one cup of coffee. I'm harmless, really, Scout's honour. Anyway, it's high time we met. I see you go by most mornings. It's not like there are a lot of runners in Humboldt." He paused. "I have to admit," he said, patting his waistline, "You inspire me."

As he stood there, Andreas's ankle throbbed, the pain almost unbearable. Maybe he did need a place to rest. He could call Mia and wait in the rectory while she came to get him, which would be better than waiting out here, freezing his ass off. "I do?" he said. "In what way? You run, too?"

"I guess we should introduce ourselves. I'm Gerry Pacholok. I don't so much run, as run herd."

"Run herd?" Andreas asked. Making polite conversation was a chore. He was only half paying attention to what the priest was saying. His ankle was killing him. He was going to have to see the doctor, put in all that time at rehab—

"Just a pun. I run herd, you know, watching my flock? Folks in Humboldt are a pretty challenging group. I can never quite corral them, no matter what I do. Postmodern morals and tech combined with good old-fashioned gossip and superstition, not to mention all that New-Age stuff. Who believes in the Deity, let alone the Church? Hey, I'm dying to talk about anything but religion. What about that coffee? Here, lean on my arm. I've got you. What's your name?"

"Thanks, thanks a lot, Father. I'm Andreas Niederhauser. I teach math in Muenster."

"Nice to meet you, Andreas. Call me Gerry. Watch out for that ice, now. Here we go."

# 35

Mia sat at her desk, enjoying the view. The sun was still just below the horizon, the night's deep blue hovering above a wash of pale yellow. She could hear Mamme fussing around upstairs in the kitchen, making coffee, gathering her things. At last the back door slammed and Mia could relax; the house was hers.

Mia was still worried about keeping the office, knowing how angry Mamme had been, but last night Dad had confided that her mother was upset about a personal matter, something Mia didn't have to worry about. As if she wouldn't worry, just because she didn't know what the problem was—that only made it all the worse. Maybe it was just hormones. Some women took ten to fifteen years to go through menopause. Was that what she had to look forward to? She grimaced. You couldn't escape your genes.

And her timing was clearly impeccable, picking right now to land in this hornet's nest. She leaned back in her chair and looked out the window, between the spruce trees and out across the orchard. The sun was a fierce dot rising above the horizon now, its long red spikes of light shooting toward her between the trees. There were half a dozen chickadees flitting from tree to tree in the dim light, black caps and white breasts outlined in pink by the glow. Two birds were perched on her mother's feeder, cracking sunflower seeds, while others dove into the wind and rose against it, landing on the swaying boughs of her backyard forest, the trees she used to call *Miette* in honour of their beloved family holidays.

Well, it wasn't a forest and it wasn't hers, she reminded herself. She was going to have to find a way to get out from underfoot. That much was for certain. She looked for the book that had leapt off the shelf at her yesterday, the Franklin connection. Where had she put it? For a minute she felt panicked as she scanned her desk. How had she lost it so quickly? She shuffled through the piles of books and papers. It was beige, she remembered that much, with a black plastic spine. At last she saw it: *A Memorial Sketch with Letters.*

As she scanned John Irving's letters to his sister-in-law Katie, she wondered if Ryan Thomson could tell her more about this booklet. It was about his many-times-great uncle, and Ryan had remembered her, even after all these years. Maybe it would be worth going to the rink, taking him up on his offer, after all. As she sorted through her papers, she came across the slip with the phone number she'd pulled from the bulletin board at the library, the one for the kittens. She dropped it into the gray ceramic bowl at the back of the desk, where at least she wouldn't lose it.

Two hours later she was just starting to wonder where her father was. He must have gone to the university, she thought, probably to avoid Mamme. As if on cue, her phone rang.

"Mia, are you up already?"

"Of course, Dad. I'm hard at work."

"I'm afraid I need you to come pick me up. I'm at the Ukrainian Catholic Church."

"The *where?*"

"The Ukrainian Catholic Church, yeah, in the rectory. Come to the back door. You could say I followed in Mamme's steps this morning: I went for the trip of a lifetime, and the good father who helped me up needs to get ready for his service now. Can we stop by the pharmacy for some crutches—and then, I guess, we'll have to hit the hospital?"

The next morning, Mia was tidying up, sorting her papers and supplies. Things had been quiet around the house, especially at mealtimes, with Mamme and Dad both stern and silent. It was so odd to see them this way, so detached, so stiflingly polite. The stress was starting to make Mia feel ill. Her stomach hurt when she didn't eat and hurt worse when she did. Somehow, though, they made it through dinner without another explosion from her mother.

She tossed a handful of paperclips into the bowl, and a little slip of paper bounced up and fell out onto the desk. She saw the phone number she'd plucked from the bulletin board at the library. She reflected for a moment as she looked at it—could it be a sign? Maybe a kitten would cheer everyone up again.

She pulled out her cell phone and dialled. A man answered, "Hel*lo?*"

"Hello," Mia smiled. "I'm calling about the kittens?"

"Sorry. All gone—"

"But I just saw your poster at the library."

"All gone," he repeated. "The first day. Cute cats don't keep."

"Really? I meant to call right away but something came up. Do you know anyone else who has any?"

"Any what?" The man sounded suspicious.

"Kittens?" Mia couldn't understand why he couldn't follow a simple question.

"No, it isn't exactly kitten weather. Most cats only breed in the spring and summer." A woman mumbled something in the background that Mia couldn't quite catch. He turned his voice away from the phone. "What's that?" She could hear a woman in the distance and then he was back. "Oh, sure. You could have her."

"Her?" Now Mia was confused.

"The mother."

"Well…I was thinking of something young and cuddly. How old is she? What's she like?"

"Well, this is her second litter. She's about a year old, I guess. Fluffy little thing. Not very sturdy for a barn cat. Funny colour, too. Has nice kittens, though. Too many. Who needs all those cats?"

"I thought you said she didn't have any kittens left?"

"She doesn't. All gingers, like herself. The ones that lived, anyhow."

"So… could I come and have a look at her? When would be a good time?"

"Well, we're home right now, will be here for the next hour or so. That work for you? No time like the present."

"Sure, that would be great. Can you share your location with me? My name is Mia. Mia Koehl-Niederhauser."

"Coal Needer-what?"

"Never mind," Mia said. For the millionth time, she silently cursed her parents and the name they'd gifted her with. "Let me grab some paper." Mia took out her notepad. "How do I get there? Fire when ready."

By the time she arrived home, Mia had her hands full, literally. Litter pan, box of litter, bag of food from the vet's, and a closed cardboard box. The box was bumping and jumping a bit in her arms, and she was struggling to fit her key in the lock without dropping anything. She was startled when Ursula opened the door from the inside and asked, "Need a hand?"

Mia said, in a rush, "Oh, thanks, Mamme. That would be a big help. Here, could you take the box? She's not making this easy."

"She? What's in here, anyway? Feels like a racoon—"

Mia set her purchases down beside the door. "It's Alphonse, my new pet," she said. "You'll love her."

"I don't recall agreeing to any new pets." Ursula started to spread the cardboard flaps to peer inside.

Mia took the box back from her mother. "Careful, Mamme, she's going to get out. Let's get inside. You were the one who said I needed some friends. She'll be good for me. You know I've always wanted a cat."

"But we have a cat. You named him: Adam, First Cat."

"Yes, but he's old now, and grumpy, and she's young and cute. Things have been pretty quiet up here lately—you're both so—no, not that I don't understand," she added in a rush. "It's just that sometimes it feels kind of lonely," she finished, wondering why, at her age, she had to defend a little decision like this to her own mother.

"That's what I've been saying. Why not look up your old friends?"

"Oh, they've all flown the coop, at least the ones I used to hang out with. The people my age in Humboldt are all married with children. It's not like we have much in common," she said ruefully, tapping the soft little paw that was jabbing up between the flaps. "Ouch!"

"She's quick, I grant you that. Probably a good mouser. But why *Alphonse?*"

"Why not? She was free, she needs a home, and she needs to be spayed. They tell me she had her first batch of kittens at six months old—permanently stunted. Besides, wait 'til you see her."

"No, no, I mean, why the *name* Alphonse? It's a female, right? You keep saying 'she'—"

"Oh, yeah, of course it's a she." She laughed a bit. "Well, I don't really know. I saw a poster for Alphonse Reifferscheid at the hardware store—you know, they're having a celebration of his life this weekend—and I sort of thought the name suited her."

Ursula stroked the buff-coloured paw that was poking through.

"Would you mind watching her for a minute, Mamme? Just while I run down and set things up in the office?" Mia smiled suddenly, her face as bright as sun glancing off water. She nodded as Mamme hesitantly started to play with Alphonse, who was batting two little paws up again and again between the box's flaps.

"But be careful," Mia warned. "Those dainty little claws are like razors. She got me a few times." She held up a scratched finger. She went from the porch into the kitchen and fetched a clean white saucer and a bowl for water, then carried all of the supplies downstairs.

As she moved around her office, setting things up, Mia was surprised to feel a rush of relief. She hadn't considered, until Mamme appeared and started questioning her, that her parents might object. She picked out a spot for the food, arranged her softest throw on the slipper chair in her study, and set up the litter box in one corner.

"Mamme?" she called. "You can bring her down now. Thanks."

In moments her mother appeared, the little cat cradled in her arms, purring like a motorboat.

# 36

The last thing Ursula had planned to do was to fall in love, but Alphonse was impossible to resist, even in those first few moments. With Mia downstairs, prepping the study, Ursula freed the little miss in an act of self-preservation, trying to stop the tiny claws from shredding her fingers. Once she had lifted her out, the little fluff-bot stopped scratching immediately and settled into Ursula's arms, purring as if there was nowhere she would rather be. Her yellow-green eyes were wide as they toured the main floor, Ursula showing her the sparrows in the Schubert cherry in the front yard, then the greedy crew pecking at the feeder through the kitchen window. By the time Mia called up to ask Ursula to bring her down, the whole litany of troubles that had seemed so overwhelming when she called in sick that morning—her fight with Andreas, his wretched sprained ankle, whatever he was really doing in the mornings, her guilt over Mamme and Annelis, even her blessed diagnosis—all of it had just lifted away.

Once Alphonse (what a name) was set down in the study, she sat up on her haunches like a little bear, still purring, begging to be petted. She was thin—Ursula could feel her ribs through all that fuzz—but feisty, and no bigger than a six-month old. Ursula thought to herself that they'd soon see about fattening her up, and maybe it wasn't too late for her to grow a little, too. As always, she couldn't help worrying. How was Adam going to react, having to share his territory, just like that? If they didn't watch out, he'd have her for breakfast. And what about Andreas, what would he say? He wasn't an animal person; he tolerated Adam, who knew who ruled the roost. On the other hand, Ursula was sure he would never interfere with anything Mia wanted.

And then an odd thought floated through her distracted mind: with his crutches, at least he wouldn't be able to run anymore. That would stop those early morning assignations, at least. She smiled at Mia, just thinking about it.

# 37

Andreas woke with a start. For a minute he wasn't sure where he was. He was freezing. While he slept, he must have thrashed off the stupid throws, but he knew that was not the reason. He had never felt like this before. For a few minutes everything was a jumble, the dream still more real than the stiff leather sofa beneath him.

*He was in water—cold, dark, deep water. He remembered taking one last look at the bright surface above before he swam down with a group of six or seven divers, all wearing masks and wetsuits. Something was stirring up the silt; the field was murky, especially in the circle of light up ahead. He couldn't let go of his fear, the darkness that lurked behind and around him as they swam. The wreck below, lit by those up ahead, looked both terrifying and enticing. Not much further down to reach it. The others were swimming in and under and around the deck, pointing to this and that.*

*He knew they'd been warned not to touch anything, so he only watched as some of the others picked up plates and cutlery, bottles and buttons, all of which they examined and then dropped back into the silt as they moved onto the next find, and the next. If the Parks Canada people, the archaeologists, were worried about damage to the pristine site, Andreas thought, they had plenty of reason, but the lure of all that tourist money must have been irresistible, at least to the higher-ups. Surely workers would have mapped and catalogued everything before they let visitors enter the wreck. Well, if not, it was too late now. A real, honest-to-God ghost ship. Andreas felt strange, lost in time as much as in space. Just then he looked over to the side, where people were gathered, pointing. A woman had appeared on the surface from out of nowhere. She was wearing a bright pink life preserver. She splashed under, but there was something wrong; she didn't bounce up; only her thrashing legs were visible in the bright water that separated them from the sky. No one tried to save her. He looked around to see if he could do anything to help. She was too far away, just flailing and flailing above him.*

*When the dive master signalled it was time to go, they surfaced in twos and threes and pulled off their masks. The air was brisk, even colder than the water. There were plenty of people to help them into the dinghies and then back aboard ship. He had no idea where he was, except that he felt as cold as could be, the rocky shores barren except for a few scattered buildings. At last he heard someone ask when she had been found, the* Erebus—*and then he knew. It was Franklin's ship.*

There was a terrible noise. His head hurt. He woke with a start. Damn it, it was his phone. It was five a.m., time to go for his run. He started to sit up, winced when his foot hit the floor. Of course, he had forgotten to change his alarm. He wouldn't be running for weeks, the doctor had said. Well, he had to do something, if only to figure out why he was dreaming of the Franklin Expedition via Bruegel's *Icarus*, the painting come to life. And why didn't that life preserver float? Why had no one helped that poor woman?

Gerry would have the coffee on at the church already. He hobbled over as quietly as he could to the chair where he had left his clothes and cautiously dressed himself.

# 38

The curling rink was dark when Mia entered, only the red EXIT signs glowing at the doorways and a bare bulb lit over the entrance to the ice. She could hear someone talking, a pair of someones, joking down on the ice. She felt shy all of a sudden—this was a dumb idea. What did she know about curling? She'd never even watched *Men with Brooms*. When she'd seen Ryan in the grocery store, it had sounded so easy—*Just come down, give it a try*—but now she felt completely out of place. She didn't have the right footwear, and they would have to lend her a broom. Feeling new in her hometown was beginning to feel old.

She was just about to turn around and leave when the lights whooshed on overhead. She turned to look as the door opened behind her. Shit. He had seen her.

Ryan called, "Hey, Mia! Glad you could make it."

She forced a smile. "Hey! Wouldn't miss it." She waited as he walked towards her. They made small talk as they went through to the ice where the others were waiting, a girl laughing with someone who looked oddly familiar.

Ryan made the introductions. "Mia Koehl-Niederhauser, my brother John, and Kathy Paslowski. Mia and I went to grade school together, if you can believe it."

"What, you went to grade school?" Kathy teased him. "That *is* a surprise."

Ryan's face flushed. "No, I mean—how many people our age do you know who've made it to Vancouver and then come back home? And yet here you have not one but two specimens who have voluntarily followed the same flight path."

"Speak for yourself, boyo," Mia said, smiling. "You may have volunteered, but—"

"Hey, c'mon. It's fantastic here. A great place to raise kids. You do want kids, don't ya?" Kathy asked. "I know your mother, Ursula, right? The Swiss lady with the buzz cut? She's such a character, really one of a kind. They don't make them like that anymore."

"Yeah, that's Mamme; she's *something*, alright." Mia shook her head. "How do you know her?"

"I'm her stylist. In Humboldt, that means her counsellor-confessor."

"Ah, right, gotcha. Sure, she's mentioned you. You're the miracle worker."

"Well, I do what I can." She smiled conspiratorially. "But she won't give up on that buzz cut, not even with my natural powers of persuasion—"

John was inspecting her footwear. "So, Mia, when's the last time you curled?"

"I hate to admit it, but I've never curled before. I thought maybe one of you could show me what to do."

"Well, there's time enough for some practice before the game starts, I guess," John said. "Here. Come out onto the ice. This is a rock."

"Thank you. I know that much," Mia blushed.

He smiled. "Good! You stand here, hold your arm like this. Swing it back, crouch with all your weight behind you, and then let go, as you slide full forward, gliding. Don't let go yet, no, try it again. That didn't go anywhere. You want more weight behind it. You guys get out there and sweep when she throws."

"Yes, sir, Brother," Ryan said sarcastically. "Who died and appointed you skip?"

"Well, if you want her to learn from the best—"

Kathy grinned at Ryan. "Let him have his delusions of grandeur. Here, grab your broom, youngster. You could use the sweeping practice, too."

Before long, Jody and Kevin and the others trooped in, and the game got going in earnest. Mia was surprised at how much fun she was having, even though she could see she was going to have to work hard just to remain upright for the entire game, as stiff and sore as her legs felt already. Sweeping was easier but had its own challenges. The only players who were serious about winning were John and Jody, the skips; it was clear that Ryan was only there to socialize. He kept the girls laughing and was willing to play the fool to do so, seeming to enjoy antagonizing his brother even more than all the attention.

When they were finished, Mia sat down and he brought her a beer. "So, what d'ya think?"

"Well, I won't be trying out for the winter games anytime soon, but hey, it's a nice diversion. Though it does feel odd to be trying so hard to throw my back out, when we could be sitting comfy over in the bar at the Pioneer. I'm sure I'm going to regret this in the morning. Shit, I regret it already."

"No doubt you do. You won't be alone, though; we'll all feel it, in every long-forgotten bone or joint or muscle in our aging bodies."

"Who are you calling aging? I'm a young woman, embarking on life in a new direction. That's my new mantra. So you must be, too."

"A young woman? Or a mantra?"

"No, idiot. Young."

"Hmmm...—Ish. See how young you feel tomorrow." He took a generous swallow of beer. "At least I'm young compared to the *old man*," he called towards John, who was standing to the side, talking to Jody.

"Huh?" John said, looking over at Ryan. "Of course you're younger than Dad, jerk. Do I need to explain the reproductive cycle to you?"

Ryan lifted his beer to him. "No, that you do not. But at least I'm not turning forty next week, like someone I know."

John shrugged. "Forty is the new twenty," he called, amidst laughter from the others.

Mia smiled and turned back to Ryan. "So if your brother is here, tell me why you had to come home to help your dad farm?"

"Oh, John couldn't farm with Dad. No, no, no. Those two have been locked in some Godawful death-grip deadlock for twenty-odd years. John farms his side of the creek, Dad farms the other, and never the twain shall meet. Now that I'm home helping Dad, John sees me as the competition. It's bizarre, really. But you know—no one gets to pick their family members."

"John seems nice, though, kinda funny. But yeah, I do know what you mean. It's been plenty weird at home since I moved back." Now why had she said that? Now she was going to have to explain.

"Oh? In what way?" Ryan looked interested.

Might as well just come clean. She needed to talk to someone, anyway. "Well, my dad and I have been driving my mother crazy, but not on purpose. Every little thing we do seems to set her off."

"Yeah? Like what?"

"Like ballistic. I've never seen her like this, ever. Now we're just trying to stay out of her way. Honestly, that's why I'm here. I needed some away time."

"Huh—and here I was hoping you were here to see me. I remember your mother; she was my chemistry teacher. Nice lady. Stern, but knew her stuff. She must be near retirement age now."

"She is, but she'll never quit. Dad has been telling her to take a leave so they can travel after his winter courses are over, but Mamme won't hear of it. Says she's writing a book."

"Ambitious! What kind of book?"

"Oh, I don't know, something for teenagers."

"Y.A.?"

"Fiction? No, no. Mamme would never make shit up. She's researching—climate change, I think. It's hard to tell what her topic is. I'm just the cleaning lady."

"So what do you do when you're not cleaning or freaking your mother out?"

Mia took a deep breath. "I'm trying to write, too. I'm a journalist, as I think I blurted out at you last week. When I can find stories or contracts."

"You mean you mislay them?" Ryan smiled.

"Hardly! I'm the organized one in the family. It's just hard to land contracts these days. I worked in Calgary last, after Vancouver, Toronto, all over the map—like a bloody ping-pong ball. It's not the gig I thought it would be, that's for sure. They promised us a master's degree would guarantee steady work."

He shook his head. "I've heard that song before. What a drag." He took a swig of his beer. "For me, it's been the opposite. When I was studying archaeology, every friggin' person I met asked me, 'Where're you gonna find a job? Hasn't all the old stuff been dug up already?' And now, hallelujah, you can't break ground, build a parking lot even, without an archaeological survey. There's gold in them thar hills," he grinned, pushing his dark hair out of his eyes. "So you've been all over the map; what did you think of the North?"

Mia felt all the pieces slide into place. Her forced move home, her bumping into Ryan in the grocery store, of all places, and now, having him ask just that question—these had to be signs from the universe; they had to be part of the plan. It was just too well-synced to be random. As Dad always said, *fortune favours the bold*, she told herself. "Now that's exactly what I *have* been thinking of! Now that Franklin's ships have been found, it's time to decode the disaster, decipher what in hell happened—like we used to talk about." Mia hesitated. "It's so uncanny—meeting you again, after all these years, and you an archaeologist now—" She paused for a moment, trying to read his face. "I saw an advertisement for a cruise that takes folks out to the wreck of the *Erebus*. I'm looking into it. What do you think—care to come with?"

Ryan smiled. "I saw that in Dad's *AMA* magazine, too! It sounds pretty sweet. But isn't it like nine thousand bucks a berth? Seems a mite steep…"

"True, but if we were to write about the trip, we could apply for a grant—"

"There would absolutely be a book in this. And now that they've found the *Terror*—"

"Let me look into the funding. There has to be a way we can see both—"

Just then Kathy came over and rested her hand on Ryan's shoulder. "The terror? You two talking about Mia's mom again? How did she like the new doctor?"

Mia felt her face flush. "Doctor? What doctor?"

"I fixed her up with my guy. She's been having trouble with her memory—she and your dad are terrified she has Alzheimer's." Kathy looked smug.

"*My* parents? You must be thinking of someone else."

"No, no. I mean your mom, alright. She's been to a specialist who's all but confirmed it. I told her she should get a second opinion. When you're so upset, like she's been—"

"Upset? You heard about that?"

"Hasn't everybody? Welcome to Humboldt."

"There must be a mistake. There's nothing wrong with my mother. She's just annoyed with me for losing my job and having to move home."

"If you say so, Mia. But you might want to check things out. It's never easy living with parents, but Alzheimer's, wow, that's tough. My grandmother has it, and, well— Mom had to put her into a nursing home. She kept turning the burner on and then just wandering away. We were terrified she was going to really hurt herself, or somebody else. You and your dad ought to know what you're getting into." She shook her head.

Mia just looked at Ryan and Kathy, who stared back, sympathetically. For once, she had nothing to say.

Kathy cleared her throat. "Well, maybe it's too late for that; you're here already. Let's hope old Dr. Chernov can pull a rabbit out of the hat." She clinked her bottle against Mia's and winked at Ryan. "Here's to miracle men."

John came over, smiling. "Hey, we should all have another beer. Let's tell Mia what we do when we aren't throwing rocks at one another."

# 39

The next morning, Ursula looked in the mirror as she washed her face, dismayed by the dark circles under her eyes, the lines on her forehead, the dated hairstyle from the nineties. It had taken plenty of confidence to let the hairdresser buzz her glorious hair into a brush cut, but she had been young then, and the girl had persuaded her that it would be hip, so easy to care for. And once it was done, she had never looked back—not until recently, when Kathy had helpfully suggested she might like to try a look more flattering to someone her age. And, following that vein of thought, she had let herself be talked into a makeover at the pharmacy yesterday. Today, her hair was so thick with gray and white, so stiff with all the hairspray the girl had used, it looked like a bottlebrush.

What a ridiculous word, *makeover*: there were no do-overs in life. She turned on the shower, adjusted the tap, and stepped in. She wet her hair, squeezed the expensive shampoo onto her palm, and massaged her scalp for a few moments. Ducking her head under the shower, she rinsed it thoroughly, then loaded the loofah with shea-butter bodywash and scrubbed herself all over. She rinsed off, twisted the tap, and seized her thick white bath towel.

What had gotten into her? Makeup was like changing your name when you married: men didn't have to; why should women? She had insisted on hyphenating her name, resisting Andreas and his charm as he tried to dissuade her. It would be a trial for all the little Koehl-Niederhausers who would people their future, he tried to convince her. Poppycock. As their only child, Mia was a spectacular speller and was perfectly well-adjusted, her lengthy last name a distinction in a field where a person needed to stand out.

Still, the makeover had been stunning. Ursula had gasped when she put on her glasses and saw the effect. She gasped again when she heard the price, but just swiped her MasterCard nonetheless. She deserved a pick-me-up. It was an odd thing, feeling old. For the first time, the salesperson asked if she were a senior, and she hadn't even dared to deny it. The girl took twenty percent off, saying conspiratorially, "We'll take what we can get." When Ursula tried to think of a witty reply, nothing came to her.

How she longed to feel lovely again. If she could conjure even the appearance of normalcy, all the effort in the world would be worth it. She towelled her damp hair and fluffed it with her fingers. What were the steps that had seemed so natural in the drugstore? She lathered her face with the special soap, rinsed it off, patted it dry, and wiped it with a cotton pad soaked in toner. The cool astringent tingled. She dabbed dots of moisturizer carefully around her eyes and worked it into her forehead, cheeks, chin, and neck. The lines plumped to nothingness, the bags under her eyes disappeared. Taking a sponge wedge out of the little plastic bag, she dipped it into the base and applied that to her eyelids and beneath her brows, stroking it onto her skin the way the salesgirl had shown her. She blended the concealer under her eyes and across her cheekbones, fanning the edges smoothly, then sponged on the foundation, stroking it carefully on her face and down her neck. She blurred the edges as best she could.

The first stage complete, she took the eyebrow pencil, made quick, short strokes to darken in her right brow, completing a pleasing arch, and repeated on the other side, then smudged them slightly with the sponge end of the pencil. She rubbed the wand in powdered beige shadow and stroked it evenly on her lids, adding just a touch of a darker shade at the outside corners. She dabbed ecru highlighter under her brows. Taking the lid off the charcoal-coloured eyeliner pencil, she drew the first line like a pro but couldn't stop her hand from shaking halfway through the second eyelid. Damn. She wiped the tiny vertical line away, dabbed on more eyeshadow, and retraced the step, smudging the lines as the girl had done with the applicator.

She forced herself to silence all doubts. Now for the tricky part. It was time for the real magic, the step the girl had said would take off ten years. She squeezed a little glue onto the back of her left hand, delicately picked up the artificial eyelashes, dipped each base in the adhesive, and applied a few lightly, one by one, to fill in her own sparse lashes. To finish, she unscrewed the mascara, scraping the applicator against the lip of the tube, and brushed it on carefully. There. That was fine. Now for a light brush-swirl of blush, a few strokes of lipliner, a smack of pale berry-coloured lip gloss. She looked in the mirror and forced a smile.

For a moment, something like hope bubbled up. Then that sensation fled, and she had to fight the impulse to scrub her face, throw herself down on her bed, and cry herself to sleep. Time had truly caught up with her—not just her mind, but her body, too. The best she could hope for now was to find her place in the herd, to be normal, no matter what ideals she was betraying. Right on cue, she could hear her mother's favourite quip: *Why settle for the mediocrity of the norm?*

She tried to imagine what Andreas would think. Would he be pleased that she was making an effort? But despite his love of all things new, he would never say he approved, no matter how much she longed to hear it. Kathy was as close to a confidant as she had. Maybe the stylist was right; maybe she was being entirely too hard on him. Perhaps he didn't know she needed him to comfort her. He was just a man; she had never asked him for anything, not since—

No. She hadn't asked him for a blessed thing. She went back into her bedroom, sorted through her closet, paused at this hanger and that. Not the deep blue tunic; not the green sheath, either. In the end, she settled on normal once more, pulling out a white blouse and a slim black skirt. She draped the heavy gold and plum-coloured scarf just so, as the salesgirl had shown her, to conceal her neck. In the girl's hands, the soft gold fringe had looked rich, luxurious. But when Ursula turned to the mirror, she felt like a fake. She refused to pursue that thought. The outfit was fine. It was the same way all the other teachers dressed; it screamed respectability, and screaming was what she felt like doing, anyway. She tried to remind herself that everything would be fine. It had to work. Because two days ago, she had lost herself in time again.

And that was one of the most ominous signs, everybody knew that.

# 40

Andreas smiled grimly as he pulled the car off the road and set the parking brake. Despite the early hour, the sky was bright, light pushing the dark up and away just as the sun drew itself over the horizon. The days were already so much longer than they had been even a month before—every year the change of seasons seemed like a miracle. And that was what he needed right now. Just one fucking miracle. He swung himself on his crutches up the path and knocked three times on the heavy wooden door. After a few moments, a booming voice called, "C'mon in!"

He hesitated. Gerry was the first person he could really talk to after all these years in town. So far, they'd talked about all the local characters, and running, and politics. They hadn't yet ventured into the personal, although Gerry was no fool; Andreas was sure the man knew there was something on his mind. They would get to it sooner or later. That was what priests were good at, right? Listening, giving advice? And since married men could become Ukrainian priests, as Gerry had, he must know what women were like.

Andreas looked around as he waited. He studied the willow bush beside the door, each branch articulated with delicate crystals. The hoarfrost was a quarter of an inch thick, all of it sparkling in the pink light. In just two months these branches would be waving long slim green leaves. God. He wished spring were here already. Would this ridiculous winter ever end?

The door opened and Gerry's ruddy face beamed out at him. He was dressed all in black, as always, but that was the only sombre thing about him. He had an apple-green-and-yellow checked tea towel over his shoulder and two bright blue mugs in his left hand.

"Andreas, you old worrywart, come in, come in. You know you don't have to knock. No one in Humboldt ever locks their door." He waved his hand, ushering Andreas into the hallway.

"Courtesy, Gerry. Just being polite. I wouldn't want to interrupt a meeting with anyone."

"And who else would be at my door at this time of the morning?"

Andreas rubbed his chin with his right hand. He smiled. "Hmmm. Lonely widowers, or the lovelorn?"

"So which category do you fit into?" Gerry turned to lead the way into the kitchen at the back of the house.

Andreas laughed grimly. "Ursula is very much alive, thank you, so that must make me lovelorn. Well, I certainly feel lost. As usual."

"You think you mean that, but I've never known anyone with a greater grasp of what he wants than you. And how to get it. You just don't allow yourself to follow your own basic instincts." He waved a hand, gesturing for Andreas to sit on one of the vinyl chairs.

Andreas ignored him, looking puzzled. "Me? You are talking about me, right?"

"I am, absolutely." He gestured again. "Sit."

"So what is it I want?"

"What is it you think you want?" Gerry looked at him briefly, then took the tea towel and wiped the insides of the mugs.

"I want to feel like myself again. I want my wife to feel like herself again. I want our Goddamned Swiss-precision marital clockwork back again. I want our daughter to find a job in her field and free herself from the old folks' home. And I don't have a clue about how to get any of us there." He sat down heavily, leaning his crutches against the wall.

Gerry poured the coffee, sat down, and smiled patiently. He pushed one of the mugs towards Andreas and helped himself to a spoonful of sugar. "This could take a cup of coffee or two. Relax, Andreas. You might just want to start at the beginning."

# 41

Despite her desperation, or more likely because of it, Ursula found herself utterly in love. Here was someone at last who was always glad to see her. She had assumed that all cats were self-serving, barely tolerant of humans, as Adam was. This was completely different. "Peaches, Peachy-pie," she called. "Where are you? Come out, come out, wherever you are!"

"Prrrrttt!" The sound came from under Mia's desk, and out popped the dainty little cat. As always, she sat up on her haunches like a baby bear so that Ursula could stroke her forehead.

"You are adorable, you know that, don't you?" Ursula set down the saucer of milk that she had brought from the kitchen. "Quickly, now. We don't want to get caught. Mia will be home any time now."

A minute or two later, Ursula heard the key in the lock at the back door. She picked up the saucer and gave the cat a little scratch under the chin. "Tomorrow," she promised. "I'll bring you milk tomorrow." She left Mia's office and went into the bathroom around the corner, rinsed the saucer, and stashed it under the sink.

"Mamme?" Mia was carrying a stack of books. "Were you looking for me?"

"No, I was just going to clean the bathroom. It looks a little too-well-lived-in. It won't take a minute."

"You don't have to clean my bathroom! I'll do it later, maybe this afternoon. Do you want to come and see Alphonse?"

Ursula smiled. "She's a sweet little thing. But why she has a man's name," she shook her head, "now that is beyond me."

"I don't know... I think it's because she's all-flouncy, *Alphonsey*. It just seemed like a sign when I saw the name." Mia opened the door to her study, blocking the opening with her foot to make sure that Alphonse didn't escape. "Alphonse? Alphonse? Where are you? C'mon out. We want to play with you."

Over her shoulder she said, "Mamme? Can you make sure she doesn't escape?"

Ursula smiled. "Of course! Look out! She's making a break for it!" She leaned down and scooped up the little cat, who had popped out from her hiding spot, dodged around Mia's feet, and made it out into the hallway.

"That was too close," Mia said. "After the way Adam snarled when he first saw her, I have no intention of letting them duke it out. We both know who would win—and it wouldn't be Alphonse. He has fifteen pounds on her and a disposition like Genghis Khan."

"She is petite. And I've never heard anyone vocalize his displeasure with more conviction. I was terrified for her."

"I'll say—and you, you were terrified, too, weren't you?" Mia took Alphonse from Ursula and held her close. "Thank goodness she knew enough to high-tail it away from him! Though running right to Dad wasn't quite what I expected."

"It *is* odd, isn't it? He doesn't even like cats, though he and Adam share some kind of grudging curmudgeonly respect. But Adam has never liked to be cuddled. He tolerates us."

"That's his prerogative. He was here first."

"I didn't know what to expect when she climbed up your father's jeans, his sweater, and just perched on his shoulder."

"I know, right? She's a canny little thing. Such a brazen act of buttering up! Why is it cats always go to people who don't like them? Maybe she just picked him as the tallest landmark. And when he said, 'Arrgh, Matey. The pet shop was all out of parrots,' as he hobbled around with her on his shoulder, I thought I'd split a gut laughing."

"It was pretty funny. She looked adorable. Peaches is clearly determined to make friends, whether we want to or not."

"Peaches? Who's Peaches?" Mia cuddled Alphonse in her arms. "You feeling alright, Mamme? Anything you want to talk about?"

"Oh, I mean Alphonse. It's just an idea, she's so fuzzy, all that fluff just the colour of a nice ripe peach. And the way she flounces that big tail around like a feather boa—so flirty with it—"

"Yeah, well, geez, Mamme." She set the little cat on the floor, where she started batting at the computer cords. "Peaches sounds like a stripper's name—or the singer's—is that really the effect you want? You sure you're okay?"

"Don't be ridiculous—of course I'm fine! But I think of her more as an old Southern belle, reincarnated. And you did say you weren't sure if you were going to stick with the name Alphonse."

"I did?"

"You did. I remember it clearly. And she looks like a Peaches. Peachy-pie!" Alphonse ran to Ursula and sat up on her haunches. Ursula stroked her from her nose to the top of her head and all down her back, as the little cat purred. "See? She comes to that name," Ursula looked over and smiled.

"Hmmm. You think that might have something to do with all the food you've been bringing her? Honestly,

Mamme, I wasn't going to say anything, but did you think I didn't know you've been smuggling her saucers of something? There's a stack of them under the sink in the bathroom."

"I just wanted to check on her, make sure she wasn't feeling too lonely."

"It's okay, Mamme, I get it. As I said, I'm glad you like her. Adam will get over himself, sooner or later, and then we'll be able to let her run around the house so you can see more of her without breaking into my space."

Ursula's face flushed as she stood up. "Breaking into *your* space? Well, I guess I should have asked. But you were out, and I hadn't seen her today yet—"

"Mamme! It's okay. You're welcome to come into my study. It's not like I'm working on anything top secret. But did I tell you? I found an old book in the library with some pretty fascinating letters from the *Terror*."

"The Franklin expedition? You're still fussing around that? Anyway, if they could get letters out, how were the men ever lost?"

"They gave the letters to passing ships, right up to the time they first were stuck in the ice. One sailor, Lt. Irving, wrote to his sister-in-law in Scotland, telling her they thought they could chop themselves out and the sailors would just drag the ships along. They weren't worried at all, even when they were already doomed." She shook her head.

"So what happened?" Ursula reached over to pet Alphonse.

"That's what's so puzzling. They went silent right after that. Years later, when the search teams came to look for them, they were all dead, all one-hundred and forty-nine of them. They found a burial cairn; identified Lt. Irving's bones by his Royal Navy Medal for Mathematics, buried with him. He must have had one of the early deaths, when they still had energy to erect a cairn. It's pretty spooky. I'm wondering about a contemporary angle—what if we're all going along, concerned about climate change but absolutely confident that we'll overcome it, when we've already authored our own disaster?"

Ursula looked up, startled. "Those who don't study history are doomed to repeat it."

"Exactly," Mia said. "So even when you have seen what will happen, how do you know how to turn your ship around?"

"That's what I was working on, *Schätzli*. That's precisely what my book was all about: how to get young people to turn things around."

"No one wants to think about disaster looming. It might be a hard sell, Mamme." She reached over and patted her mother's arm. "Let me know if there's anything I can do to help."

# 42

Andreas hesitated, rubbing his finger along the chrome edge of the chipped imitation-marble tabletop. "She won't even talk to me anymore. She's curt with Mia, too. She'll say, 'Pass the beans, please,' or 'Have you paid the water bill?' but never anything that's important. She has this look in her eyes, as if she doesn't trust us, doesn't trust me. She's wary, Gerry, always on guard, looking for any excuse for an explosion."

"Have you asked her what's wrong?" The priest passed the plate of arrowroot cookies.

"She'd never tell me. And just whose side are you on, anyway?" Andreas took a biscuit and dunked it in his coffee.

"I'm on your side, Andreas. And Ursula's, and Mia's. You know that." Gerry leaned forward, his arms resting on the table, sipping his coffee.

Andreas smiled, shaking his head. "That doesn't seem fair. You're my friend, Gerry. You haven't even met the women. You don't know what they're like."

"I know all the Ursulas, all the Mias, the Andreases. People just want to feel loved by those they love. As an equation, it's pretty simple. Why do you think Ursula doesn't trust you?"

"You mean this time?"

"*This* time? You're an old hand at hurting your wife?"

"That's not what I meant. But she is mad at me most of the time, these days."

"That's probably true. We put the people we love on pedestals, and then, once they turn out to be mortal, we zero in on their weaknesses, wound them the same way, over and over and over again. It's the original sin, I guess. It's in our genes. So what did you do this time?" Gerry leaned back in his chair, rested his hands on his belly.

Andreas shook his head. "That's just it. I don't know. If I did, I'd fix it. I try to be affectionate, I make small jokes, even tolerate the new cat she let Mia get, but it's as if she's constructed some gigantic barrier between us that makes the old Berlin wall look like a picket fence. She's always waiting to catch me doing something that means I don't love her, at least in her mind." He rubbed his jaw.

"Sounds like she wants to protect herself. But from what?" Gerry took a biscuit.

Andreas was silent for a moment. "From me. From my failed protection of her. She told me that I don't put her first. But she makes that impossible. Like the first blow-up— she was furious that I didn't stop Mia from reorganizing her bookshelf. How could I know that Mia was going to pull out all her ratty old bookmarks, re-shelve everything according to the blessed Library of Congress system? I thought she was just cleaning up, you know, doing a little dusting. It needed to be done; it was a terrible mess. I tried to tell Mia that Ursula liked to keep them in her own order, but my colleague called, and I got distracted. I just forgot. In any case, believe me, I thought Ursula would be happy to have the help."

"It's not me that has to believe you."

"Of course not. But I'm serious. She went fucking ballistic on us, excuse my French. Ape-shit. She tore into me as if I had planned it." Andreas shook his head.

"And? You hadn't?"

"Christ, no. Yes, I thought the bookcase was an eyesore, like Mia did. But if Ursula would clean up her own stuff—" Andreas ran his hand through his hair.

"So why didn't she want her bookshelves cleaned?" Gerry took a sip of coffee.

"Well, she claimed she had them in order, you know, for her precious 'research project.' She says she's writing a book, if you can believe that, when she's always going on and on about not being able to remember anything. But she remembers well enough every bloody time that she doesn't remember, if you know what I mean. The shelf was a disaster—it was so disorganized, that's all. Mia spent all day straightening it out—"

"But they were Ursula's books, right? And she had them organized in her own way?" He swept his arm towards the open doorway, beyond which lay the priest's study. "Like I keep mine?"

Startled, Andreas looked into the room; it was dominated by one large, cluttered bookshelf. Books stood tightly packed on the top three rows, while others lay horizontally in front, in irregular stacks, scruffy papers of all colours sandwiched between. The lower three shelves were empty, except for a few scattered piles of loose white handouts. It was top-heavy, a disaster waiting to happen. Anyone pulling a book from the top shelves could tip the whole thing over. But Gerry had the right to deal with his own messes, so Andreas only squinted jokingly at his friend and said, "Hey! Looks just like home. Are you related to my wife?"

"Hardly, unless she's Ukrainian. But if someone re-shelved my books, I'd kill them," he smiled pleasantly. "It's not disorganized if you know where things are. I need them to be in the order they're in. If someone moved my stuff around, I wouldn't be able to find a thing. It's my system; my wife says keeping clutter is just part of getting older."

"That's what I keep telling her! Forgetting is normal at her age. She doesn't have dementia. The neurologist all but ruled it out. He said he was ninety-eight, well, ninety-five percent certain she doesn't have it. What she does have is an enormous sense of entitlement—and—and—a temperament like Attila the Hun." He shook his head.

Gerry narrowed his eyes. "Hold on a minute. You told me she's a hypochondriac. But your family doctor referred her to a specialist?"

Andreas threw his hands in the air. "Clearly you don't know Ursula. When she wants something, no one can stand in her way. Poor Dr. Au didn't have a chance."

Gerry shook his head. "Poor Dr. Au is a gatekeeper, responsible for public resources. I've known him for ten years. He's a very serious guy, not about to waste the tax-payers' money on specialists that aren't medically necessary. And have they done an MRI?"

"How did you know she has to have an MRI?"

Gerry shook his head. "Never mind. Have they?"

"The waitlist is ridiculous. Six months to get in to see a neurologist, two more months for an MRI—or longer. They're always saying that early detection is crucial, but that seems impossible."

"It does seem that way sometimes."

"In any case, she's fine. She's burnt out, that's what the neurologist thinks."

"Hmmm. Okay, so when you started telling me about all this, you said she had completely melted down, unlike anything you've seen before?"

"Unlike anything since Mia was little and she needed some time off. That's what I keep telling her. Retire—before somebody fires her, if she's acting at school like she is at home. At least take some bloody time off. But no, it wasn't the only time. She had another explosion a few days later."

"Same issue?"

"No, new issue." Andreas grimaced, shaking his head. "But I told her we were going to do it—Mia needed a study. We were just clearing out the spare room and happened to give away a bunch of stuff she wanted to keep."

"Ah. You breached her rights. Same issue. But I take it you and Mia have always treated her this way?"

"What are you talking about? We were saving her the work of cleaning up."

"As I said, if someone rearranged my things, I might kill them. Or at least fantasize about it. And I'm a priest."

"Of course you're a priest. Isn't that why you're defending her?"

"Hardly. No, believe me, Andreas, I feel her pain. You disrespected her things, her wishes. And it seems that maybe, just maybe, you aren't acknowledging her fears."

"What fears?"

"That she may have dementia. You're not taking her seriously. I should know. My favourite aunt has it, and depression, changes in personality, new bouts of rage—she has all those symptoms."

"She's always been a mercurial little thing…"

Gerry spoke gently, his voice firm. "And even if your neurologist is ninety-eight, ninety-five percent certain she doesn't have it, that leaves a two-to-five-in-a-hundred chance that she actually does have it—and for someone as young as she is, that's pretty damned terrifying. For all of you."

# 43

Mia was up early again. The days were starting to get longer, with the sun starting to peek over the horizon already. She couldn't stop thinking about how things had been lining up: the Irving letters, the cruise; it was such synchronicity that Ryan had seen the same magazine, read the same ad. There really was no time to waste if they wanted to go up North this year. The cruise line was booking for late August. Fall came early in the Arctic, so that was their window of opportunity before ice and cold made travel ill-advised for Southerners.

Information was easier to find than expected, though, about the problems the search teams were facing. Most of these related to disputes between the Inuit who owned the sites where the wrecks were found, the teams of archaeologists working for Parks Canada, and the British, who owned the lost ships legally. These last, despite their promise to sign the wreckage over to the Canadians once they were found, had claimed their right to cherry-pick any items recovered from the wreck that were worthy of display in British museums. There were plans for an interpretive facility in Nunavut, but debate waged about whether the Inuit should expand their pre-existing centre or build the new one Parks Canada hoped for. The North really was the holy grail of Canadian topics—never more relevant than now, with truth and reconciliation and the desire to make amends for the horrifying systemic mistreatment of Indigenous peoples. And new research showed that the effects of climate change were rapidly worsening in the Canadian Arctic, which was warming at three times the rate of the rest of the world.

Even the Conservatives were admitting that climate change was a real thing. In contrast to the three long years that Franklin's men had been frozen solidly in the ice, the Northwest Passage had been open all last summer, and that cruise ship, the *Arctic Palace*—clearly some twenty-first century marketer thought a more cheerful name than the *Erebus* or the *Terror* would be a good idea—was working with Parks Canada itself. The plan was to take passengers out in boats to survey the wreck of the *Erebus* in the shallow water where it had been found.

The price was more than an ordinary Canadian would have on hand: base fares were nearly nine grand, even if you wanted to share your cabin with three others. Dad had promised to cover her expenses, but she had told him that wasn't necessary. She wasn't about to tell him that she had applied for a joint grant for herself and Ryan. There would be plenty of time to break that news, if and when they succeeded. It was such a long shot, really—a pretty outrageous ask. With the help of the cruise website, she had carefully detailed the budget for the whole shebang: not just the cruise, but the flights to and from, mandatory insurance against illness and/or evacuation, money for personal needs, additional expenses in the event of delays or itinerary changes, daily gratuities for the ship's crew, the doctor's fee for confirming you were safe to travel, any medical charges on board ship, possible fuel surcharges, and like an ironic little cherry on top, a small Discovery Fund fee.

Even if they got the grant, even if they could get up there to see the actual site, she still had to convince herself to learn how to dive. She was terrified of deep water, and not fond of the cold or dark. Maybe she was crazy to even think of it; maybe that dream had been right: the lights were on, but there was nobody home, except that it was hinting at her, not Mamme. To top it all off, the government website presented a stern warning:

"The region surrounding the Wrecks of HMS *Erebus* and HMS *Terror* National Historic Site offers spectacular scenery, wildlife, and opportunities to experience Inuit culture and learn about northern places. But there are a host of dangers associated with travel in this northern wilderness. The remoteness of this area and limited rescue capability increase the risk of the challenging natural hazards. All visitors must be prepared to deal with extreme and rapidly changing weather, unpredictable river crossings, high winds, and travel in Polar Bear Country. You must be self-reliant and responsible for your own safety."

She was surprised to feel a shiver run through her as she read. Had the sailors on the Franklin Expedition had similar warnings before they signed on? Irving wrote that his father had recommended he choose between Australia and the Navy. He chose Australia, tried to make a go of it, but didn't like the struggle and went back to the Navy. Yes, she could write without going up there: Irving's letters would reveal more about the day-to-day life of the explorers than the contested wreck could for many, many years to come. But you couldn't describe a place without experiencing it. And she knew from the lighthearted tone of his last letters that Irving and his mates had really had no idea that every single one of them would perish. She, at least, should know better, and she could hardly ignore the irony of the document found in the cairn with Irving's bones, its ghostly *All Well*.

And yet, it certainly felt like everything was falling into place. It had to be, this time.

# 44

Ursula shifted uncomfortably on one of the cold folding chairs in Dr. Chernov's waiting room, reading emails on her cell phone. Her students were nothing if not brazen, she had to give them that; there was no end to the plaintive, badly-spelled pleas about dying grandparents and lost dogs and other impending catastrophes. Their chemistry labs were due this week, and report cards the next, and already there had been half-a-dozen requests for more time. If only she *were* in charge of time, she could grant herself luxurious ribbons of the stuff, proper time to repent. How was she going to make things right? She'd tried to demonstrate her desire to make amends to Andreas. She just couldn't find a way to get past the barrier he'd built between them.

They were trapped, both of them moths against glass, clumsily bumping at one another through the opposite sides of a picture window, batting and smashing their papery wings, caught in the illusion that they could reach the other side, connect with one another, if only they tried hard enough. Maybe there was no way to fix things, not after what she'd done. She sighed as she scrolled through her email. At last she heard the doctor clear his throat, and she looked up, her face still frowning as all thoughts vanished.

"If you would come this way, please?"

She stood and followed him down the hall to his office. By the time she'd finished describing what had happened, she was all worked up again. "This just proves that my husband has not listened to a single thing that I've said all these months. What did he think, that I left those books stacked just so on a whim? That I could simply recall the names and titles and pages—despite my condition?" She paused, shaking her head. "I've always made my living with my mind; my memory is my lifeline. Now, more than anything, memory is my enemy."

Dr. Chernov looked up from his notes, suddenly attentive. "That last sentence—say that again." He peered into her eyes.

Ursula hesitated, tried to remember. "Memory—is my enemy?"

"Precisely! Notice that you recall the important ideas perfectly. We say what we mean; the trick is actually to *hear* ourselves. So why is it, what is it, that you can't bear to remember, Ursula?"

She snapped back, "There's nothing I can't bear to remember. I simply forget everything that seems important."

Dr. Chernov held her gaze as he spoke. "When we have something we want to forget, our mind accommodates. It refuses to discriminate. If you don't want to remember one thing, it will obligingly keep memory, all memory, at bay. It's blatant self-protection."

Ursula started to rise. "Thank you very much, Dr. Chernov. When I want therapy, I'll seek the services of a psychologist." She zipped up her jacket and started towards the door.

Dr. Chernov stood, too, stepping out from behind his desk as he spoke. "From a holistic viewpoint, we know that emotional troubles often manifest as physical disease. So I ask again: what is it that you want to forget? And why push away any and all offers of help?"

Ursula could barely keep her temper. "You're not offering help, you're bullying me, like everyone else! Why will no one believe me? I can't stand not being able to remember what I've read, what I've heard, what I've thought! I can't stand it! How can I be expected to function like this?"

Dr. Chernov walked towards her. He put his hands on her shoulders, steered her back towards her chair. "Precisely. And that is what we must talk about." He let go and gestured for her to sit again.

She had no idea why she sat down.

He spoke gently. "You're upset because you feel you have lost months of work?"

"Feel? I *know* I have. I've been working on that project for ages—not months. When Mia left home, I needed something to do to preserve my sanity. Andreas lounges like a sea-lion on the sofa every evening, barking at commentators, surfing through television programs that don't interest me in the slightest. I started to read, just news items online at first, and then I realized that I couldn't ignore the science of climate crisis just because I wasn't an academic anymore—someone has to make a difference, now, or it will be too late. I decided to write a book, persuade high school students to push for real, sustainable change. It's more urgent than ever. But all my work is gone—I can never read and collate all that material again. Not with my memory."

Dr. Chernov nodded, his face serious. "Okay, now we're getting somewhere. Bear with me: think exactly about the words you've just said. You 'needed something… once Mia moved away.'"

"What does that have to do—"

"Just humour me, please. Just for a little. You said, 'to preserve my sanity.' Why would having your daughter leave home make you crazy?"

Ursula waved her hands. "It's just an expression. It was a shock, an adjustment. All of a sudden, I had so much time to spare. Andreas said it was empty nest syndrome, but it's more than that: I needed to use my mind creatively. It had been such a long time since I'd had the chance to do that."

"But, surely, your teaching—?"

"Please. I am a realist. Teaching school is tremendously hard; you have to be a subject expert, a referee, a warden, an interpreter, a guidance counsellor. The stress never, never ends. I needed to express my creativity differently, as I used to do."

"The creativity that you used in your graduate work at university? Or as a mother?"

She hesitated. "Both—I guess. I needed to do something that no one else was doing, to justify my existence."

Dr. Chernov leaned forward, his fingers a tent on his desk. His eyebrows raised. "That sounds ambitious. In what way?"

"Don't you remember? I told you about my project. The environment, mass migration, mass extinction—"

"Yes, yes, but those have been discussed in scientific circles for some forty or fifty years. What made it imperative that you personally validate your life—all of a sudden?"

Ursula sighed and looked out the window. Flakes were floating down now, the world a snow globe shaken by some unseen hand. She spied a tree in the distance. "Yes, it's been talked about for decades, but nothing has stopped. Nothing anyone says seems to have any effect—who's listening? I had to try to make a difference. I wanted to motivate the young, to get them to seize the reins away from the Baby Boomers, to create change before it's too late. And then I found out my father was ill."

"Ill? In what way?"

Ursula looked at her hands in her lap. "He had some strange symptoms. He had gum disease. He was losing weight. In the beginning, we thought it was anemia, that he wasn't eating properly. My mother died when I was a young woman, and Babbe lived alone. But then the tests came back: it was cancer, it had metastasized to his bones and his liver. They couldn't do anything for him."

"And when did you learn this?" Dr. Chernov said gently.

"Two years ago, this coming June." Ursula lifted her head and looked into the doctor's face. "He—he died that year, in December."

"I'm very sorry." Dr. Chernov's eyes held hers. She could see his compassion. The snow swirled against the window behind him.

She said, "Thank you," but couldn't bear his gaze. She didn't want his sympathy. She looked past him and focussed on the yard outside. That was an apple tree out there—she was sure of it.

"Were you able to be with him?"

The apple tree was bare, almost black, in the afternoon light. She forced herself to focus on the conversation. She was not going to miss *this* diagnosis. "What? Oh, yes, I spent his last summer at home, in Basel. Andreas stayed here, of course; he teaches—well, he used to teach—courses run year-round." She paused, looked down again.

"And?"

She lifted her eyes. "And my father died two weeks before Christmas, one week before I was scheduled to fly back to see him. By the time my siblings realized we were losing him, it was too late for me to get there in time."

The doctor said nothing at first. He held her gaze. "That must have been difficult."

Ursula nodded, her face a mask.

Dr. Chernov leaned forward slightly. "Now, think back. When did your trouble with your memory begin?"

She shook her head. "Honestly, what a question! I can hardly remember when I started to forget!"

"You can. Think hard."

She paused for a few moments, tracing the lines on her palm. "I remember I had a terrible time doing report cards that June. I had so much to do, getting ready for the trip, trying to make sure everything would run smoothly at home, getting my marking finished, getting the garden established for the summer. It took so much longer than usual to do what I needed to do. I couldn't think. I was so distracted. It was incredibly stressful."

Dr. Chernov nodded. "Of course. And how were you when you came back?"

"Much as you would expect. Heartbroken, grieving, disbelieving—full of shock."

"So, what did you do?"

She paused, her eyes widening. "What could I do? I went back to my job. Andreas made me go to my family doctor to get something for my nerves: an antidepressant, and something for anxiety. But you know that. It's in my history."

"Hmmm… And the medication—did it help?"

"I was able to sleep. But it didn't take away my anxiety. If anything, I felt fuzzy, more out of control. I had to do something. My father was dying. I was afraid I'd never see him again." She shook her head.

"How terrible." Dr. Chernov pushed the tissue box towards her.

"It was." Tears were not an option. Ursula stared out the window.

"And Andreas? He flew over with you for the funeral?"

The snow was piling up in the little Vs where the branches met the apple tree. "No, he did not. At Christmas, flights are prohibitively expensive, especially on short notice, so we decided he would stay here, have Christmas with Mia, keep things running at home. I was fine. It's not as if I was alone; I had my brother and sister." The little drifts of snow against the black looked like dried apple blossoms.

"Have you stayed in touch with your family?"

"They're very busy, of course. We're all busy. But they packed up his household, and my sister sent me some mementoes. Just his old clothes, knickknacks, books. That's when this latest trouble began. As I told you, it was my own fault. His things arrived unexpectedly, and like a fool, I put off dealing with them, just stored them to go through later. I remember I was getting a migraine. But then Andreas gave the room to Mia for a study, and they donated the boxes to the thrift store."

"That was the reason for your first explosion?"

"No, my second. As I said, the first happened when I found that Mia had reorganized my books. But you've got to believe me: I am not that type of person. Outbursts are unheard of in our home. It's a completely new symptom." She pulled her gaze away from the tree and met his eyes.

He looked back, studying her, then jotted a few notes on her file. "It may be a new symptom of an old problem. You've gone through a lot without any help. Why not take some time off? And in the meantime, make sure you go for the MRI ordered by your specialist. We want to be certain you don't have changes that might indicate physical ailments."

"What kind of physical ailments? A brain tumour?"

"See how you zoom in on the most terrifying idea, one I didn't even suggest? I'm almost certain you can't remember day-to-day details because you can't bring yourself to remember your loss; your memory is already overburdened attempting to keep grief away. And, as you know, certain antidepressants and anti-anxiety medications can impair memory. Don't go off them, not until we have the full picture. Withdrawal symptoms now would only make things worse. What is important is that you have the MRI."

Ursula sat still, stunned. "Why? What do you think it is?"

"Again, see how you search for the worst possibility? You can't tolerate the feeling of being out of control. You need there to be a physical reason for your memory problems. I'm almost certain you're fine. Let the neurologist read the MRI. He may order a PET scan, too. Just go to your appointments and relay anything he tells you back to me."

"But what if I can't remember what he tells me? Last time—"

"Ursula. You are a grown woman with an advanced degree. Ask the doctor for a written report, but don't tell him it's for me. Many doctors won't share their findings with alternative practitioners. And now you *must* take it easier. If you can be kinder to yourself, that will help you get along with your family. Why not start a journal, a place where you can vent your fears and frustrations? Keep track of your dreams and feelings."

"I have a journal. But I fail to see how I'm going to be kinder to myself or anyone else; I never know when I'm going to explode."

"It's precisely because it's already happened that you'll know. When you start to feel that angry, just go to your room or take a walk. Think about what's setting you off, then write it down in your journal. You can do this. Come back in four weeks and let me know how it's going."

Ursula glanced out the window again, but the snow had blown from the apple tree and it was bare, even as the day's gray light was fading.

# 45

Mamme must be running late again. She seemed so preoccupied these days, spending such a long time getting dressed in the mornings. Mia could hear her, rushing around in her room then hurrying down the stairs. She came into the dining room and gulped the cup of coffee Mia poured for her. She waved away the porridge and fruit she was offered. "No time for breakfast this morning, thank you, *Schätzli*."

That was not a smart way start to the day. Mia frowned.

"Have you seen my USB key?" she asked. "It has my lecture on it, my PowerPoint. It was with my book bag, and now it's gone. It was right here, in the middle of the table—"

"Hmmm...no, I have no idea, Mamme. Maybe it fell to the floor?"

"Not unless someone knocked it there."

They heard a noise from the living room. Adam must be batting something around over near the window. When Ursula went over to inspect, she saw that it wasn't Adam, after all.

"Peaches, you little wretch! That's my stick! Stop that—"

The cat just picked the USB key up in her mouth and ducked under the sofa.

Ursula kneeled down and reached underneath. "There you are, missy. Give it to me." She reached again but quickly withdrew her hand. "Ouch!! Stop that, you little monster! I don't have time for this. Give it to me! Mia, come control your animal—"

"I'm sorry, Mamme. She must have been a writer in a previous life. She loves anything connected with writing, runs off with all of my writing implements—pens, pencils, erasers—and now apparently she's a computer expert. I'll keep her in my study after this."

"That was the plan, was it not? But never mind, it's my own fault. I should put my things away. It drives your father crazy when I leave work on the dining-room table. Here, you hold her and I'll retrieve it—"

"Hey!" Mia shouted. "Stop biting me, damn it. Have you got it yet, Mamme?"

Ursula nodded and straightened her back, sat on her heels.

"And you, little Miss Alphonse, you are going back down to our room. So much for the freedom experiment." Mia started to carry her away. She held the cat firmly to her chest, stroking her.

"You're still calling her Alphonse?" Ursula stood up, bracing her hands on her knees. She stood and scratched the little cat's chin.

"Of course! What else would I call her?"

"I thought you hadn't decided yet. She's so much more of a Peaches…"

"Peaches? You're still stuck on that idea? Dad insists on calling her Après Chat—or Apricot."

"I'm sure he does." Ursula pursed her lips. "He does pretty much what he pleases these days."

Mia looked at her mother sideways. "What's that supposed to mean? Are you still angry with him? I thought it was kind of witty, really. You know, After Cat, a sequel to Adam, First Cat? And she is apricot-coloured."

"She looks like a Peaches to me. Here, Peaches!" The little cat squirmed and turned her head.

"Of course, she looks at you when you use that voice. But there's no way I'm setting her down to see if she goes to you now, unless you want to spend the next few days rounding up your things again. I'll take her downstairs. C'mon, Alphonse."

"And I'd better get going. I was late already, and little miss hasn't helped. Oh, and Mia—maybe you could do a load of wash for me sometime today, just the gray towels? I'll throw them in the dryer when I get home."

"No problemo. I can do that, too. I'm good at throwing in the towel—as you know." She grimaced. "Consider it done."

"You know that's not what I meant. Are you—"

"I'm fine. I'm going to get dressed and start work, as soon as I have the little thief locked up again. I have lots of things to do. Just get out of here, will ya?"

By ten-thirty a.m., Mia was deeply engrossed in the Irving booklet. The letters from Irving to his friend Malcolm and his sister-in-law Katie certainly seemed genuine enough, sincere and youthful, even naïve. His main lament about the Navy was that most of the men were not religious. *Dad would appreciate that*, she muttered. The lieutenant wrote that he was lonely without companions who shared his beliefs. They were in the land of the midnight sun, some of the men happily hunting around the clock, while others worked at chopping the ships out of the ice so those with ropes could pull them along. Irving found a few spiritual companions at last, and together they strove to save their souls. Mia found it haunting that in his very last letter, the last words before his connection to the world went forever silent, he was clearly enjoying himself. He joked about Franklin's earlier trip, where the old boy lived by boiling and eating his boots and other pieces of leather, yet neither Irving nor any of the men sensed the imminent danger facing the entire crew. How could so many people be so oblivious?

Something about that thought brought Mia back to the present. Given her mother's inexplicable moods these days, Mia would be the one in mortal danger if she didn't do what she had promised. Setting the open booklet face down on her desk, she went to gather the laundry. Following her mother's new system, she collected the used gray towels, replaced them with fresh yellow ones. It was a bit odd, changing colours with every wash, in strict rotation. Surely Mamme could just remember when they'd done the laundry? Or maybe Kathy had been right, and there was something really wrong? No, Mia decided, it had to be old-fashioned perfectionism. Mamme was nothing if not in control. Mia finished the bathrooms on both upper floors and went down to the basement.

When she opened the door to the laundry room, she could hardly get past the stacks of boxes returned from the Good Neighbour store. Her mother couldn't be happy about giving up so much real estate in this already tight workspace. It was Mia's fault they were here; well, to be accurate, it was Dad's fault. He was the one who had been so sure Mamme wouldn't mind if Mia took the storage room for her study. What a mistake that had been.

She squeezed past with her basket, measured the detergent into the washing machine, turned the water to hot, and selected the coloured cycle. She added the towels, closed the lid, pushed the start button, and went back to her study. Fifteen minutes later, when she heard the first spin start to whirr, she realized she'd forgotten to add the fabric softener. Damn it. She dashed down the stairs and poured the thick blue liquid into the dispenser. Why couldn't her mother use dryer sheets, like everybody else? But she knew well enough that there was no arguing with her, least of all about advances in technology.

As she turned to leave, she noticed that one lonely box was sitting on the table beside the dryer, flaps half open. She looked around, laughing at her own furtiveness. No one was home to see her. What was so precious about this stuff? She and Dad had looked through the boxes that day when they cleaned out her study; they'd seen old clothes and textbooks, mementoes of school and family vacations. But when she bent down and peered into this box, she was even more puzzled. She hadn't seen this. There was a tall glass cloche. She couldn't resist lifting the cover to touch what stood inside: a doll, if you could call her that. It was a miniature, really, an exquisite model of a young woman about five inches tall, dressed in an elaborate evening gown of fine black silk and elegant black shoes.

Mia touched the doll's head with a gentle finger. The dark hair was pulled into a tiny chignon at the nape of her neck. It felt like fine human hair. The doll had a sweet face, with large dark eyes and pursed pink lips. Mia gently flexed the jointed limbs. She looked in the box again, and when she lifted the next layer of tissue paper, she found a piano, a miniature baby grand. Mia ran one finger lightly over the keys and a charming tinkling scale sounded. She bent the doll at the hips and knees, seated her on the bench in front of the piano. She fit perfectly. The washing machine stopped for the first rinse cycle. In a few seconds, it started to fill quietly. Mia twisted the key on the underside of the piano and a fine waltz filled the room. She would have loved to have this kind of toy when she was a child. But if they were Mamme's, why hadn't Groossbappe sent them to her years ago?

In the bottom of the box, there was a collection of other dolls, each in its own clear plastic cylinder. One by one, she took them out of the box. The first wore an embroidered peasant blouse, a ruffled brown skirt, and a pair of sandals. Another was dressed in a scarlet flamenco dress and strappy high heels. She held two pairs of tiny black castanets that clicked when Mia touched them. The next was a French beauty in an elaborately embroidered blue-satin gown. A blonde wore a Nordic ski outfit, and another sported sunglasses and a mod mini-dress cut from the Union Jack, clearly from England. At the very bottom there was a magazine, the headlines in Hochdeutsch. Mia didn't try to decipher it—she couldn't take her eyes off the images on the cover. Each half featured the same familiar girl with a mop of dark hair. In one, she was wearing a lab coat over sweater and slacks, carrying a stack of charts; on the other, she was in a long dark gown, playing a grand piano in a spotlight on a darkened stage.

Mia heard the washer stop spinning with a clunk, and the room was silent again. Carefully she put the dolls into their containers and wrapped the piano up again, putting everything back in the box as if it had never been disturbed. The only thing she hadn't had time to look at was a small journal stuffed with loose papers, everything held together by an elastic band. When she opened it, there was a postcard on top; letters on thin blue paper stuck out here and there from the journal like bookmarks. The image on the postcard, Bruegel's *Landscape with Icarus*, made her pause.

She'd studied this piece in art history, the old master's painting of a sunny day with a jaunty ship. A peasant was patiently ploughing a field with a horse on the hill above, completely oblivious to the wretched end of a winged young man, Icarus, who had plunged headfirst into the clear green-blue water, his legs still thrashing. At the rocky shore a man bent, looking down, just as ignorant of the boy's predicament as the shepherd with his sheep who gazed up at the hills, leaning on his staff, his back to the fallen boy. She remembered the professor had read the class a poem by Auden, "Musée des Beaux Arts," written about this very painting. The professor had assured his students that, as painter and poet were showing, "The everyday world is so full of its own distractions, we mortals

225

can barely contemplate our own sorrows, let alone anyone else's, or take the time to wonder why the gods might suffer us to destroy ourselves and one another."

She turned the postcard over and admired the flowing handwriting. She didn't bother to try to read it; it had been so long since her mother had tried to teach her the old language. She'd ask her to translate them, tell her what the letters were all about. They must be important in some way, or why would Groossbappe have kept them? Mamme would love to wander down this memory lane. She gathered the journal and its contents and set it aside, pulled the soggy towels from the washing machine and tossed them into the dryer.

Was it odd that Mamme was still so affected by Groossbappe's death? A year had passed already. It wasn't as if he hadn't lived a long life. They'd known he was terminal six months beforehand; they'd all had time to prepare. Surely Mamme would have felt worse if he'd lingered, old and sick and in pain? Mamme wasn't a stranger to loss—she had survived most of her adult life without her mother. Mia hesitated to speak up, and Dad wouldn't be much support, not with the trouble between them. He smiled and joked as usual with Mia, of course. The world would have to end before *he* showed any fear or concern. But the used towels in the main-floor shower proved that he wasn't sharing their bedroom. If her mother was ever going to make peace, to *direct energy outwards* (as she always said strong people do), there was no time like the present. All she needed was a little nudge. Mia took the journal and headed back to her office.

# 46

When Ursula entered the garage, she was stunned. Her car was missing again, after she'd told Andreas last night how much trouble she was having finding parking for his monstrosity of a truck. Yet here it was, as on every other day. He must be taking her Honda because it was an automatic; it would be difficult to work the clutch with his sprained left ankle. She was furious that he had ignored her and just gone out, off on one of his mysterious assignations. He had to be meeting someone. What doubt could there be? She wished he would at least have the decency to tell her the truth.

Reluctantly she climbed in, pressed the electric door opener, and in seconds she was underway. But when she reached the highway, a semi whooshed by in front of her, covering her with slush. She flicked the windshield wipers to high, but they couldn't keep up. She tried slowing down; the idiot behind her just passed. With all the slush, she couldn't see clearly. Fuming, she wondered why they were having such an early thaw. She tried to spray the windshield with wiper fluid, but there were just a few splats and the annoying whirr of the pump. She pulled over onto the shoulder, cursing Andreas. She was really going to be late now. *Why would you be so distracted as to allow your washer fluid to run out, Mr. Perfect?* she wondered. It wasn't like him to forget; he was meticulous. In any case, his precious vehicle was going to be filthy tonight, that much was certain. She had no intention of washing it.

She marched to the front and refilled the reservoir, slammed the hood shut, and tromped back. But as she sprayed the windshield when she pulled out, something was still wrong: there was just a half-hearted splatter of drops that only cleared the windshield a little. Well, she'd have to make do. Class started in ten minutes, and she was damned if she would be late this morning.

Noreen waylaid her as she hurried down the hallway. "You didn't forget about the field trip, did you? I emailed you; your bus was here ten minutes ago, and the driver is livid. We'd better get the students out there pronto."

Ursula blanched. How had she so completely forgotten the trip to Saskatoon she'd planned months ago? It had never even crossed her mind—not this morning, not yesterday. How could her memory be slipping again, after all Dr. Chernov had said to reassure her?

"Okay," she told herself. "Snap out of it." She'd been preoccupied with Peaches this morning; she'd been distracted. But why so completely? The most frightening thing for her was that she hadn't felt the slightest inkling that she was forgetting anything, let alone something like this. She turned to Noreen and said crisply, "Thank you, Noreen. Of course I remembered. I had trouble in traffic. Please go tell the driver we'll be right there."

The hour-long bus ride gave her plenty of time to wonder and worry, and the visit to the Saskatchewan Science Centre dragged on forever. By the time it was over, Ursula was ready to weep, except that was not an option. Her head pounded, and there wasn't a damned thing she could do about it, trapped in the bus with thirty noisy teenagers for the long ride to Humboldt. At last she was back in Andreas' damned truck, making her way home. A parcel van passed her, spraying her with slush. She used the windshield washer but all she heard was that empty whirr. She stifled a scream. She'd filled it only this morning—that much she remembered—but there was no denying that she had already forgotten that she needed to take it to a shop for repair.

Shaking with frustration, she pulled into the Petro Canada and parked over near the air hose. Maybe one of the attendants could help her. She sat still for a moment, rubbing her temples. What a day. What a month. All she wanted was to get home and lie down.

The corner of her half-closed eyes caught a flash of something brown in the bottom right corner of the windshield, but when she looked closely, she saw nothing. She rubbed her neck, watching. There it was again: something was definitely moving over on the passenger side of the hood. A tail appeared, a long gray tail, and a sudden flash of colour: there it was, a deer mouse. With a strange mix of curiosity and revulsion, she half-admired the huge ears, the tiny black eyes, the sniffing nose as the little thing blinked up at her from just beneath the edge of the hood. She couldn't believe it: a mouse, in Andreas's vehicle. Ursula wondered if she were hallucinating. Maybe Dr. Paul was right. She *was* losing it.

For a moment she felt lost. Then she straightened her shoulders, shook her head, and got out of the vehicle. She called to the young man working the gas pump. "Could you help me for a moment, please?"

He walked over. "Sure, ma'am. What can I do you for?"

"I think there's a mouse under my hood," Ursula smiled. "Or there was a minute ago. I just saw the cheeky little beggar. And my windshield washer pump isn't working. It's a bad day to have no way to clean the glass."

The evening sky to the west was already pale yellow, highlighted by wisps of glowing pink cloud. The streetlights were starting to come on. Ursula stood and watched as the young man lifted the hood and poked around. "Nothing in here now, ma'am. Looks fine to me." He looked at her curiously.

Ursula wanted to turn and leave, but she wouldn't give in. She reached under and lifted a hose, pushed another aside. "Look!" she said. "There's a nest under there. And look at those holes in the line! No wonder the fluid won't pump."

He whistled. "You'll have to get that looked at. What's the name?"

"It's my husband's vehicle. Andreas Niederhauser."

The young man went into the office and came out a few minutes later. "We don't have any line the right size on hand tonight. 'Course you're gonna want to get rid of your livestock."

"Livestock?"

"The mice."

"Ah. Well, my husband can take care of that. But how am I going to get home tonight?"

"Can't you just drive?"

"Not if I can't clean the windshield."

"Hmmm. That'll be quite the trick, 'less you've got a spare hose somewhere."

"Let me look. My husband is always prepared, that's one thing you can say about him." She pressed the latch to the glove compartment and shredded Kleenex and bits of paper mixed with mouse droppings tumbled out in a flurry. The owner's manual was in shreds. Ursula asked herself what in the world had been preoccupying Mr. Clean to the point where he let things get so out of hand?

"Nothing in here, anyway, apparently," she said, straightening. "Look. Do you have some electrician's tape you could wrap the hose with, just for now?"

"Good idea." The boy smiled and walked away. As he passed the gas pump, he greeted a waiting customer, a pretty young woman. Ursula wanted to scream as she watched him unscrew the gas cap, lift the nozzle, set it in the tank, click the handle to lock it, and saunter into the office. At long last, he came out, but instead of returning to Ursula, he stopped at the pump, removed the nozzle, hung it back up, and replaced the gas cap. He washed the young woman's windshield, side windows, and lights. He waited for her to go into the office and pay, then watched her drive away.

At long last he came over to Ursula, who was still standing there, tapping her boot. Reaching into the engine, he wrapped tape around the ripped hose. He took the jug she had brought from the crew cab and filled the reservoir. "There," he said. "That should get you home. Can Tire will be able to fix it for you."

Ursula got in and turned the key. The engine revved, and she flicked the washers. They sprayed perfectly. She lowered the window to thank the young man. Andreas could get the real repair done himself. The sun was gone, and darkness hovered in all but the southwest corner of the sky. She turned on the lights, backed up, and drove out into the street.

# 47

Andreas pulled into the garage. He opened the door of Ursula's Honda and got out. He still felt awkward walking with the cane, but it was better than crutches. When he limped into the porch, he heard the clothes dryer running downstairs, and as he was sitting down to take off his boots, the machine stopped. Hmmm. Someone was doing the laundry, and he would bet real money it wasn't his wife.

He rubbed his hand across his chin. Could Gerry be serious, suggesting that Ursula might actually be ill? Or could the priest really be playing the devil's advocate, pulling Andreas's leg, pretending to side with the little demon? She hadn't complained about having any trouble teaching; she was a grim automaton these days. Funny that for so long he had thought her seriousness and strict sense of propriety were sweet. She'd seemed so shy that first day they'd met, a flustered little wood nymph, falling at his feet. *The trip of a lifetime.* And they had had a good life—until all of a sudden, they didn't.

Naturally someone in Gerry's position would want to keep marriages together, but Andreas had absolutely no intention of giving in this time. If and when Ursula got over her mood, when she apologized properly, he'd see if he could find it in himself to forgive her. There was nothing he could do to speed her up. He hobbled down the stairs to the laundry room, using his cane and the handrail to brace himself. Yes, he was right. Mia must be doing the laundry. As predicted, she was already well on her way to becoming Ursula's servant. He leaned his cane against the dryer, pulled the towels out, and loaded them into the basket. He couldn't carry them upstairs, but at least he could fold them; that much he could do for her.

As he turned to leave, the sun was shining in through the high window, glinting off something hanging on the wall beside the stacked boxes in the corner. It was a photo of apple blossoms on the old tree, the one Ursula been so in love with. Had he seen the picture before and just ignored it when he'd brought her precious boxes back? Or was it some new statement of his wife's resentment? He looked at it, the symbol of the first disagreement that had troubled their marriage, and he wished more than ever that he had found a way to tell her. She'd been adorable when she brought the tree home, so bubbly and full of pride at her bargain, but the plain truth of the matter, aside from the obvious, was that it didn't fit. Why she cared so much about this particular tree was a complete mystery to him. Whatever else she was, Ursula had always been practical. She was direct, often to the point of insensitivity. It wasn't like her to keep anything that wasn't useful. But surely this photograph testified to the fact that she had never forgiven him for not planting the thing. He hobbled over to look more closely at it, this trophy to his failure. Such spectacular pale pink blossoms, and here and there, even a few fuchsia-coloured buds, maybe a centimetre or two in diameter.

Mia came bouncing down the stairs. When she saw him, she asked, "What's with the pretty photo, Dad?" She picked up the basket of folded towels. "The laundry room seems like a strange place for décor."

"Your mother has always had odd ideas. Not all the time, just now and then, out of the blue. But Mamme, once she takes a notion, is like an elephant. There's no point hoping she'll ever forget. It's a picture of the tree she tried to over-winter down here, and she was all the more disappointed when it died anyway. It happened before you were born; I thought she was over that particular loss long ago. But never mind. We know well enough to leave her blessed things alone now, don't we? So, how has your morning been?"

"Uneventful. I'm reading and searching online, writing a bit, you know the drill. Trying to figure out the story. Half the battle is staying true to the known facts; the other half will be researching my educated guesses, figuring out what's true. Both are pretty hard feats. Fonzi is keeping me company."

"Fonzi?"

"Alphonse. Après Chat to you. The little menace."

"So who's going to take care of your protégé when you go up North?"

"Well, that isn't settled yet. The trip's horribly expensive. But if, just if, I can get a travel grant, Mamme says she'll take care of the cat for me. She's always down here playing with Fonzi anyway, sneaking her saucers of milk."

"Mamme? How maternal! I'm amazed; I wouldn't have thought she'd be interested in anything feline. She never does a damned thing for Adam."

Mia looked sideways. "Whoa, that's pretty harsh. What's up? You two still bickering?"

"Your mother has a lot on her mind these days."

"I'm sure she does, with you sleeping in your study."

Andreas hardened his expression and looked away. "Mia. Don't trouble yourself. Your mother and I have some things to work out. You'd best stay out of it." He reached over to squeeze her arm. "So, tell me about your work. If you want, I'd be happy to read what you've written."

"Thanks for the offer, Dad, but no. You can read it when it's finished, like everyone else."

He arched a brow and shook his head. "Well, sure, okay. But you've never minded my input before."

She sighed. "True. But this time I don't know what I'm doing. I have to feel my way. To the layperson, writing history seems so easy. There are characters already, and a plot—you don't have to make shit up. But trying to do it justice when no one knows what happened, really—it's like you have to intuit each detail through a hundred and seventy-some years of misinterpretation and mist. It's certainly not the kind of thing I'm used to, which is why it fascinates me, I guess. It will be ages before we know what grade of garbage it is. Be grateful you don't have to plow through it."

"If you say so, Mia. But don't write too much before you go up North. Like most things in life, the reality will be completely different than what you first expect."

Later that evening, Andreas was in the living room, reading his tablet as he lay in his recliner, both feet elevated. Mia had gone out curling again, and Ursula was busy cleaning the kitchen. He could hear her bustling about as she wiped the counter and washed the dishes.

Suddenly, she spoke to him from the doorway. "Andreas, do you have a moment?"

Deep in an article, he didn't respond.

She raised her voice. "Andreas. You have to get the mice out of your truck. They've eaten your owner's manual. It's disgusting."

What a ridiculous idea. He held his peace, said nothing.

She spoke still more loudly. He could see her in his peripheral vision, edging into the living room. "They've chewed through the washer fluid hose. I nearly had an accident today. I had to ask a boy at the gas station to tape it up. Are you listening to me?"

Just to get rid of her, without deigning to look up, he said, "I'll look into it."

She snorted. "You'll have to do more than look into it. That fix isn't going to hold. With all the warm weather we've had, it's absolutely slushy."

"I *said* I'll look into it." He scrolled through the article he was reading. He could feel Ursula just standing there, staring at him from ten feet away. He said nothing more.

At last she said, "Do whatever you please. Just be sure to leave my vehicle at home tomorrow." She turned to walk away.

Surprised at that, he raised his eyes. "You know I can't work a clutch with this ankle."

"Then you'll have to stay home." She crossed her arms across her chest.

That was ridiculous. "Why? What's the problem?"

"I just want my car; I need my own vehicle. Your six-a.m. rendezvous will have to wait."

"Rendezvous?" His frown broke into a broad smile. "Ursula. I would hardly take your car for some sort of romantic liaison, if that's what you're suggesting. I simply have coffee with a friend."

"Well, your friend will have to wait. Doesn't she have a car?"

"There is no *she*."

"So you're seeing a man?"

"Ursula. I'm not *seeing* anyone, not in the sense you're implying. And if you must know, he's on your side. He thinks you're right to be worried."

"About you? Well—"

"Not about me."

"What are you talking about?" Her face darkened. "What did you tell him?"

"About your 'condition,' as you call it. Your memory troubles." He shifted himself to an upright position. At least now he could look her in the eye. "His aunt is dying of Alzheimer's. Apparently, inexplicable rage is one of the symptoms."

"Inexplicable? Inexplicable! Oh, Good Great God in Heaven! Now you're telling people our private problems, the ones you don't even believe in? You talk *about* me to this person, when you won't even be honest with *me*?"

"Who says I'm not being honest? We're talking now, aren't we? You just always seem..." he paused.

"So what?"

"So angry. So pissed off. So ready to tear a strip off me," he said, shrugging and looking back down at his tablet.

"Andreas! You are not an idiot, and neither am I. Don't act like one. Of course I'm angry! You're lying to me, you take my car, and now you're telling tales about me to someone I've never met or even heard of—"

Andreas rose to his feet, bracing his hands on his chair. He picked up his cane and hobbled painfully across the floor to the kitchen door, where Ursula was standing. He pulled himself up to his full height, towering above her. For a long moment he was silent. Then he said, "For the last time: I am not lying to you. I am not gossiping about you. So why are you so upset? What's eating you?"

"You really have to ask?"

He turned as if he were going to walk away, then he swivelled back on his good foot to face her. "Okay. No, I don't have to ask. You want to know what I think? You really want to know? You're annoyed about being stranded with the truck because I took your car. I can understand that. It's your car. And I hate it when there's no washer fluid, too. You've left it empty more than once when you've taken my vehicle. But I'm the one who has the right to be angry. You spat in my face, for which you have yet to apologize—"

"Apologize? Why in God's name would I apologize? If I did anything unreasonable, you drove me to it. And when did I ever leave you without washer fluid? It was your mouse—"

He closed his eyes just for a second, and then opened them and said, "Ah, yes, the blessed mouse. Now you're hallucinating. Just do what you will. I'll take my own vehicle in future."

"And how are you going to do that?"

"With difficulty. Not that you care."

"You're absolutely right. As always. I don't care at all." She brushed past him and climbed the stairs to the bedroom. He limped back to his chair.

As she stomped up the first flight, he could hear her muttering loudly to herself. *Absolutely, Mr. Perfect, tell me why I'm here—in this Godforsaken place, alone, without the consolation of the slightest privacy?* He had to crane his neck to hear the next words. *I love you, you idiot,* she hissed. *Even in my dreams.*

He almost couldn't believe he'd heard her right. She slammed the door to their bedroom.

# 48

Ursula woke up early the next morning, still angry enough to chew nails and spit rust, determined to show Andreas that she was serious. If she was alone in this marriage, then alone she would be. She bustled around, and by 7:00 a.m., she had almost finished cleaning and organizing. She stuffed the heavy duvet into a fresh cover, pushing it into the corners and then neatly drawing the crisp blue-and-white over the rest. She perspired a little as she wrestled the bulky thing into place. There were already clean sheets on the bed, and the pillows were waiting to be laundered, along with piles of winter clothes from the closet to be washed and stored away. Since Andreas was still refusing to come back to their bed, she was claiming the room as her own, as sanctuary.

An outsider might have thought they were both completely civil. He said things like, "Would you pass the butter, please?" or "Would you like me to change the laundry over?" but still, he had made it clear last night that he did not intend to offer one single word of apology. She found it unnerving, the way he could play the strong, silent type, pretend he'd done nothing wrong. Words were his medium:

he relied on them to render everyone and everything pliable. At least now she knew she was correct: he wasn't running in the mornings. Instead, it seemed, every day he managed to hobble out to the car, yes, *her* car, and disappear to meet with this new friend. How that infuriated her. And although she had tried to get him to open up, she couldn't just come right out and ask him with whom he was meeting. If she stooped to ask such a question, that would only provide him with an opportunity to lie—or to mock her, or to pretend he didn't hear. Well, he would hear her message loud and clear when he saw his things.

There had to be another woman.

She moved briskly, sorting the whites from the darks and the coloured clothes. Did he expect her to tolerate his misbehaviour? Or to let him divorce her after nearly forty years of marriage? Trite as it sounded, she *had* given him the best years of her life, even though things had not turned out the way she had once thought, that harmony of souls and minds and bodies she believed they'd shared when they were young and vital. But surely grownups knew that marriage was a negotiation, a finely balanced dance? There had been so many good years, really good years. So why, when she needed him now most of all—

She spied her suitcase in the back of the closet and took it out. She had forgotten it was still packed, back from the day he had destroyed her book collection, the day she'd almost left him. Idiot. Honestly, what had she thought that would solve? She was hardly going to give in and hand him his freedom now. But until he came to his senses, she would have the bedroom. They'd have to carry her feet first from the house to get rid of her. She pulled the clothes from her bag, sorted them, hung up the jeans that weren't wrinkled, tossed the tops and the blouses and dress pants into the pile on the floor. She sorted the whites into a basket and carried them downstairs to the laundry room. Mia's office door was closed when she went by. She could hear her, though, talking to the cat. It must be nice to have someone to talk to. Ursula wasn't surprised that Andreas seemed to be philandering at last. She should be used to that possibility; looking back, she wondered if she had been afraid of it ever since that first summer here. There was a good reason so many of the local women had wanted them to visit, and it wasn't to engage *her* in scintillating conversation.

How could she have been so happy for so long? She hadn't seen the signs, even when it came to their property, hadn't even asked herself whether they were imagining the same space. They both loved the idea of building a winter-hardy orchard. But, as it turned out, she had dreamed of a place that would burst with colour and variety, a poetic space of whimsy that they would add to over the years, built with trees and shrubs that the universe sent them to find, one at a time, like the little five-grafted one, the winter-blooming tree. He, of course, always had to be the expert, the academic. Once he got out the graph paper and the horticulture books, she should have seen that what he had in mind was symmetry and order, mathematical precision. *She* was the botanist, yet he ordered the specimens. And that second spring, as the dry blossoms blew, why hadn't she seen how passive aggressive he was? By then she had been pregnant, hardly in a position to contemplate ending the relationship. And after Mia came along, they'd been so busy. So happy. A child needed two parents, and her own position in the marriage was too complicated to contemplate. She'd told herself it was just a tree, after all.

Only lately, since they had started bickering, had Ursula come to suspect that they were entirely different people. She had looked to Canada for its freedom, its lack of regulation and old-fashioned hierarchy. She was so tired of all the old ways in Switzerland, where there were rules, strict rules, and, sure as taxes, someone would be certain to turn you in if you dared to commit the slightest infringement. At least in Canada, you could do your laundry or wash your car any day of the week, any time you pleased. Why would she ever have left Basel, why give up her family to set up life in such a small place, just to be bound once more by rules? There should have been absolute release here, freedom. Yes, people here gossiped, and did plenty of that, but you didn't have to engage in it. For a moment she wondered what they were saying about Andreas now on coffee row. She would be the last one to hear it, either in Basel or Humboldt. She tossed in the detergent and measured the fabric softener, dropped the clothes into the machine. She cranked the temperature to hot, set the cycle to white, slammed the lid, and strode up the stairs.

As she entered the kitchen, she looked out the window at the actual orchard, its clean lines, its perfect precision. She snorted as she hauled the vacuum out of the broom closet and lugged it toward the stairs. She panted a bit as she struggled to her room. She would settle things. She paused a moment. Settle, that was the word. Why *had* she settled for a life that was so much less than what she'd hoped? Andreas had called the tune, mastered all the idioms—even changed his accent—and welcomed the new technology, ordered every blessed new gadget. Despite all his adaptability, he was still Swiss in one fanatical way: he demanded that things be kept just so, clean and lean and efficient, as if they were still living in his mother's house. Only rarely did he condescend to help. That was almost enough to make her abandon her cleaning, just to spite him. No, she was doing this for herself—let him see how he liked to have *his* things rearranged.

She zippered her empty suitcase and shoved it back into its spot in the closet. She piled his books, his shoes, his slippers, his dirty socks and underwear into a laundry basket and deposited it all in his study. Back in the bedroom, she pulled his clothes from the chair and dug through the hangers, stomping over with armful after armful, which she left piled on his bloody expensive leather sofa. Back in her room, she took out the drapery attachment and started to work. Always so fixated on having the house immaculate, the man must have thought the gods sent their daughter to be his personal servant. Right from the first, the bookcase fiasco had had Andreas's name written all over it—and so did the new "office." Mia had never liked cleaning. She hated chore days, Saturday afternoons after their Baseldytsch and Hochdeutsch lessons, when Ursula had insisted that she help. Andreas had seized the chance to get his own way without lowering himself to ask Ursula to tidy up. It was just like him, such an indirect jab, perfectly planned and executed. He must have been surprised when she dared to object; he hated confrontation, as he knew she did. Well, this time, she wasn't going to back down or change her life for him, not anymore. Finished, she unplugged the vacuum and stomped with it all the way down the stairs.

# 49

That evening, when Mia entered the kitchen, her mother was standing at the sink, peeling a sweet potato. She gently set the old magazine on the counter beside her, then pointed at the twin images: the young woman in a lab coat, carrying a stack of charts, and the other, an elegant girl playing a grand piano. "Are these you, Mamme?"

Ursula looked over. "Where on earth did you find that old thing? I had completely forgotten about it." She set down the sweet potato, rinsed her hands and dried them, then picked up the magazine. "Yes, that was back home, when I was in Waldner's lab. The first, the only time I ever found myself in the news: *Young Women in Science.*"

"It sort of jumped out at me when I was in the laundry room. I was sure it was you. I hope you don't mind?" Mia looked sideways at her mother.

Ursula seemed bemused. "Was I ever that young? Look at that hair! It was so odd, being noticed then. Everyone knew my father, the surgeon, and my mother, the pianist: she was truly world-class. Her friends were utterly shocked when she retired, she told me. The unwavering instincts she had for music, for art, for the way people should live their lives. She insisted that all her children learn to play the piano and to paint and to pursue life to the fullest, every minute of every day, whether we thought we wanted to or not."

"So? Where's the piano?" Mia teased, touching her mother's forearm.

But Ursula ignored the joke. "If anything, this article showed me what I had to do. You can't build a successful career with a divided heart; she of all people should have known that, but it was always her plan that mattered. She taught us to live 'wholeheartedly,'" Ursula stabbed quotations in the air with her fingers, "as she used to call it. It was not until after she died, three weeks after this article came out, that I understood. And by then, it was too late."

"Too late for what?"

"I had made my choice, so I kept to it, but—you've got to understand. My father, my brother and sister, we all needed to grieve her loss privately. It was what people like us did."

"People like who?"

"We didn't show our feelings. We didn't know how," Ursula grimaced. "I was so lonely, it was incredible. It was a terrible winter, storm after storm, followed by the grayest May on record. In one odd way, I was grateful for the bad weather. I felt as if my pain were causing it, the whole natural world grieving with me. There was nothing to do but lean into my work. Only my father seemed to care or understand, but of course I couldn't tell him what had happened." She could hardly bring herself to think about it. "It would only have added to his pain."

"Tell him what?" Mia crossed her arms and leaned on the counter.

Ursula closed the magazine. "It isn't something I can talk about. That was the worst year I ever knew, until this one. I couldn't stand the chatter, the smallness of the gossip."

"But you're so strong; you got through, you met Dad—"

Ursula shook her head. "You don't get through a loss like that. You learn to carry it. For a long time, I thought your father was helping me do that." She picked up the sweet potato and the peeler and started back to work. Clearly, she was through talking.

Perplexed, Mia looked into the backyard, to see what Mamme was looking at. There, out the window, was the crazy robin, shaking in the wind on the nearest apple tree.

# 50

Andreas was leaning heavily on his cane, standing at the repair counter of the local garage. "What do you mean? I phoned yesterday. My appointment is for ten-fifteen."

"I'm sorry, sir. There's no record of an appointment at that time. What did you say your last name was?"

"Niederhauser—N-I-E—"

The young man interrupted. "That's fine, sir. Susan must've forgotten to write you in. She does that sometimes. She's still new. Gen Z, eh? It's like they all have Alzheimer's—none of them can remember the simplest thing. We can take you in anyway, if you can wait half an hour or so."

"I guess so. Thanks."

"Help yourself to coffee. Fresh this morning."

Andreas limped over, looked at the coffee in the pot, and decided not to chance it. The stuff looked like hi-test; it was thick, opalescent, with a sheen that probably meant it had been sitting there since seven. He sat down on one of the hard plastic chairs and sorted through the sections of yesterday's *Star Phoenix* scattered on the low coffee table. He picked up the first section. Might as well enlighten himself as he waited.

An hour later, he pulled himself up and limped over to the repair counter. "Surely they can't still be working on my vehicle?" he asked the same young man.

"Excuse me?"

"My truck. You were working on the windshield washer hose. They told my wife a mouse chewed through it—"

"What was your name, sir?"

"Niederhauser—N-I-E-D-"

The young man flicked through screens on the computer. "No one by that name booked in, sir. Maybe the appointment is under a different name? Your wife's?"

"Listen, you booked me in an hour ago."

"An hour ago? No appointments on the book for ten-fifteen, sir. Were you a walk-in?"

"No, but you said Susan had forgotten to write down my appointment. Niederhauser. Andreas Niederhauser. You typed it in yourself."

"N-E-E-"

"No, N-I-E-"

"Well. There you are. N-E-E-derhouser. We're not finished with the strut boots yet, sir. That'll take another hour, at least—"

"Strut boots? I needed my windshield washer hose replaced!"

"Your strut boots have been on order for a while. They just came in last week. They're putting them on now."

"Listen to me, please, listen carefully. Have you lost your mind? I did not order strut boots. I do not need strut boots. Is the washer hose repaired or not?"

The young man fidgeted with the computer. He peered at the screen, then turned to the door and went through into the garage. After a few minutes he returned, and said, "Yes, the windshield washer is repaired. But they've got the vehicle all taken apart—your strut boots will only take another half an hour—"

"For the love of God! I do not have time to wait for something I didn't order. Please have them put my truck back together now."

"But you'll have to pay for the labour, anyway, sir."

"I will absolutely NOT have to pay for something you had no permission to change. Is that even a real part? A strut boot? It sounds like something someone invented for non-mechanically-inclined customers—"

"Oh, it's a real thing, sir. You ordered it three months ago. Here's your signature. Would you like to speak with the mechanic?"

"I do not want to speak to him or to her or to any-fuck-ing-one else. I want my truck, and I want it now. Please. If it isn't too much trouble. God in heaven."

# 51

When Mia brought out the dolls and the piano and the postcards, Ursula tried not to start another fight. Still, she couldn't stay silent. "What are you doing, Mia, looking in my boxes again? What possible good can come of digging through all my things? Have I not been clear?"

"Mamme, relax. I just wanted to know more of your stories. Please? These look interesting."

Looking at Mia's earnest face, Ursula relented. Letting her share the past might actually be a good thing. Soon enough, her mind—everything that made Ursula herself— would be completely gone, and it would be up to Mia and Andreas to remember. Maybe Mia had a right to know as much as she could tell her about what her family was like. *But please, God, please don't let it be genetic—*

Mia handed her a postcard of old buildings first. Ursula took it in her hands, staring at the image before turning to the back. "That was one Babbe sent me from Brussels, forty-two years ago. 'Everything is so much nicer than I expected, after all the stories. Your mother is completely charmed by all the Bruegel pieces here. The weather continues pleasant and warm.' Look. It's dated the summer before my mother died."

Mia put her hand on Ursula's arm. "About that, Mamme. How did she die?"

Ursula pretended not to hear. She couldn't talk about her mother—not to Mia, not to anyone. "Let me see that one, the one with the botanical gardens, with all the tropical plants and water lilies. The Viktoria-Gewächshaus, in Basel. It was one of my favourite spots. Ah, yes. It's even dated June 1978, the year before I met your father. Four years before we emigrated to Canada."

"But you two were happy then, right?"

"Of course, we were happy; we were in love, even though I was grieving my mother, and the stress of grad school was overwhelming. But yes, of course we were happy. Your father was always so gallant. And, of course, I was so young—"

Mia looked sideways at her mother and said, "Not *so* young. You must have been twenty-five or -six, right?"

"I mean, I was too young to know that the dream we thought we shared was a mirage."

"In what way?"

"It's an odd thing, really. I don't know how to explain it." She paused. "Whenever your father and I went hiking, our strides matched, seemingly without trying. He shortened his step, and I lengthened mine, and somehow, even with his long legs and my petite ones, we shared a common rhythm. But it's taken me nearly forty years to see that if he doesn't want to do something, there is absolutely no way to make him do it. Not even when something really matters to me. It actually wasn't until about a year ago that I noticed that he just says *yes* and then doesn't do it. But that realization showed me the fate I had chosen. For the whole of my life."

"That's pretty dramatic, Mamme. Your life's not over yet."

"Isn't it? How dare I challenge his ideas?"

"He said that?"

"I just said he did not. Your father is never rude. Obstinate, Yes. Stubborn, absolutely. But rude? Not to save his life. Misdirection is his game. The first time I almost saw it, I persuaded myself it didn't matter. I just watched him procrastinate. But at last I've figured out the obvious: I'm such a fool. I never wondered why I was so attached to the memory of my five-grafted apple tree. He never got around to planting it, but then, when winter came, your father suggested we carry it indoors, and I was sure he meant that he would plant it the next year. The strangest thing was that it bloomed in the basement, even set small green fruit. For all those years I thought it was a symbol that miracles could happen."

"What apple tree—the one in that photo in the laundry room? So why wasn't your tree planted?"

Ursula turned her head, looked out the window. "When it was spring again, I asked your father to haul it upstairs and he seemed happy to do so. But when he set it back on the deck, in that same place it had spent the entire summer—in that moment I saw it. When the dry blossoms blew, something in me blew away with them, although I never let myself admit it. Looking back, I see that as clearly as if he had screamed the words at me. He was never going to plant my tree."

"But you didn't tell him how you felt? How do you know what he was thinking?"

"With your father, everything fits neatly in boxes. To him it was just a tree. In my mind, everything is interconnected: there are signs. That tree represented my freedom, my creativity, my ability to contribute to the marriage. And I know now that none of that was important to him. He saw the sign, the winter-blooming tree, and ignored it. It bloomed and leafed out with almost no light; it set fruit with no bees to pollinate it; and yet he never saw its potential, the potential of *my* ideas. I was so sure it meant we'd get a second chance. But he had already decided that he didn't want to do it, and so he procrastinated about what I wanted until it no longer mattered."

"He didn't know what it meant to you, and frankly, I don't think he knows he hurt you, either—in fact, I'm sure he doesn't."

"Mia. You already knew about this? You two have been talking about me?"

"Only about the tree—"

"Listen. There is another difference between your father and me. He loves to gossip. I do not. You've seen him; he's the big man, the storyteller. He chats up every person he encounters—waitresses, gas station attendants, cashiers, doctors, lawyers—it doesn't matter a bit to him. He'll say anything to charm a stranger."

"But you've just been talking about him—isn't that gossip? How is he different?"

Ursula stood up and went to the sink. She stood there a few moments, her hands clenched on the counter. At last she ran water on the dishcloth, wrung it out, and hung it up. She turned and looked into Mia's eyes.

"Mia, listen to me. Don't get involved in our troubles. A child's place is not between warring parents." She set her brandy glass in the dishwasher, rinsed her hands, dried them on a tea towel, then took the postcards from Mia's hands, bundled them in an elastic with all the letters.

"I'm hardly a child, and I'm not between you. But I can see how unhappy you both are—maybe you're not seeing the real miracle."

"*You* are the miracle, Mia. You are. Please don't tell your father what I've said tonight. This is between us. If he were interested, he would have asked me himself by now. You'll only make matters worse."

"But he is interested! He's just confused. You've got to talk to him. Give him a chance."

Ursula felt as bleak as ever she could remember. "You have no idea how many chances he's had," she said, shaking her head. "You're the one who's confused. I'm going to bed. Good night. And I mean it, Mia—stay out of it, for everyone's sake. Just leave my things alone." She shook her finger sternly and walked away.

At two thirty-four that night, Ursula awoke and looked for Andreas. She was alone, of course; there was nothing to do but lie listening to the still house, the wind outside the only sound as it rushed through the trees. The gusts sounded like surf. The clock radio glowed silently on the empty side of the bed. She was lonely, lonely, lonely, and she couldn't tell a soul. She reached up to rub her eyes, then dropped her hand beside her pillow.

That was odd. She could feel something there, a little bundle. She turned on her bedside lamp. It was a pair of socks, her socks. Clean ones, still folded together.

She hadn't the faintest idea when she would have put them there, or why.

Now she was losing it, entirely.

# 52

Mia was waiting anxiously to hear about their grant. The application had demanded a detailed itinerary and budget; the competition was daunting, and she didn't imagine there was a snowball's hope in hell that she and Ryan would receive funding, but still she allowed herself to ache for it. If only she could get back out on her own, away from the anger that permeated everything here. And although it didn't look like any cruise she'd ever seen—it was spartan, a trip for adventurers, not partygoers—following Franklin was one thing she'd—they'd—always wanted to do, and now that it was nearly within reach, she wasn't going to give up. Making the trip, writing the book, working with Ryan—those were once-in-a-lifetime opportunities. She wasn't going to end up like her mother, angry and old and full of regret—or worse, like her grandmother, if she had been able to translate Groossbappe's journal correctly. The last thing her mother needed was to learn about *that*. She'd hidden the journal deep under her mattress.

There was still one detail, that panic-inducing detail, she knew she had to face if she wanted to dive to the wreck. She had to conquer her fear of deep water. She looked online for courses. She could go to Edmonton for a three-day beginners' session on scuba-diving that was being held at West Edmonton Mall over the Easter long weekend. The price was prohibitive, but far cheaper than flying to some exotic place like Aruba and taking lessons there, where the warm water would do nothing to prepare her. Dad said he would be happy to lend her the money for the course, and she had an old classmate from grad school who lived in Edmonton near the mall. How dangerous could diving in an indoor pool really be? She e-mailed Melissa to see if she was interested in putting her up (or putting up with her) and received a quick reply: "Awesome! That would be fab. What time will you be here?"

Just then a little orange paw batted out from behind the computer, and Mia tapped it lightly. They swatted back and forth for a few moments, then she closed the laptop, scooped Alphonse up, and put her on the floor. You had to watch out: she was tiny but oh-so-pointy. "Just like Mamme," she told the little cat. "Just like our Mamme."

# 53

Andreas was restless. He was laying on the damned couch, thinking about Ursula's stubbornness, the constant little digs she'd been making. He knew she had seen him sweat all these years, endure the trials of teaching mathematics on-line or driving all over the province for courses, the strain of committee work, the endless year-round cycle of sessional duties. She couldn't fathom his other troubles, the ones he hadn't wanted to worry her with, his sky-high triglycerides and blood pressure, the stress surrounding the cutbacks, the never-ending drudgery of teaching four terms a year—which was still less stressful than having the courses he thought of as his assigned to faculty members. It was a wonder he hadn't had a bloody stroke already. He tossed and turned. Mia had to be right. Ursula thought all her problems were *his* fault.

He wondered suddenly what that noise was, that droning moan, like a gigantic mosquito in the distance. After a minute it came to him: cattle, lowing, their mournful mooing snaking down the valley from some farm up in the hills. It must be weaning time; the farmer was doing what had to be done, separating cows and calves for the first time. But the racket didn't make it any easier to go back to sleep. He felt like bawling, too. At last he drifted off. In the dream he was back in their battered rowhouse in Saskatoon, seated in its microscopic living room.

*He was reading the* Saskatoon Star Phoenix *after supper while some newscaster—Peter Mansbridge?—was rattling on and on. Ursula walked into the room and switched off the television, coming over to settle beside him on the sofa, drawing her slim legs up beneath her, graceful as a little cat.*

*"Hey! I was listening to that," he objected, looking down at her with mock sternness. He gave her a little pinch.*

*She pinched him back, and then flattened her hand on his arm. "I'll turn it back on in a minute. I just wanted to tell you what I've decided." She was smiling, but there was something wrong. He could sense it.*

*"That sounds ominous. What? You're not leaving me—" he teased, trying to make her laugh.*

*"Don't be ridiculous. You're not getting rid of me now, not after I've changed continents for you."*

*"For me? I thought this was a joint decision. But okay! I'm all ears."*

*"Then listen, All Ears." She paused. "I went to the university today, to the Botany Department, and looked over the list of professors. And what do you think?"*

*"I bet you're going to tell me—"*

*Her smile disappeared. She shook her head. "They're men, every single one of them. The whole ill-begotten pack."*

*Was that all? He shrugged. "So what? You'll be the first woman," he said, as he turned back to his newspaper.*

*She took his chin, turned his face to hers. She was suddenly grim. "I'm not joking, Andreas. It's never going to happen. I'll never find a tenure-track position, I know it. We've been fools to think I would. And here, now that the economy is a wreck, with the recession—"*

*She was overreacting; she always did. He removed her hands from his face and looked back at his paper. "You're being a bit melodramatic, aren't you, Schätzli? Something will come along. It has to."* He turned the page.

*"Nothing says it has to. I've made up my mind. I'm going back to school."*

*He glanced at her. She was serious. He paused for a long moment, controlling his frustration, then said evenly, "Well, sure. Why not? You have time."* He turned another page. *"If you think we can afford it. Tuition won't be cheap."*

*Her voice rose. "You're missing my point. I have no future here. My doctorate might as well be newsprint. I could clean windows with it for all the good it will do me. And anyway, I saw an advisor today."*

*He looked up.*

*"I've made up my mind. I'm going to become a high school science teacher. It will only take two years. I can work retail, take three courses during the regular term, study spring and summer session, too."*

*Andreas looked at her in disbelief. "Two years?"*

*She nodded.*

*For a moment they stared at one another, then he lowered his gaze, and turned the page. "Okay. It's a great idea."*

*Ursula said nothing. After a minute, Andreas glanced up. "Isn't it?"*

*She paused, then said firmly, "We can't go on like this."*

*His voice rose in exasperation. "Like what? Schätzli, don't be a martyr. I'm working. You're working. We're fine. Things are just a little tight, that's all. We'll find real jobs, don't worry."* He held out a section of the newspaper. *"Here. Take a look at the classifieds. You'll find something better. You've just got to keep at it."*

*She ignored the paper and crossed her arms. "Well, I'm not going to keep at it. I'm going to do something."*

*There was a long pause, then he gave in. "As always, I bow to your practicality, Ursula. You've dreamed up a new reality, just like that, where you'll have more time and less work. It's ideal for you."*

*"What are you talking about? Are you saying I don't have what it takes to be an academic?"*

*"No, no, of course not. Have you been listening to me at all? I just insisted you'll find a tenure-track job. Teaching school is your scheme. Leave me out of it. But you'll have summers off, and Christmas and Easter. You won't have to publish. It's a good idea—and it will be helpful later, when we have children."*

*She stared at him, her face blank, flushed. For some reason she still wasn't satisfied. This whole conversation was maddening. He looked down at his paper and closed the section he had been reading. He reached over and picked up a new one, rattling it as he flipped it open. Ursula said nothing, just rose from the couch and stalked out of the room. He registered the fact that she had gone into the bedroom, but he decided to ignore it. After a few minutes, he got up and turned the television set back on. She would get over it; she always did, given enough time.*

Andreas woke up, blazingly angry. Now they were fighting in his dreams, too? Could she actually have told him all of that and he'd ignored it? Or forgotten it all? The leather sofa was so bloody uncomfortable. The full moon was shining in through the window. It was just a dream, only his mind's way of making sense of her, the miserable mood she was in, her passive-aggressive, controlling moves, shutting him out of his own bedroom. It wasn't some sign or portent. Surely she hadn't told him all this, then or now. But what if it was the truth? That was ridiculous; there was no such thing as telepathy.

It seemed so real. Could he really have been that clueless? He would have seen that she wanted him to stop her. He dismissed that idea. Surely she had no reason to expect him to step in and rescue her—when had he ever been able to do that? Aside from that first day on the hill, when she had been physically incapacitated, they both knew that nothing could never stop her from doing a single thing she wanted to do.

But for the first time in his life, he lay there and wondered.

# 54

Ursula fell back to sleep, exhausted.

*The next thing she knew, she was standing fifty feet back in a cave that overlooked a gloriously sunny stretch of beach. Just beyond the entrance, to the right, she could see large, dark rocks and a steep cliff, foaming waves crashing and smashing against them. She knew it had to be the ocean, though she'd never been here before. Yet everything seemed so familiar. She felt like she was inside a picture she'd seen somewhere but couldn't place. The water erupted rhythmically into tall bursts of spray as the waves dashed on the rocks. The cave's floor was smooth; the sand felt cool but dry on her bare feet. Ursula had a strange sense of foreknowledge, as if she were watching a rerun on television. She knew that as long as she stayed in the cave, she was safe. She was deeply certain of that, even though the tide was coming in and the beach in front of the cave was flooding higher and higher with every burst that rushed over it.*

*She thought about running down to the beach before the tide took over. She wanted to feel the sun and the spray and the energy of the scene before her. But just as she had that longing, an image stretched across her field of vision: there was a great cliff of water out to the left of the cave, waiting for her. The water was twenty feet high, held back as if suspended by a force field or some magic spell, a wall ready to crash on her if she dared to leave the cave. At the moment, all forward motion had stopped; the heavy wall of roiling water was cut in mid-air. She was safe as long as she stayed inside. When she again entertained a thought of leaving, she saw that wall of water looming high, the one that would crash over her, drown her.*

*A peasant farmer, talking with a shepherd, walked a huge horse and a herd of sheep past the cave and down the beach. Just then, a winged child dressed in white tumbled through the air towards the bay. The two men didn't even look as the boy fell, limbs flailing, into the water, his great feathered wings sucking him under the surf, his thrashing legs the only sign that such a marvel had ever existed. Ursula ached to go and rescue the child, but she felt even more certain that if she dared, it would bring the wall of water crashing down upon them both. And so she could only watch, trapped, safe inside the enormity of her danger, as the child was sucked under the waves.*

*An old wooden ship bobbed in the harbour, scores of men in dark pea coats walking about on deck, working the sails and rigging, yet no one saw the child or realized his peril. The child's legs stilled, then disappeared. And still no one noticed a thing. Ursula dropped heavily onto the sand, bent double in the cave, and hugged her knees as she would have liked to hold the fallen child. An enormous iceberg floated by, the side nearest the cave lucent green and glowing in its height, and within minutes another came, and another. The giant floating cliffs melted into spray as they crashed on the beach, and then an old-fashioned diver walked out of the foam towards the entrance to the cave. Soggy wings protruded from his shoulders. He took off his helmet.*

*It was Mia.*

# 55

In the end, Andreas gave in. He laughed at himself for doing so. He could imagine her snorting, "What a cliché," and it was, he knew—the penitent husband's return—but surely even Ursula would appreciate the gesture. Gerry had been adamant. He had to give Ursula a sign, some token, to persuade her that he really was on her side. He'd argued that surely Ursula was so angry now, she was beyond tokens, but Gerry gave no ground: Andreas had to demonstrate his goodwill, defuse the hair-trigger tension, before something broke completely, once and for all.

But when he reached the florist's, the door wouldn't open. It must be frozen shut, he thought at first, then he saw the paper taped to the large shop window: *Closed for Family Emergency*. Jesus Christ. It was locked. What about *his* emergency? Small-town life was *unbelievable*. You couldn't do something nice, even when you wanted to. The only other place that might have what he needed was the grocery store. He got back into his vehicle and drove all the way across town. When he'd found a parking spot and battled his way through the bumbling shoppers and their awkwardly angled carts, the selection was dismal: battered-looking frills of yellow or white chrysanthemums, which Ursula despised for their bitter scent; limp orchids with drooping, lonely buds; plain-Jane African violets; tall leftover Easter lilies—the flowers you gave your grandmother, nothing romantic about that. He walked back and forth in a dither. And then he spied them: rich, velvety, just starting to open, clearly raised in Brazil at this time of year, probably where the rainforest had been decimated. If she guessed that, she would have a fit; he couldn't buy something that wasn't good for the planet. But hadn't she bought her beloved apple tree at a grocery store? Gerry had been pretty emphatic. He had to do something.

Twenty minutes later, he arrived home, cradling a green-paper package. He hummed as he took down their best tall vase. As the chatty cashier had instructed, he filled it with lukewarm water and stirred in the powder. Stem by stem, he held each under the tap and sliced two inches off. Lifting this one and moving that, he fussed until the arrangement was perfect. He took a minute to think, popped the card he had written into the bouquet, and centred it in the middle of the dining-room table, where Ursula would surely see it when she came home from school.

Satisfied, he strode downstairs to find Mia in her study. The door was ajar. She was typing on her laptop, a soft penumbra of light falling from her studio lamp. Après Chat was curled up in the corner of the desk, snoozing atop a pile of papers.

"I'm going to make a special supper for your mother tonight, something to cheer her up. Do you have any ideas? Has she mentioned anything she's been craving?"

"What? No, sorry, Dad. To tell you the truth, I'm not her favourite person right now. We had words; she's pretty ticked off at me. Maybe I should go out? Give you two some alone time?"

"No, no. That wouldn't help at all. She'd only wonder what we were up to. But what are you talking about? Words about what?"

"Oh, you know Mamme these days; it wasn't anything. She's in some funk. Everything I do means absolute betrayal to her, one way or another. I just asked her about Groossbappe's things, you know, the ones in the boxes, and we ended up talking about you—"

Andreas frowned, ran his hand hard across his jaw. "Seriously, Mia, does that seem like a good idea, especially right now? Mamme is stressed out. You know how she feels about her things. She has more on her plate than we could imagine—so Gerry assures me."

"Gerry? Oh, right. Your priest?" Mia raised an eyebrow.

"Yes, my friend, the priest," he smiled sternly.

"So Mamme's been talking to him? How did you get her to do that?"

"No, I've been talking to him. He says she's carrying the world on her shoulders."

"How original. And really? You're talking to a stranger about her? I'm pretty sure that will piss her off when she finds out. And he knows this how?"

"He knows how to read people. I just tell him what she says or does that I can't understand, and he interprets. I had to talk to someone, for God's sake. He's a good listener; he seems to understand her in ways that never occur to me. It's like she's speaking some secret language..."

"She is pretty unpredictable, getting angry at us for cleaning."

"Exactly. Her explosions made no sense to me. Gerry says we invaded her space, not once, but twice. But, to complicate things, he also told me his aunt was diagnosed with dementia, and rage is one of the symptoms. Mamme is panicked, he says, terrified that she's losing her mind. She's frantic about her poor memory, yet it may be the anxiety that's causing the problem."

"Her poor memory? She's terrified of losing her *memories*, that I can see. Her father's things. But her mental abilities are pretty damned formidable."

"She can't retrace her steps. Apparently, she had her books grouped in some way she can no longer reproduce."

"But neither of you ever said a thing about that. How could I have known?"

"You couldn't, of course. But Gerry says she blames me for not stopping you. And what's worse, she's right. I could have—"

"That's hardly fair. I'm not some delicate little flower people need to protect—"

"Of course not. But I should have *protected her things*. It wasn't your fault. I pointed out that they were a mess, but I could have told you to leave them alone. I knew she was going through a difficult time, being tested for dementia."

"What? Dementia? I didn't believe Kathy when she mentioned it. I thought it was just good old Humboldt gossip—"

"Gossip? There shouldn't be any gossip. I haven't told anybody."

"Hello, *Gerry*? Calm down, Dad, I'm just bugging you. Kathy is her hairstylist, surely you remember that? She's the one who told me. Anyway, it's ridiculous. You're both naturally absent-minded, forgetful people. You live in your heads, you always have. And normal memory loss starts at age twenty-five."

"Hey! Speak for yourself! Nothing wrong with my memory, thank you. I know it seems insane, but she insists she mixed up the months this winter, thought it was November when it was February. And that is one of the symptoms, losing yourself in time. And she does forget appointments and meetings, so now I just keep track of things for her…"

"But Dad, that sounds serious. The doctor sent her to be tested?"

"I know. I thought Mamme was being ridiculous, but Gerry says it's not that unreasonable, given her behaviour lately. For God's sake, don't tell your mother that Kathy is talking about her—" His voice dropped to a whisper, and the cat stirred, lifted its head to Mia.

"So, you really think she might be ill?"

"I don't know what to think. We have to show her that we love and support her." He reached out to scratch the cat's chin. "At least that's what Gerry says. It sounds right to me."

"God, Dad, if she does have it, it's early onset. That shit is genetic: I could have it—"

"Calm down. Nothing is for sure; we don't have all the results yet. The neurologist did cognitive testing and seemed to think her memory is normal, even after I called him to tell him about her explosion. But she might be having a breakdown."

"But he wasn't certain, you said."

"I know, I know. That's what Gerry says, too. And her memory has always been phenomenal, not normal. But all that could be explained by stress."

"What stress? My return to the family nest?" Her eyes narrowed.

"Sweetheart, don't be foolish. It isn't about you. She loves having you here, we both do. But she lost her father, for one thing, and you know how close they were." He folded his arms across his chest.

"That was ages ago, a year and a half."

"Sixteen months. In terms of loss, that's nothing. Gerry says that grief really doesn't kick in until after a year, and even then it's not cut and dried. It doesn't hit people until they're dealing with the day-to-day, then some little thing happens and they realize that they can never have that connection again. She's just started to feel the permanence, the dozens of things she can never tell him."

Mia glanced at her phone, lying on the desk, and nodded. "And he did call every day."

"Exactly. Every single day. He was her confidant, not me. I thought I should have that privilege, but Gerry says I have to earn it. He says I'm emotionally unavailable."

"Unavailable? What are you talking about? You're the most available father who ever was. You always make time to listen to me—" Mia reached out and touched his arm.

"Just because I'm okay as your old man doesn't mean I'm a stellar partner. I do get tired of listening to her complain about her students, their inability to memorize, their lack of attention to detail, blah, blah, blah." He shook his head. "I can't stand it. *No negativity*, right?"

"That's what you always say."

"And right now, Mamme specializes in the negative."

"You mean she shouldn't vent?" Mia shook her head, her ponytail waving. "Gerry wasn't kidding—you aren't being very supportive. If you know she's in pain, why can't you empathize with her? You always have time for my problems."

"Ah, but your problems are interesting. You have a career to build, places to go." He smiled. "Our lives are pretty humdrum compared to that."

"This all came on after I moved home."

"Poppycock. We saw the neurologist a week before you arrived. I distinctly remember Mamme stalking out of the doctor's office because I forgot to tell her that you were moving home before I told him."

"God, Dad, you didn't! Jesus. But if it's stress, why does she—you—still think she has dementia?"

"I'm crossing my fingers that she doesn't. And I bet it's easier for her to believe that the doctor was wrong than to admit that she's stressed out and needs help. You know Mamme: she has to do things her own way, in her own time."

"And you and Gerry have figured all of this out?"

"Gerry, mostly. I just supply the data; he provides the analysis. I couldn't think like your mother does if I had a thousand years and my life depended on it. He's helped me realize that that's what keeps marriage interesting. The little woman keeps me wondering what she'll do next. But who knew I needed a priest to explain her to me?"

"Some atheist. And I'm pretty sure she'd better not hear you call her *the little woman.*"

He smiled, squeezing her shoulder. "Even I believe in luck. And now if that luck is going to continue, I'd better get supper started; can't miss my window of opportunity. When you're finished here, come up and see what I bought her."

# 56

It was after three and Ursula's classes were over for the day. She was seated at the front bench doing paperwork: scanning the morning's quizzes. Jared hadn't finished his, and most of the answers he'd scrawled were incomplete or incorrect. Why did students never ask for help before the exam when they so clearly needed it? She would have to email him to set up an appointment.

When she looked at her day planner, she couldn't believe her eyes. There, in her calendar, in her own black pen, was her notation: she'd already seen him, from noon to twelve-fifteen, that very day.

Panicked, she tried to think back. She couldn't remember the lunch hour at all; everything was swirling around. What had she said to him? Did he ask for help? At long last, she faintly remembered calling him aside when the bell rang, but after that she had no memory, none at all. Her mind was blank. They must have talked about the quiz, but—what had she said? It wasn't as if she could ask him. The strange socks in her bed, and now this? Her condition was definitely worsening, and fast. She picked up her phone and called Dr. Chernov.

Within two hours she was seated in his tacky waiting room, wondering what to do. Six months ago, she was a fully functioning individual, a working professional with a book underway, a husband she loved, a well-adjusted adult daughter. She was an accomplished educator, looking forward to retirement; she had everything to live for. Now, she was losing chunks of time; writing her book was an impossibility, and with the way she'd treated Andreas—and Mia— She shut her eyes tightly. After this, there was no doubt. She had to have dementia.

Dr. Chernov opened the door to the waiting room. He looked a little less dishevelled than usual. "Ah, Ursula. Come this way, if you please." He smiled encouragingly.

Ursula rose and followed down the dim corridor. His office was as dingy as ever. They settled themselves on the chairs and he folded his hands. "So," he smiled. "What is it I can help you with today?"

"I have proof now that I'm losing my mind."

"Yes, that's what you said on the phone. What's happening?"

"I lost track of what I was doing, completely, today. I went to make a note to meet with a student and discovered I had already met with him, not two-and-a-half hours before. And I don't remember a thing about it. Not one single thing."

"How do you know you've met with him if you don't remember?" He smiled patiently.

"It was written down. I went to see when I would have time to meet with him and there it was, already in my calendar. We met today at lunchtime, and I have no memory of it at all."

"Hmm. So, you were distracted—or you may have had an absence seizure."

"A seizure? Surely I would know if I'd had a seizure?"

"Not necessarily. You would lose track of a period of time."

"Well, that I did." She shook her head. "But, as you say, I have been distracted, it's true. You can't believe the dreams I've been having, such awful dreams."

He looked down at the chart for a moment, then back into her eyes. "What kind of dreams?"

"All kinds of dreams, disturbing ones. In one of the first ones, I actually tried to kill myself. And let me tell you, it was a relief, an enormous relief."

He leaned forward and reached out. "Ursula, suicide isn't the solution you're seeking, or you wouldn't be here telling me." He patted her hand. "You wouldn't harm yourself—it would devastate your family. And suicide is a permanent response to a temporary problem; let's find out what's really frightening you. Now take a deep breath, and describe your dreams to me, one at a time, in detail."

By the time she had finished, Ursula was flushed and distraught. Dr. Chernov leaned forward across his desk and offered her a box of tissues.

She waved it away, saying, "It's no use. As much as I want to, as much as I need to, I haven't cried for forty years."

"What do you mean?" He leaned forward, resting his arms on the desk.

She waved her hands. "My mother died in a car wreck. At first, we couldn't believe it; we couldn't take it in. Yes, the roads were icy, but she drove that way every single day. She was a skilful driver, she loved driving. And there were no skid marks, no debris on the road, no injured wild animals, nothing to indicate she would have had to swerve. It was a mystery. I couldn't cry that day, and I haven't been able to shed a tear since." She wrapped her arms across her chest.

"So why do you think you didn't cry? Were the two of you not close?"

"We were extremely close, so close we drove one another crazy. I don't know the science of it. I don't know anything these days—but I simply could not—cannot—"

He wrote something down, sat there tapping his pen for a moment, then looked up. "Do you want to know what I think?"

"Of course. That's why I'm here." She raised her brows and tilted her head, exasperated.

"You are confronting the fact that everything is outside of your control. You're dying for control. That's why you dream of death, attempting death. Right now, life seems over, but you are experiencing some relatively major transformations. Change is pivotal to your growth as a human. Without this cold spell—"

"This cold spell, as you call it, is God-in-Heaven terrifying."

"Yes, I'm sure it is. That's why you're dreaming of water and ice. You want to run from the tears. All those moose and deer you've been seeing, even the hallucinations you may have had, are a kind of waking dream, and rather than act on what your mind is telling you, you dream about yourself, alone, out in the wilderness. Can it be a coincidence that your mother died on an icy highway and you dream about animals falling through the ice?"

She shook her head. "A dream would hardly be that literal."

He caught her gaze and held it. "Some dreams are precisely that literal. You were an academic. You gave up your career. You have a large and beautifully wild soul, but you keep it confined by practicality. You feel like a draft horse. In your dream, domestic animals drown. Only those comfortable with their own wildness can safely follow their path across the ice. Maybe that moose was Andreas, or Mia. That's why it was able to walk across the frozen dugout where the draft horses had drowned. And your dream about jumping—you say you felt peace, but if you wanted to die, why change your mind? Why would only part of you end up back safe— and why on a cliff?"

"It can't be as straightforward as what you're implying. I never dream of my mother. I was in Basel, in the botanical garden, then it turned into the jungle—"

"Exactly. In dreams we wake to our most fundamental truths. Your dream took you from your favourite civilized space, a living museum, to the wildest place your mind could imagine, but even so there was ice and a frozen ship, there in the jungle. Your subconscious wants you to understand. That's what dreams do; they teach us about ourselves. The child you tried to hold inside you drowned, and no one around you even noticed."

"The child didn't drown in every dream. In the cave dream, she walked out of the waves towards me. In a diving suit. The child wasn't me: it was Mia."

"Of course. You want Mia to survive. You love her; you see her as capable. But you didn't save yourself because you wanted to live, only to avoid further punishment, and the winged miracle child still fell into the water."

"Well, when you put it like that—"

"You mentioned Bruegel's painting. The daring, dreamy part of you, the one like Icarus, drowns. Just because you wanted to see Mia walk out of the waves doesn't mean that you were willing to save yourself. There's a reason your mind chose that particular painting. It's a study of people who are too self-involved to see the one suffering, even when his existence is miraculous and his fall so very devastating."

"But Icarus flew too high—isn't that what my mind is saying to me? I should know better. And Mia saved herself. That's the miracle. She's terrified of deep water."

"*You* dreamt that Mia saved herself. Why won't you take credit for any of the good that you do, such as teaching your daughter to find the power within herself—to live her dreams? You love Mia, yes, but your subconscious also wants you to love yourself. What doesn't show in the painting is that Icarus's father, Daedalus, built the boy's wings and cautioned him not to fly too high. What might that mean to you?"

Dr. Chernov paused, waiting for Ursula to raise her eyes. When at last she did, he said gently, "That dream, and everything else we've discussed, tells me you can't bear to think clearly because there are just so many things you won't let yourself remember." He looked at the chart. "I'm certain I'm right. When did your neurologist schedule your MRI?"

"It's later this month. The Tuesday after next."

"You're not having any other symptoms? Headaches?"

"As a matter of fact, I do have migraines. But I've had those for years."

"Where, exactly?"

"In my head."

He smiled. "Where exactly in your head?"

"Right here," she said, pointing. "Again and again."

He stood up, placed his hand on the spot she indicated. "Just there, all the time?"

Ursula paused, then said, "The Internet says a pain in one spot could mean a tumour."

"I think we can exclude Dr. Google from this differential. You have too much on your mind as it is. Have the MRI and we'll go from there," Dr. Chernov smiled, as he turned to open the door.

# 57

When Ursula arrived home, a delicious aroma wafted out to greet her. She ducked her head into the kitchen, and there was Andreas, wearing the striped apron and reaching into the oven, turning the beef in the roasting pan. Mia was at the sink, washing dishes.

"Ah, Ursula! You're just in time. We were starting to worry about you. Want a hot potato? Here, catch!" He took the serving spoon, pretended to toss a crispy roasted potato at her.

"What are you two doing?" Ursula asked, looking in amazement from one to the other. "You're in an awfully good mood. You're up to something."

"We thought it was time for another little family feast. Mia suggested *Lummelbraten*, and it seemed like a good idea to me. Why don't you go get changed?"

As Ursula passed through the dining room, there, on the table, were twenty gorgeous red roses. She could feel Andreas watching her through the doorway. She took the envelope marked "Ursula," and pulled out the card, written in Hochdeutsch: "For my little wood-nymph, may it be spring, now and forever. Forgive me. —Andreas."

So, he was trying—something. But wasn't it she who needed to apologize? She was too tired, too shaken up after her visit to Dr. Chernov, to worry about that now. Maybe just this once she could accept the gesture at face value, assume it was meant without subterfuge, *without malice aforethought.* She nestled the card back among the stems, cupped the curve of the buds lightly with her hand, and breathed in the fragrance. She crossed the room and started up the stairs to change, wondering what had happened, but too exhausted to worry anymore.

Dinner was a delight, full of celebration and news-sharing. The beef was pink, the red wine sauce savoury, the carrots and celery, the roasted potatoes—all was perfection. Apparently, zebras could change their stripes: Andreas was attentive and talkative again, and Mia, always so petrified at the thought of deep water, was going to West Edmonton Mall over the long weekend to take a course in diving.

"Really, Mia? Diving? Are you sure?" Ursula's eyebrows rose.

"I'm as sure as I can be. I applied ages ago for a travel grant to go up North to see the Franklin ships. But no diving, no visit to the wreckage. It's the thing I've always wanted to see, but I never really expected they would be found, let alone be within my reach. It's that simple. *You* should understand..." Mia paused.

Ursula looked puzzled. "Well, I understand that you have always been fascinated by Franklin—"

"No, I mean, you're full of fear, and yet—you're unstoppable. You couldn't have done what you've done," Mia said, "unless you could conquer your fears."

Ursula's face flushed. "You two have been talking about me—"

Andreas put his hand over hers. "I was just telling Mia about a dream I had of you, Sweetheart, about the day the truck took out the corner of the gas station. You defended the entire town from the flying debris with an umbrella."

She tilted her head. "I did what? How on earth would I do that?"

"It was a dream, Ursula. You had this hot-pink umbrella—the colour of your new ski jacket—and you held it out in front of the bystanders. All the brick fragments and rubble just bounced off. Then you nonchalantly folded it up and returned it to the hardware store, as if it were nothing unusual at all."

"What an odd dream. Why would you think that?"

"Apparently, you're not getting the credit you deserve, and my subconscious recognizes that." He smiled and refilled her glass of wine. "You've been protecting me, or all of us, all of our lives, I think. I just didn't get it."

Ursula's eyes widened. "I always try—"

"Absolutely. I didn't understand how hard you try, every day, not until lately."

They looked at one another for a moment, then Ursula, uncomfortable, said, "I've been having strange dreams, too. Dr. Chernov insists I'm trying to work out my fears—loosen my tears."

Mia and Andreas looked at one another, then at Ursula.

"Dr. Chernov? A rhyming doctor? You never mentioned him before. And what tears? You *never* cry—you're not the weepy kind, Mamme."

Ursula paused. "He's the new doctor I've been seeing, a holistic one, a homeopath who works with dreams and psychology, too. Kathy recommended him." She took a sip of her wine.

"A homeopath? That *is* new. And? What dreams are you having?"

"Oh, crazy dreams, nothing that would interest you. He thinks I'm going through some sort of transformation. In botany we called it *vernalization*. Some trees need a cold spell before they bloom. It's affecting my memory. It's like I'm dreaming all the answers."

Andreas smiled. "Oh, you already have all the answers; you have an exceptional memory, Ursula. And Mia and I have been having strange dreams, too. Quite the coincidence. But you're just going through what normal people do, at any age, in the era of the Internet."

Ursula smiled back but shook her head. "You know I don't believe in coincidence, Andreas. It's more likely a sign. But what does that have to do with the Internet?"

"I read about it in the *Star Phoenix* last week, when I was getting my truck fixed."

"Oh?" she said. "Then you got rid of the mice?"

He nodded. "Indeed, I did. But I left illuminated about the current problem of memory loss; the article said that, faced with so much information, the brain rejects whatever can be looked up again, just ditches whatever seems less relevant, and sometimes that turns out to be stuff it should have saved. Even twenty-year-olds have trouble remembering. Apparently, it's an epidemic."

"So you're aware that you forget, too?" Ursula tilted her head in surprise. "Is that why you're always reminding me *we discussed this*? To remind yourself?"

"That's my job. I just keep you on track. We're advanced players, Gerry says."

"Advanced players? What on earth does that mean? And what does Gerry know about us?" Ursula's smile faded. She set down her knife and fork.

"Look, you've been talking to Dr. Chernov. I talk to Gerry. What's the big deal?"

"The big deal is that Dr. Chernov is a professional. I've never been able to get a straight answer out of you about this Gerry. Who is she?"

"A professional? Homeopathy? That's a little sketchy, wouldn't you say?" Andreas raised his eyebrows.

Mia looked from parent to parent. She jumped in.

"Mamme, Gerry's a man, a priest. A Ukrainian priest who picked Dad up when he fell in front of his church."

"A priest? *You've* been talking to a priest?"

"Yes, I've been talking to a priest. It turns out he's quite a nice guy."

"Is that so?" Ursula's face was taut.

"We mainly talk politics. He's one of the best-read people I've met here. He's counselled a lot of people, and what I say is kept in the strictest confidence." He smiled in that charming way that always made Ursula suspicious.

She sniffed. "One would hope."

"And what does Dr. Chernov say about your condition?"

"Much the same as Dr. Paul. He wants me to have the MRI, just to be sure. My headaches might just be stress—or something neurological."

Andreas looked grave. "Yes, absolutely. Gerry warned me about that, too." He reached over and patted her hand. "I know it's hard not to know, but I have a good feeling. You're going to be fine, once we clear up your stress." He looked sideways at Mia. "And speaking of things in the near future, you were going to tell us about your trip. You'd leave and return when—? And who's going to take care of the little Après Chat?"

"You mean Peaches," Ursula corrected.

"Fonzi," laughed Mia. "Honestly, you'd think three grown people could share a reality long enough to agree on a single name for one cat. I should have the last word. She's mine, after all."

"What wise parent ever gives their children, even their grown children, the last word?" smiled Andreas, gracefully. "And have you asked the cat? Besides, we're the ones who have to take care of her while you're away traversing the frozen wastes."

"If I get the grant."

"We'll find the money if you don't. Following your

dreams is more important than anything, especially when you're young. But we have to agree on a name. She must be so confused," Andreas nodded. "I agree with Mamme."

Ursula smiled, "She looks like a Peaches, a little flouncy Southern thing with a peach-coloured feather boa. Après Chat, Apricot, is too intellectual. Cats don't get puns. And I can't picture her in a leather jacket, like the Fonz—"

"Alright, alright," Mia said, laughing. "I give up. Peaches it is. Why not? She is a peach—besides, you'll call her whatever you please, no matter what I say. I know it."

# 58

Ursula drove to the Ukrainian Catholic Church and parked on the street. It was high time she met this priest, this Gerry, who knew so much about her. She went in at the front door, walked through the narthex, steeled herself, then pushed open the double doors into the nave. The big church was completely empty, so, uncertain what to do next, she walked quietly to the front and sat down in a pew. There was no sign of the priest. She hadn't been in a church in decades. She tried to relax, collect her thoughts.

The silence was profound but not oppressive. She could have sworn she felt the century-or-so of prayerful congregants wrapped around her. There was a sense of comfort in the quiet, like the feeling she had found in the Buddhist temple she had visited in Saskatoon, or in the chapel where they had been married. Such stillness, a held breath. She wondered whether Andreas felt this presence when he came here, and if so, what he made of it. She was so lost in her thoughts that she almost didn't notice Gerry when he came through the door from the rectory.

At first, he went about his business, pulling dead flowers from the arrangements, tidying the front of the church. Eventually he made his way to the pews, straightening the prayer books and hymnals in their holders. By the time he had worked down the other side of the aisle and up to the row where Ursula was seated, she was waiting for him.

He put out his hand, and said, "I'm Gerry Pacholok. You must be Ursula Niederhauser."

Surprised, she said, "I am, indeed. But how would you know that?"

"I know your husband. Andreas has told me a little bit about you. I know that you like fuchsia and that you're five feet tall. Besides, you're not of my flock. Not too many strangers drop by. I wondered when we might meet."

Ursula's face flushed to match her ski-jacket.

"Why don't we have some tea?" he said, putting out his hand. "Andreas is a great guy. I'd like to get to know you, too."

"Whatever he's told you about me, you might take it with a grain of salt. The man does love to hear himself talk," she said, as she rose and followed Gerry through the church and into the rectory. He took her jacket and hung it up on a hook near the door, then led her to the Arborite kitchen table. He waved at a chair, indicating that she should sit, and went to the stove, filling the enamel kettle and setting it on the burner. He took down a blue teapot and withdrew two mugs from the cupboard. "Earl Grey or Red Rose?"

"Earl Grey, please." Ursula took a deep breath. "Andreas tells me you believe I might have dementia."

"Ah, yes. I was concerned for you." Gerry turned to her and smiled.

Ursula shook her head. "*Concerned* is not the word for it. My world is falling apart. I can't remember what I'm doing from one moment to the next, my mood flips like a light switch, and now I've started to lose track of time. I've done things, irreversible things—" She stopped, her face flushing again. "And now I'm prattling to a stranger."

"I can see how this is very frightening for you. There's a good chance, though, that your problems are real but not from dementia."

"Then what? I've started losing chunks of time—"

"Could you be stressed?"

"Of course, I'm stressed! Who wouldn't be?"

He nodded. "That's very true. But were you worried about something when your memory problems started? Have you been through any increase in pressure recently, something that would set this off, some loss, a trigger—"

Ursula was silent for the briefest of moments. Then she said, slowly, "Nothing unexpected. But my father passed away a year ago last December."

He paused to look at her. "I'm very sorry for your loss."

"You already knew about this. Andreas must have told you. What else did he say about me?"

"That he was worried about you, that you seemed not to slow down or give yourself time to grieve."

"There is no point in giving in to grief. My father was old and suffering."

"That doesn't make the final separation any easier, does it?" He shook his head.

"*Final* separation? Don't priests believe in an afterlife? No wonder you get along with Andreas! But no, nothing makes death any easier, but I should be able to handle it. I have forty years of experience. My mother died when I was in my twenties. And I had an older sister I never knew, who died before I was born."

He looked intently at her. "How awful. What—"

"Annelis drowned, and Mamme died in a car crash. Both completely unexpected." Ursula knit her fingers together in her lap and looked down at them.

"And that must have made it all the worse."

"With Annelis, it's complicated. How do you miss someone you've never known? But I always felt responsible. With Mamme, I had my work to keep me busy, and then

I met Andreas. It was so odd, falling so in love while being in such pain."

"Losing your father at Christmas must have brought all that back? And added a new dimension to it? The pain must be unbearable."

Ursula looked up, straight into his eyes. He held her gaze, waiting.

"That's not the neurologist's theory. He thinks I have MCI."

"MCI?"

"Mild Cognitive Impairment. Age-related loss of mental function. It's the one medical diagnosis that has been established. The specialist confirmed it."

"That would be stressful, too. Stress and grief can sabotage the strongest mind. How are you sleeping?"

"You mean—? He told you about that, too? Because we—it was the first time in almost forty years that we ever slept apart... And now we've made up. He's moved out of the study."

He smiled gently. "I'm relieved to hear it. But are you sleeping well? Do you feel rested in the morning?"

She looked at him, surprised. "I've been having the strangest nightmares—dreams about wild places, wild creatures, mythology..."

"Andreas mentioned some pretty odd ones, too. Do you talk about them with him?"

She shook her head. "He doesn't believe in dreams as portents. Where I see signs and messages, he only sees coincidence. He could dream my thoughts and still he would think it a pure fluke."

"But that doesn't mean you're not entitled to your own interpretation. How do you feel in your dreams?"

She widened her eyes. "So alive, so aware, so terrified. Dr. Chernov says I need to feel my own strength."

"I don't know him, but I like this guy already. *Feel* is the operative word here. You have the strength, you've proven that. It's time to let yourself share what you've been carrying all alone, feel those profound losses that are manifesting as anger. Tell me more about Annelis. And your parents? What was it like, growing up in your family?"

They talked for almost two hours. Ursula was late getting home again, but she was thoughtful, less agitated than usual, when she came in, and Andreas and Mia cheerfully greeted her. Andreas was wearing the striped apron, melting grated Emmentaler into white wine for fondue, and Mia was tearing a crusty baguette into pieces for dipping. The table was set with all their best pieces, and the roses were in full bloom, luxurious and crimson and velvety, six full days after Andreas had brought them. Ursula took a moment to go over and inhale their scent.

At last, Ursula lay in the cold machine. She was trapped in a tight plastic mask, inside a tight tube, the only bit of freedom the little mirror that reflected a slim slice of the outer room. The MRI whizzed and whirred, popped and banged, went on and on, making a surreal cacophony of random banging noises and telephone rings that reminded her of a John Cage performance. She heard the technician call over the intercom again, "You okay in there? We're almost halfway now. It won't take as long as you think. Keep relaxing, Mrs. Koehl-Niederhauser. Stay still."

When the technician had asked, "You okay in small spaces?" she'd said, "Absolutely. I love small spaces." The lie had floated easily from her lips. She wondered why she would have said that, but then it came to her. She remembered hiding behind her father's chair as a child, her favourite spot, while her parents went around the house, pretending not to know where she was. "Where's Ursula?" they'd call. "Where's Ursula?" And then she would pop out and they would cheer with delight.

*I love small spaces, I love small spaces*, she told herself over and over and over.

She knew she mustn't let herself think about another fifteen minutes in there—

"Sorry! Something's not right. I'm going to get you out of there. Hang on."

"I'm fine, fine. Don't worry about me," Ursula lied, relieved.

The technician slid her stretcher out of the MRI. "You seem to have broken the machine," she joked. "I'll have to restart it."

"What do you mean, I broke it?"

"The computer just shut down for some reason. It does that from time to time. I'll have to get the program up again. That will just take a few minutes. In the meantime, you can rest out here. Enjoy the freedom."

Ursula felt anything but free. She lay there, knowing she was out of the machine, but with the mask still on she was definitely trapped. She tried to think pleasant thoughts. She was out on the mountain, hiking along...

"Mrs. Koehl-Niederhauser? You awake? We're up again. Here we go. We're back in business. You okay?"

"I'm fine. Never better," Ursula lied again.

Maybe if she kept saying it, it would be true. If she kept thinking it was alright, everything would be fine. Isn't that how Gerry said positive thinkers got through rough spots?

The jackhammer sound started again, then a long pause. An old-fashioned telephone rang, paused, rang again. There was a mysterious ticking. Ursula tried to meditate, to focus on relaxing her hands, her feet, her limbs. Breathe in, breathe out, slowly and evenly. But the noise made it hard to focus. Time dragged on and on. Ursula could hardly stand it. *I love small spaces*, she kept saying to herself.

Finally, at long last, the technician said, "Let's get you out now."

When she opened the mask, Ursula asked, "How long was I in there?"

The technician consulted her phone. "Altogether? It's been about an hour and a half. If only Ethel hadn't given up and quit there. Sorry about that."

"It's not your fault. It was just much longer than I expected."

"Yes, sorry. It should have only been about half an hour or forty minutes. But when Ethel shuts down—"

"Who's Ethel?"

"That's what we call the old girl. Here, let me help you sit up. Take it easy now. You might be dizzy after being still so long."

"Thank you. I'm fine, really. And the results?"

"The scans will have to be read and then sent to your doctor. He'll let you know if there's anything to be concerned about."

*Oh, there's always plenty to be concerned about,* Ursula thought. *But we never know the half of it.* And, as Gerry says, if we're lucky, we never will.

# 59

Andreas sat protectively beside Ursula on the stylish teal sofa, quietly holding her hand. The doctor rapped on the door and entered, holding the door for the nurse, who set down the tray of coffee. He noticed that this time Ursula ignored the carafe and turned to face Dr. Paul, who was just sitting down in his Eames recliner, reaching for his tablet.

At last he spoke. "Well, Ursula, how are things going?" he smiled.

"That's kind of you to ask. I think I'm a little better lately. But can MCI be episodic? Can it just go away?"

"Who told you you have MCI, Ursula?" The doctor looked puzzled, consulted her chart.

Andreas jumped in. "No, no, *Schätzli*. Dr. Paul described MCI to prove you *don't* have it. You heard him. We both did."

Ursula reddened, looking from man to man.

Andreas was firm. "He ruled it out."

The doctor shook his head. "Well, that's not entirely true, either. We can't rule anything out; we can't say it will *never* happen, only that it appears not to be happening now. However, I did *not* tell you that you have MCI. Don't you remember?" He scanned the chart again, then looked over at her.

Ursula paused, embarrassed. "To tell you the truth, I lost focus while you were talking. The whole day was such a workout." She corrected herself, "Work*up*. That was what the team called it, if we can call those young people a team. They didn't seem to know what the others were thinking."

"How would they? Telepathy is not a thing—" Andreas joked.

Ursula set her mouth. "They couldn't repeat what I'd said when they were taking my history. And you know how I feel about tests. I was so cold I was shaking. All those puzzles and drawings and pronunciations and mathematics, as if I didn't still remember all that I learned as a young person. As I tried to tell them, that isn't my problem: what I learned long ago is fine. It's learning new things or paying attention to what I'm doing at any given moment, that's where I have trouble."

"That's interesting," Dr. Paul said. "Go on. It could be significant."

"I couldn't learn those strange word associations." Ursula paused. "And the nurse was so young, she yelled 'dear' at me as if I were old and deaf."

Dr. Paul and Andreas exchanged a glance. Ursula was shaking her head. Andreas put his hand on top of hers. "To the young, anyone over forty is over the hill," he joked.

"Forty?" the doctor corrected. "More like twenty-five." He smiled. "But you seemed so relaxed, Ursula. I think I remember you just sat there and served the coffee—"

"I had to do something."

"I reviewed the nature of the tests with both of you," Dr. Paul said.

Ursula shook her head. "Andreas kept asking for more details, the significance of this metric and that, all the norms and standard deviations. That's my problem: I can't concentrate. It's like when I listen to the weather. I drift off, and by the time I come to, the announcer is finished, the report over, except for the latest storm heading for Newfoundland."

"But Ursula, surely you heard me say that it was unlikely you're suffering from dementia. I was clear. And now we've had the MRI—"

"I heard you ask about menopause." She shook her finger at Andreas. "Then before I knew it, the doctor started talking about mild cognitive impairment."

"But I wasn't talking about you, not at all." Dr. Paul frowned.

"You were. You said that one in six people will go on to develop dementia—"

"Yes, people with MCI! Why would you think I was talking about you?" The doctor looked puzzled.

"Who else would you be talking about? You recommended retirement, a support group. And I'm still having new symptoms. The other day I found a pair of clean socks by my pillow—I lost track of time when meeting with a student—"

Andreas knew the answer to one of those mysteries. "I left those socks on your bed. They were in with my laundry."

"You left them by my pillow?"

"Not on purpose; they must have bounced when I tossed them onto the bed. But I bet I know what distracted you in the last appointment. You heard Dr. Paul say, 'with academics, when the disease takes hold, it's like they've fallen off a cliff.'"

"I don't recall hearing any such thing." Ursula was adamant. "And I'm hardly an academic."

Andreas took her hand again. "Ursula, in your mind and in your heart, you *are* an academic. I wondered what effect that expression would have on you, but you didn't even flinch. You must have blocked it, Sweetheart. Those are the words he said. And of course you couldn't listen after that."

Ursula turned to Dr. Paul, saying woodenly, "My mother died, driving off a cliff. It was an accident."

Dr. Paul looked carefully at her. "That would explain your loss of focus. But, Ursula, as I said last time, the cognitive tests showed no sign of MCI or dementia. For a woman your age, taking antidepressants and sleeping meds, your comprehension is strong. From what's been said, anxiety appears to be the problem."

"But what about the MRI?"

"The scan was fine. There were some nonspecific changes, nothing indicating disease or any tumours. Just the normal changes we associate with aging."

"You're saying I'm alright?" She looked from man to man. "I have been feeling a little better…"

Dr. Paul smiled. "Well, I would recommend, again, that you reduce your stress. No doubt talking with a therapist would help. But no, there are no signs of dementia at this point. Now that we have a baseline, though, we can re-evaluate you in a few years if you are still worried."

"Worried? You mean I could still be ill?"

"Any of us could become ill, Ursula." He smiled. "But the diagnosis is that you do not have MCI, much less dementia. You have been underestimating the effect of your stress. Keep active, exercise your mind and your body as much as you can, get enough sleep, eat well. Don't forget to laugh—often." He rose, came over, and shook their hands. "And good luck to you both. After all you've been through, retirement should be the best time of your life."

# 60

Ursula was silent in the truck, and Andreas seemed to sense that he needed to let her be. She could still hardly believe that she didn't have dementia—it was such an enormous relief, but so much to take in. Yet that didn't fix everything: she still hadn't confessed what Dr. Chernov and Gerry had helped her see. Both men had warned her that if ever she and Andreas hoped to find anything like the fine harmony they once had, she would have to risk sharing her heart with him. True, Andreas had been better of late, more respectful, even supportive, but she hadn't been able to be honest with him yet. She was terrified that it would spoil things between them forever if she told him why she had been so angry, that he had hurt her in those ways.

At last they were home. They walked in silence into the porch, took off their coats and boots, and went into the house. Ursula checked her phone. She had turned off the ringer in the doctor's office and had forgotten to switch it back on; there was a text from Mia, saying she was out with friends. The time had come, then. Before Andreas could turn on the television, Ursula led him to the sofa. For a moment she looked away out the living room window, staring at the single tree on their front lawn, the Schubert chokecherry. She didn't feel ready, but she summoned her courage anyway.

"It was the oddest thing, today in the doctor's office, realizing I had completely missed the diagnosis. All I remember about that first appointment is thinking back about my little tree and how you let it die. That was the moment I realized that you had *never* loved me."

Andreas looked as if she had struck him. "Ursula! What an awful thing to say!"

She shook her head. "I've spent a lot of time looking back lately, and it seems as though we've always wanted different things. You want to be Canadian; you barely speak Baseldytsch, even when I do, yet you insist on your Swiss love of order. You couldn't even plant a single tree of my own choosing because it wasn't on your diagram."

"Ursula, *Schätzli*. That's what you're talking about, that apple tree?"

"Yes, my five-grafted apple tree."

"You've got it all wrong, Sweetheart. That wasn't it at all. I didn't want to embarrass you by saying so, but there was nowhere we could plant it."

"Because you wouldn't make room. It wasn't perfect, like your specimens."

He took her hands and held them. "I was so sure you'd figured it out—the branches were too thin to support themselves. Espaliered trees have to have their branches tied horizontally along a wall or vertically on a special type of wire fence. We didn't have a place for that. It broke my heart; you were so proud of the little tree. How could I admit I wasn't able to make it work? The kindest thing was to let you forget about it. And you seemed so happy. I was sure you understood."

"That's just it—I couldn't understand why you wouldn't plant it. But you're right about one thing: I took the only choice left to me, to pretend to forget, after I'd asked you and asked you, and you never made time."

"Sweetheart, that wasn't it at all. The weight of any fruit would have broken the branches—they needed support."

She shook her head. "*I* needed support. I identified with that tree: I had to try to live in those dark desperate conditions when we first arrived in Canada—and I tried and tried—and failed. The move meant I had no choice but to teach high school; my doctorate meant nothing here. And I had broken my mother's heart for it. She died for nothing."

"You have your career, you have Mia, and me—we're not nothing—"

"You're not hearing me. Gerry says I have to feel my pain, to share it with you. The tree bloomed, and some of the blossoms even set. But by the time spring came, the whole miracle, that winter-blooming tree, just gave up and died as it sat there on the deck, waiting all summer. As I did, when I started my Education degree and gave up on my academic career."

Andreas shook his head. "This is so odd. I dreamed this conversation, or something like it—but you wanted to teach school, you were so eager to have the summers off, get away from publishing—"

"That was your idea. What else could I do? We were desperate for the money. I didn't know how long it would take for you to find a position in a university. If it had been in a larger centre, maybe—but here? What else was there for me?"

"But you were an academic—"

Ursula shook her head. "Not here. I had no opportunities at all. I couldn't keep deluding myself, not after your position at the U of S disappeared."

"I thought you were happy, not having to research, not having to publish. There's no such thing as déjà vu—but I swear I dreamed we had this conversation, I know I did. What happened when you went down to the department?"

"The professors were all men. Every blessed one of them."

"That's so strange. That's what I dreamed."

"But Andreas, why would I start my book, then, if I was so happy not to research or publish? And still, there again, what I wanted—what I *needed*—just didn't matter. So you didn't value my project, protect it."

"Now, that's not fair. I've explained why I didn't stop Mia—"

"But if you'd cared about me, you would have found a way."

"Again, unfair. I did care about your writing. I was going to tell Mia that to leave your things in the order you had them, but the phone rang and I simply forgot. I got sidetracked. You've got to believe me, Ursula. I just forgot."

"You forgot."

"Yes, *Schätzli*, I forgot. I wouldn't hurt you on purpose."

Ursula looked out the window into the darkening sky. The streetlights were starting to come on. She took a deep breath, not looking at him. At last she said, "Even the people who love you most can do what they know will hurt you. My mother drove off a cliff. Deep down, I've always been afraid that it was because of something I said."

Andreas was emphatic. "What are you talking about? It was an accident, the coroner ruled on it. You told me that, right from the beginning."

"You know she was a concert pianist, but did you know she wanted me to be one, too? We were always so close, all of us. I broke her heart, my family's heart, too. And it was all for nothing. It was the last thing I ever said to her." Ursula hesitated a long moment, then said, "I told her I was giving up the piano for good. I couldn't put in the hours I needed to practise and still study botany. It was too much. I had to choose how to spend my time, and I chose my *Habilitation*, my advanced botany studies. And then after she'd died because of my choice, I abandoned it."

"But surely she just wanted you to be happy? That was what mattered?"

"It mattered, of course it did. But she always wanted me to be a pianist. She wanted me to choose her world over science, she wanted me to replace Annelis—but we never spoke of that. I was so furious at being torn apart that I said I would never play again."

"And?"

"And she said some awful things, and I said worse, and then I left. I knew she was incredibly upset, but still I went; I was too proud to stop. Of course, once I was gone and had cooled off, I felt like an idiot. I needed to apologize, to find some way to compromise. I would have made time to play, if it was that important to her. But I never had the chance to tell her."

"Because?"

"She went over the cliff that afternoon." Ursula grimaced, her eyes bleak. "After the inquest—the year we moved to Canada—a witness came forward. Babbe never wanted me to know, but, as the executor, Norbert decided I should have all the facts. After Babbe's funeral, he finally told me. It was an incredible shock."

"But why didn't you tell me? No wonder you haven't been able to think straight—"

"The witness said he saw her just drive over the cliff, and that was that. She didn't even brake when she went over the edge. See? I can't even cry for her, my own mother, dead because of me. My bull-headedness. She was right. I have no heart, no loyalty. There could never be love inside of me." She shook her head.

"Ursula, you know that isn't true. I wasn't going to tell you this, but I think you should read your father's journal. He and your mother had a terrible fight after you left, before she went out. He asked her to ease off, to let you live your own life. He tried to calm her down, but she was furious. He was certain the accident was his fault."

Ursula blanched. "You know this how?"

"Mia read his journal and showed it to me. You can be proud of her, using her Hochdeutsch," he said wryly, "and hiding it afterward, trying to protect you."

Ursula stared at him, then looked out the window. "Gerry was right: neither of you have any sense of boundaries, that's for sure. I can't believe she went in my things again. And how awful to think that Babbe felt the same guilt I have, all these years. But this was my fault. This is the first time I've even been able to say it out loud: I drove her to it."

"Sweetheart, you didn't drive her anywhere. You're giving yourself a false sense of control. If it were your fault, you could change the outcome, but of course that's not possible. You didn't cause this, nor your father. It was a terrible, impulsive mistake."

"She never made mistakes; she was such a strong person. Every single thing she did was perfect, except on that one day. It was my fault, all my fault." And even as she said those words, Ursula started to weep, tears rolling down silently first, then in great gulping sobs. Andreas put both arms around her and held her close as she wept and wept and wept. Evening deepened into night, and still the two sat together, Andreas holding Ursula tightly. At last she stopped, and still they sat together, the room dark around them.

An hour later, the doorbell rang, and Andreas got up to answer it. It was Gerry.

"I had a feeling you folks might want some company tonight. I brought dinner."

# 61

Summer was in full swing by the time Ursula and the other student artisans held their show. People wandered the long aisles of tables in the school gymnasium. Each had set their wares out on display, and Andreas and Mia took their time, stopping to admire the rich hues and unusual forms. When they reached the potters, there was Ursula's table, her new friend Dorothy standing beside her, their plates and platters and mugs gleaming in the long rays of sun through the high windows. Ursula looked cautiously from her husband to her daughter.

"Hello, you two. It's so nice of you to come. Have you seen anything you like?"

"I've seen lots of things I like. But I especially like those—" Andreas said, gesturing at the navy blue and white set on Ursula's side of the table. "And I'm determined to have them. I'm willing to pay your price."

"You might regret saying that," Ursula smiled. "We have an Arctic expedition to finance from the sale of these dishes, now that I'm retired."

Mia beamed. "Not so fast, Mamme. I had an email yesterday. You were so busy with the show that I didn't want to bother you, but we got the grant, after all."

"Mia, *Schätzli*!"

"Congratulations! That's wonderful news," Dorothy smiled, her kind lined face glowing.

"We'll be leaving in mid-August. It'll be a world-shaking trip—a career-maker, I hope. And with the latest technology, we won't even have to eat our boots," Mia grinned.

"That's what Franklin said," Ursula smiled. "Be careful—" she stopped herself. No more negativity. "Sorry, Mia. You were saying?"

"It's probably not a bad thing I've put on weight, with all the rich food you two have been feeding me. If we get lost in the North, at least I'll have some reserves."

"Where? You haven't put on a kilo."

"Anyway, you're not going to get lost, Mia—your mother would harness the cats and sled up North to fetch you." Andreas squeezed her arm. "If she can tear herself away from her research—"

"I know, right? Seriously, you can't imagine how much I'm going to miss you, both of you. It's been so nice, being home."

"But you'll be back—"

"Of course, I'll be back, but I have more news, good news, from last night. Apparently, there's a spot for me at CTV when I get back. After I heard about the grant, I thought things were going my way, so I took a chance and emailed old Schmidt—remember him? He's the one I worked for in Vancouver. Well, Melissa told me he's in Saskatoon now, so I filled him in about the trip up North. They just want me to cover a mat-leave, starting mid-September, but you never know…"

"Once your foot is in the door—" Andreas smiled and hugged her.

"I'll wear my steel-toed boots this time," Mia grinned.

"So you'll be only an hour away. *Schätzli*, this is excellent," Ursula reached over and hugged Mia across the table.

They were still talking a few minutes later when a tall young man stepped up and wrapped his arm around Mia's shoulders.

"Ryan! What in the world are you doing here?" Mia blushed.

"My aunt has a table over there." He pointed near the door. "I couldn't help but notice all that hugging from across the gym. Now that the curling's over, I never see you anymore. Do you have time for coffee?"

Mia smiled. "Of course! That would be great. Perfect timing. And I have news—we got the grant! I'll tell you all about it. Where should we go—the Pioneer—or the Windsor? Maybe we need something a little more rough-and-ready, now that we'll be explorers…" She turned to her father. "I hate to bail on you, Dad, but Ryan and I—"

Andreas exchanged glances with Ursula, then smiled back at Mia. "No worries, Sweetheart. I can amuse myself."

"Good luck with your show, ladies. See you later, Mr. Niederhauser." Ryan nodded, and turned to Mia. "What date did you say the cruise leaves?"

"August 17," she said, pulling up a screen on her phone and passing it to him. "Here are all the deets." Their voices faded as they made their way through the crowd.

Andreas looked across the table at Ursula. "I wonder what they'd think if they knew the two of us have been chasing Franklin in our dreams, too? Maybe there's something to your déjà vu, or the collective unconscious, after all."

"You? Déjà vu? That's extraordinary, Andreas." Ursula peered up at him, and for just a moment she could see apple blossoms around his smiling face.

If he could change, so could she—and it was long past due. Ursula savoured the sunshine as she quipped, "And an optimist might just say that this could be the trip of a lifetime."

# Acknowledgements

I can never thank SaskArts enough for the two grants that allowed me to finish the first draft and then later to polish this manuscript. I am enormously grateful to Access Copyright for the grant that allowed me to work on the project with the marvellous Guy Vanderhaeghe for ten intense days during the 2017 fiction colloquium at Sage Hill.

I owe deepest thanks to so many people, including beloved friends, Fr. Lawrence DeMong, OSB, Elizabeth, Shaun, and Al Harms, Val Koroluk, Roni Muench, and Barb Robinson. I am deeply thankful for the fabulous writers who have encouraged me, namely Kimmy Beach, Sheri Benning, Sandra Birdsell, Gail Bowen, David Carpenter, Méira Cook, dennis cooley, Elizabeth Greene, Carol Gossner, Hazel Kellner, Sylvia Legris, Shawna Lemay, Joanna Lilley, Jeanette Lynes, Dave Margoshes, Anne McDonald, Arlene Mighton, Loretta Polischuk, Dee Robertson, Dave Sealey, Leona Theis, and Lisa Vargo. And I am so grateful to all the wonderful crew at Palimpsest Press, especially the amazing Aimee Parent-Dunn, publisher and editor extraordinaire;

Theo Hummer, copy editor and so much more; and Ellie Hastings, designer beyond compare.

And finally, I am so thankful for our family: Nicole and Brian, Jean and Melissa, Hildi and Fred, Maureen and Reno, Rosie and Matt, Matthew and Angela, Beth and Owen, and, with every breath, Michael. You make all things possible.

Barbara Langhorst's *restless white fields* won book awards for poetry in Saskatchewan and Alberta. Her first novel, *WANT*, was shortlisted for the Regina Public Library's Book of the Year Award. She is a writing instructor and mentor, and has just moved back to Edmonton after nearly twenty years in Saskatchewan. She lives in Edmonton.